'So many characters with so many secrets and deviant behaviours make this debut mystery by James Marrison a real winner. The author's complex plotting, haunted characters and gorgeous descriptions of winter are an absolute joy to read even as the action takes one suspenseful turn, then another and then another to an unexpected denouement. When it seems as though all the clues have been resolved, Marrison saves one last shocking revelation for the final chapter . . . expertly setting us up for the next book in the series (I can't wait!), Marrison writes lovingly of his new hero, Guillermo Downes, a detective plagued by demons both internal and external, yet determined to expose murder most foul whenever and wherever he can'

curledup.com

'An assured debut which promises much for the future'

crimefictionlover.com

'A masterful novel . . . the protagonists are wonderfully portrayed. Downes is a bit of a mystery, a man born in Buenos Aires of an Argentinian mother and an English father. What led him to leave his homeland and make a life for himself in this small English town? Perhaps the answer will be revealed in the next novel in the series, something I'm eagerly anticipating'

marilynmysteryreads.com

## ABOUT THE AUTHOR

James Marrison is a journalist with a Masters degree in history from the University of Edinburgh. He now lives in Buenos Aires, which provides the inspiration for his lead character, Argentinian-born detective Guillermo Downes. *The Sleepless Ones* is James's second novel, following on from *The Drowning Ground*.

# The Sleepless Ones

## JAMES MARRISON

PENGUIN BOOKS

PENGUIN BOOKS

UK | USA | Canada | Ireland | Australia
India | New Zealand | South Africa

Penguin Books is part of the Penguin Random House group of companies
whose addresses can be found at global.penguinrandomhouse.com

 Penguin
Random House
UK

First published 2016

001

Copyright © James Marrison, 2016

The moral right of the author has been asserted

Set in 12.5/14.75pt Garamond MT Std

Typeset in India by Thomson Digital Pvt Ltd, Noida, Delhi

Printed in Great Britain by Clays Ltd, St Ives plc

A CIP catalogue record for this book is available from the British Library

PAPERBACK ISBN: 978–1–405–91750–6
TRADE PAPERBACK ISBN: 978–0–718–17933–5

www.greenpenguin.co.uk

For Clarisa

*'Tis the restless panting of their being;*
*Like beasts of prey, who, caged within their bars,*
*In a deep hideous purring have their life,*
*And an incessant pacing to and fro.*

*The Dream of Gerontius*, John Henry Newman

# PART ONE

# Prologue

It had been a huge relief to be out of London, and now, looking at the country lane outside the pub, he wondered, and not for the first time that day, why the hell he hadn't come out here sooner. A bit of fresh air, that was all he had really needed. And, of course, to be working again after being stuck inside, feeling sorry for himself. Pathetic, and not like him at all. But, really, just to get out of London had been enough.

He had felt it the moment he left the city behind: there had been an immediate loosening of tension. His thoughts had become less bleak. It was the beginning of an unexpected optimism, which had grown all afternoon as the strain of the last few months gradually lifted.

He drained his pint and ordered another one, glancing through his notes as he waited. His mind began to hover around the edges of the story. A few hundred words of background and the pictures, but none of it would be any use unless he could confront Miller and tell him what he thought he knew.

He had got some more information from the barman, who spoke like a well-heeled university graduate and looked like he spent half his life in the gym. God only knew what he was doing all the way out here in this awful pub and he didn't ask. He talked about Miller and got the impression of a morose regular with a nasty temper who scared everyone half to death after he'd had a few. He thought of the story as he fed some pound coins into the slot machine.

Would the story make it through without absolute proof? Or would they hold it until it was watertight? Would someone else get wind of it? And where was he going to try to sell it first? For years, the story had been here. Waiting. There was a sense of sudden excitement which he immediately suppressed, because with the excitement came the old journalist's fear that it would all be taken away – that even now some bright spark in London was staring at a computer screen or digging in an archive and making all those small connections. Perhaps even now they were reaching for a phone or walking across a newsroom towards the editor's door.

He got up and walked back to the bar. The road outside had become very dark. He was now feeling anxious about going out there again. He paid and left, hurrying through the rain towards his car. He got in and drove, slipping quietly out of the car park and on to the main road, and in no time at all he had reached the lane. He parked the car on a verge halfway down the hill and decided to go the rest of the way on foot to walk off the beer before facing Miller.

Miller's farmhouse was set back from a lane that turned off sharply and then disappeared from view amongst the

4

fields. Darkness clung to all the windows and the doors except for one, downstairs. The warmness of the pub and the glow of the village quickly faded into a dull, faraway glimmer as his footsteps thudded along the tarmac.

Down below, the farm stretched out. It was as he had imagined it would be: a ramshackle shell of a place. Some barns. A ragged garden at the back. Broken tarmac and frozen pieces of old machinery which looked like bones in the dark.

The grim landscape seemed to beckon him forward. He had been holding his breath, he realized suddenly, and now he exhaled deeply. The beginning of apprehension rose like a thread was being pulled from the bottom of his stomach as the farmhouse stretched out and grew bigger.

He reached the gate and tapped nervously on the edge of it while he waited for someone to come out to confront him. He called out, but there was no reply. For a whole minute he leant against the gate, but he could see no one. The wind sent a few leaves skittering across the fields as he walked towards the front door. The rain fell.

He rang the doorbell twice, walked through a small unkempt garden and then peered through a back window into the kitchen. He rapped on the window. Listened, but there was nothing.

He found that he was pushing against the door. Then, ever so carefully, he pressed down and pushed the door handle. The door swung open silently on its hinges, and he stepped in. There was a smell of fat coming from, he supposed, the stove. On the kitchen table were some plates and a few glasses. Someone had turned the volume off on the TV but a fire was burning in the grate. He ran his hand through his hair as he stood in the middle of the kitchen and listened, then closed his umbrella. He called out. But there was only silence.

'Mr Miller!' he shouted. 'Mr Miller! Is anyone at home?' He called out again. 'I'm sorry about barging in like this, but I was wondering if I could just have a quick word with you. It's important.' Maybe he should go outside and wait for him. The silence of the house suddenly seemed fraught with a waiting kind of menace. He stood absolutely still and waited a little longer, listening. A wide band of orange light poured through the door to the hallway and faintly shone on the kitchen floor. He took a few steps further in. Again he called out, his voice echoing loudly into the silence.

He stood by the kitchen table, feeling hesitant. His own fear flickered. He should leave. Yes, he would come back in the morning, that would be the best thing. He turned on his heel and pushed the back door open, deciding suddenly that he'd had enough. He had never meant to get this far; had never really imagined that he would be standing alone here in this house. He pushed open the door and then very suddenly turned around. He crossed the kitchen before he could change his mind.

The lights from the hallway cast only a single yellow glare on to the corridor's dusty carpet. He was standing poised in the kitchen doorway when he got a whiff of something acrid from the end of the corridor. The smell came to him ever so slightly and then almost immediately became much stronger. He took a step further inside the hallway.

The door, blown by the wind, suddenly slammed shut behind him. A smell of . . . burning? He peered in more closely and saw a faint orange glow reflecting against the wall. Again, it dawned on him ever so slowly where he was. He was in Miller's house. Standing *right* in the middle of it, and the distance between him and his car suddenly seemed very great. He stood completely still.

Then he took a step forward, towards the stairs, and rested his hand on the smooth curve of the banisters. A shadow rose, flickering along the floor, and then the tiniest plume of coiling smoke pushed its way across the hallway and was gone. The smell instantly became stronger.

Carefully, he moved further inside the house and began to edge his way along the corridor. He pushed open the door of the living room. It was full of heavy, old-fashioned furniture. The fire was lit in here as well, but it burned much higher in the grate and the television was on.

Suddenly the room seemed too hot. The glow of the fire was now a glare and the flames flickered greedily in the room while the smoke poured black and thick through the chimney's throat. Something was in the fire. But he didn't really want to look at it. The back of the armchair in front of the TV blocked it. With some effort, he looked away from the fire and out of the window. He wanted to go and throw the windows open. But he

7

couldn't move. He caught his own wild-eyed reflection in a window-pane and thought, Christ what am I doing? *Get out. Get out. Get out.* The flames threw a sudden bright shadow on to paint peeling from the walls.

An expression of sudden and acute disgust crossed his face as the smell filled his nostrils and the logs splintered and sent out sparks on to the hearth. His mind turned away from what he was seeing, and he started to think about other fires that had been lit in this very hearth in long-ago dead days. The coals glowing, then cold. The last trace of smoke billowing up and out to a day no one alive now remembered.

He approached the back of the chair, almost watching himself do so. Digging into the dark material at the back of the chair was a rope. He had thought, as he had seen tongs and a roasting spit, that Miller had been cooking something in the fire, but when he looked closer he realized it was a piece of meat which was burning in the grate. Then he saw a burnt towel lying on the floor. He turned back and finally looked at the man sitting in the chair.

A scream rose up in his throat and got caught there. It was Miller undoubtedly – he recognized him from the pictures he had seen – but older now. The man's arms were tied around the back of the chair. His eyes stared upwards towards the ceiling. Blood soaked his shirt, reached all the way down to his lap and collected in a large pool around his muddy boots.

Miller's face had been beaten to a pulp. His nose had been split wide open. In the gaping mouth, a ragged stump of flesh was visible behind his teeth. Someone had used the tongs to reach in and pull out his tongue. Pulled it out by the root and then flung it into the fire, where it now lay, burned to cinders. Perhaps Miller had been made to watch, and the last thing he ever saw was his own tongue burning in the grate.

The noise of the fire suddenly seemed to roar in his ears. Sweat was pouring from his face and down his cheeks and all the way down his neck and his back. He wiped his forehead roughly with the sleeve of his coat. The room was full of the smell of burning meat. He looked down. Miller's eyes were like two pieces of black polished glass. The reflection of the fire seemed to grow in brightness and spread until two identical balls of flame bloomed large, as if Miller's eyes blazed darkly into his own. He turned away. And, even as he did so, he was thinking about the story.

It would be his redemption. The story widened and expanded and he knew right then that all of it had to be true. All his past sins would be forgiven. He could go back. They would *have* to take him back. He thought of his mobile. Of course. And he began to check all his pockets one by one. It wasn't there. He'd left the damn thing in the car.

It was then that a door leading to a hall on the other side of the room began to open. He let out a weak shout of sudden and muffled shock. His mouth moved but nothing came out apart from a low, pathetic whimper. He raised his hand to stop them, to explain. They were looking right at him. Both of them. Their eyes looked almost impossibly dark. Almost like Miller's. They had been there all along.

The fire made a dull thundering echo that grew the longer he stood there. He could feel the flames rising in the fireplace, but he just stood there in dazed fascination, unable to tear his eyes away from them. They took a few steps forward; he backed away, not wanting to see them. A few steps and then a few more. He bumped into a small table, almost tripping over, managed to hold his footing, slammed hard into the wall of the hallway and then started to run. They waited for a few seconds. And then they started to run too.

# I

When I saw Russell and Varley walking out of the station and towards their car, I decided to go with them and got in the front passenger's seat. I told them I needed some fresh air and could do with the ride, and they didn't argue. We drove slowly through Moreton-in-Marsh, and Russell put his foot down as we left the town. They told me where they were going and I nodded and didn't say a word.

I stared out of the window. We drove and I thought about Powell, still unable to believe it in a way. The rain pouring down the windscreen and amongst the trees made everything worse. It hadn't stopped raining for almost a week. Powell was gone. I tried to make it sink in, but I still could not quite take in the magnitude of it. I would never see him again, and my last memory of him would be his frail shadow and the brown walls of the small waiting room and his son, Alex, pacing up and down outside.

Varley moved forward in the backseat. He was young with pale blue eyes and a thin face. He looked, as always, slightly surprised and taken aback. 'The car's been there around a week. So we're just going to take a quick look at it and see what's up. That's all. So we won't be out there long. No one reported it to begin with. You know, they probably thought it had to be there for a reason, or someone would have come along sooner or later to take it away. Not many people about because of the holidays and the New Year. Then a few people started to notice it, and then someone had a proper look. Anyway, no big deal, sir. I can't imagine that we will be out there long. Of course we can stay longer if you like. I mean, if you want to go off on your own somewhere. That would be fine . . . I mean we'd understand, sir. If that's what you think you might like,' Varley added awkwardly.

Varley kept on talking, but I didn't pay much attention. There had been an oppressive air in the station all day after word had got round about Powell. And they had both seemed relieved to be heading out and leaving the sombre mood behind them – until I'd decided to come with them, that is.

The car was parked on a verge halfway down a hill, on a lane which dipped down into the hills. It had a slumped-in look to it, as if it had been sitting in that place just a little too long. Varley got out and started to inspect it, peering through the windows, while Russell, still sitting in the warmth of his car, entered the number plate into the computer and waited for it to come up. It did so almost immediately.

'London,' Russell said to himself with distaste and stared a little longer at the screen.

Routine. The kind of things police constables do all the time. I reached for my umbrella, got out and stretched my legs, glad to be outside despite the rain.

'Someone smashed the window,' Varley said sadly.

'No alarm?'

'No. Bit of an old banger,' Varley said. 'Hardly worth it. Kids probably. Just messing about. They didn't nick the radio you see.'

Russell began to stroll down towards the farmhouse, a clipboard in one hand and an umbrella in the other. He hummed a Christmas pop song. I turned away and wandered around and had a look at the village, but there wasn't much to see. Then a few minutes later I sauntered back towards the car. Varley was standing at the top of the hill, and I stood next to him, staring down.

Russell was running. He was in his mid-forties and he had for as long as I had known him sported a big walrus moustache, but just before Christmas he'd shaved it off – a present, I'd heard, for his wife, who had been begging him to get rid of it for years. It looked like he hadn't run in a long time and had almost forgotten how to do it.

'What's he playing at?' Varley said quietly. 'I bet you a tenner he doesn't make it to the top of the hill.'

'You're on,' I said.

Varley hesitated and then looked at me and said, 'I was sorry to hear about Powell, sir. I know that we've been expecting it, but it doesn't make it any easier, does it? The same thing happened to my gran. Last year that was. I'm going to try to make it to the funeral if I can. Len,' he said, bestowing one of the highest English compliments, 'was a good bloke. He were always nice to me anyway.'

'Thanks, Varley,' I said meaning it.

13

Russell's belly jiggled above his belt as he ran. Then he gave up and started walking.

'I told you,' Varley said.

I reached into my pocket and handed him two five-pound notes; Varley took them and put them in his pocket.

'Silly sod's gone and left his umbrella somewhere,' Varley said. 'And where's he left his clipboard?'

Russell took a deep breath and then, with a great deal of effort pushed on. He reached the top of the hill and paused again to catch his breath. Varley looked on, amused.

Russell wiped the water from his eyes. 'There's a . . . a . . . There's a . . . Oh, Jesus. Hold on a sec.'

Russell bent over, gasping for breath, and stared at his shoes. Then he straightened up. 'You'd better come and have a look, sir,' he said.

## 2

Brewin stood over the dead man in the kitchen while his assistant, Fiona, stared at the small cuts on his fingers. Brewin had put on a few kilos over Christmas and the straight, white boiler suit made his belly more pronounced. He folded his arms over his stomach and the papery material of the suit rustled. He looked too big for his job, as if his hands would be too clumsy and thick-fingered for the minute work needed to inspect and later dissect a corpse. His brushed the top of his flattened nose with the back of his thumb and sniffed loudly. Then he moved nimbly around the body on the floor and kneeled, taking in the mark below the victim's chin before standing up and self-consciously feeling his belly with the tops of his fingers as the white suit strained against it. Fiona watched him, half smiling.

'I know, I know. Another damned diet, Fiona.' Annoyed with himself, he let out a long sigh and, catching me looking at him, said, 'Not a word from you either, Guillermo. I get enough of all that from the damned doctor.'

I peered around at the wreck of the kitchen. Overturned jars of coffee, rice, sugar and pasta were in the sink. Crockery lay in shards, and a smashed bottle of beer was in the middle of a puddle on the floor.

Shelves and chairs had been upturned. The contents of boxes and crates had been tipped out, pots and pans thrown on their sides. Whole shelves had been ripped right out of the walls.

It wasn't just the kitchen. The whole house had been searched from top to bottom. The chaos continued all the way through the hall, where clothes lay strewn along the carpet. Old books and the pages of magazines and newspapers were scattered on the stairs, and shoes and boots and more clothes had been hurled downward and now formed a dirty heap by the wall. Pillows, mattresses and cushions had been ripped open: feathers mixed with torn-open packets of food and shards of glass. The smell, though, was the worst part: it coiled its way around the entire house, creating a gagging stink. It was inescapable.

There was a heaving sensation in my chest when I looked down at the body on the floor. This was quite natural and would soon go away. Already I was fixing on the underlying feeling I had: the impression that they had left behind them. It was a kind of careless contempt. Contempt for both men. The man lying on the floor had been taken care of very efficiently, as far as I could tell. Then, after they had gone through his wallet, they had just tossed it at his feet.

I peered down at him. He was heavyset but not as big as Brewin and with thinning brown hair. He had a fairly solid jaw. It looked as if he had fallen over as he had tried to get out through the back door. There was a great deal of blood on the floor and around his neck and around the table legs, as he had clearly tried to get up. Falling, he had hit his head with a huge amount of force against the table and somehow knocked over a chair, but most of the blood came from somewhere beneath his chin, where he had been stabbed, and more than once by the looks of it.

'No sign of the weapon?' I said, straightening up.

'No. None.'

'But, like I say, more than one assailant, we think,' Brewin said. 'Maybe one assailant for this fella here but two for the other victim in the living room.'

I nodded and looked around a little longer, thinking about the two bodies lying here amongst this chaos for days. The man we were looking at had been taken care of with brutal, unhesitating efficiency.

'As he was trying to crawl away – in a clockwise motion – they lifted him up so that his head would have been around here,' Fiona said and pointed to a level just above her waist. 'They used a knife and repeatedly stabbed him. The wound that actually killed him was just below the chin.'

I nodded, a low feeling of apprehension in my gut. Everything looked chaotic, with all the mess and the blood which had pooled on the tiles. But the killing itself was actually quite neat. They had grabbed him under the chin, where they could get a good purchase, and then cut him so that the blood would flow away from them. No blood on their clothes that way.

'You can see that he tried to get up. There may have been another attempt to stand up. But a few more seconds after that he would have lost consciousness altogether. And a few moments after that . . .' Fiona shrugged.

'He was dead,' Brewin said, unable to resist having the last word. Brewin sighed before motioning for me to follow him.

We headed through the hallway, into the living room and stopped at the chair. The other victim was in his early forties with a mop of black tangled hair which was streaked with grey. He was wearing faded jeans and a red-and-black chequered work shirt and heavy work boots. He had a big, powerful-looking body. Forearms packed with lean sinewy muscle poked out of the frayed cuffs of the sleeves behind his back. Everything about him seemed to make everything else look too small, and the chair he was tied to seemed like it might crumple under his weight. There was a look on his face. Contempt hiding his fear. He was wearing a cheap digital watch which looked childish compared with the size of his hands, and poking just above the collar of his shirt was the tail of an animal which twisted along his collarbone.

'We'll do the autopsy first thing tomorrow on both of them,' Brewin said. 'But I don't think it's going to tell us much that we don't already know. There're a few defensive wounds on this chap as well. But they're different. To begin with, they weren't done by a knife. It looks like he was kicked and punched. Probably outside, judging from all the mud on his clothes and the blood stains at the side of the house. Then they brought him back inside and tied him to this chair. There's no front window in here – only a back window. So they had plenty of time to do exactly what they wanted to him. But not for as long as they wanted.'

'Wanted? What do you mean?'

'Well, I think they made a mistake, Guillermo. Outside. They were searching for something, right? They got rid of that other fellow quick enough in the kitchen there. That's a very, very neat job they did in there. That one in the kitchen . . . I don't even want to think about it right now. It was quick, but that makes it worse and you know as well as I do why that is.'

'They know what they're doing.'

Brewin nodded. 'Quite. So they've probably had practice. But they made a mistake with this poor bugger and he paid for it.' Brewin took a step away from me, to the other side of the chair. 'After they brought him back in here, someone pulled or yanked more than once at his hair, causing trauma to his scalp. There was a specific reason for that, I think.'

'Go on.'

'I think by the time they brought him in here he was unconscious. There's a few scrapes along his knuckles, so they might well have got more than they bargained for outside. And the pulling at his hair could have been an attempt to try to revive him and snap him back into consciousness. They might have been angry with him too by the time they got him into this chair. But the fracture here on his head may well have started an intracranial haemorrhage – a slow bleed into his brain. It could have occurred when they attacked him outside and he fell or when he was kicked. He might have been slipping in and out of consciousness the whole time.'

'But the beating's not what killed him?'

'No.' Brewin shrugged, looking gloomy and tense as he stared towards the grate. 'You noticed the towel I suppose?'

I nodded. I hadn't got the finer details straight in my mind when I first saw him. The towel was a small incongruous detail compared with the rest of the room, which was in the same state of chaos as everywhere else. The towel had been tossed near the hearth.

'His lips and the inside of his mouth are covered in third-degree burns,' Brewin said.

I looked down at the victim's face. I had suspected this but had not wanted to think about it. I felt a kind of wild despair when I forced myself to realize what they had done to him.

'Burns are always the worst to look at,' Brewin said. 'He died of neurogenic shock. Insufficient blood flow throughout the body. It would have actually been quick once the worst part was over. I know it doesn't look like it right now but the moment that thing over there' – Brewin pointed to the tongs – 'touched his lips, he would have opened his mouth. No choice. Then they reached in. As soon as the edges made contact with the inside of his mouth, he bit down so hard on to the metal that he cracked at least three of his front teeth and maybe broke his jaw as well.'

I looked at the fire-tongs. Probably they hadn't planned on using them. More likely the idea had come to them when they had seen the implement lying next to the grate. Perhaps they had goaded each other on and left the tongs to heat up as they threatened to use them on him. Then one of them had actually gone and done it. It could have worked that way.

'If it was someone he knew, he must have realized he was in trouble straight away, right?' I said.

Brewin grunted.

'But he wouldn't or couldn't tell them what they wanted to know,' I said. 'He probably expected no mercy and got none.'

'It was a punishment, you think, Guillermo?'

'Could be.'

I turned around, thinking. There could have been other ways to do it. They could have rung the front door and then rushed him. But out in the dark they would have had more of an advantage. So they knew what kind of man they were up against and planned it beforehand.

I headed down the corridor and tried the front door. It was locked and bolted from the inside. And there was a lot of dust on the threadbare carpet. So they knew he would not have used the front door when he came home but used the back. They had been here before and maybe even watched him from far off.

The towel near the hearth was light blue and dainty and looked innocuous enough until you saw the charred burn mark running like a scar all the way along the top edge. They had probably fetched the towel from the bathroom so they could pick the tongs out of the fire when they were

21

hot enough. It had probably been the only way they could get his mouth open. After they had pulled out his tongue, they had thrown the tongs towards the fire. There was an efficiency here all right, but there was something else too: a sickness coiled up right inside it.

# 3

I looked around the house a little longer before heading outside. It had stopped raining after what seemed like days. But then suddenly it started again. The wind picked up, slowly at first, pushing leaves which swirled in widening circles along the path. I saw Irwin, tall and angular with a large Adam's apple and beaky face, heading towards me.

'Any luck?' I said.

'The one in the kitchen,' he said, peering through the window, 'well, that's George Finn.'

'This is his house?'

'No. Finn's a journalist.'

'Local?'

'No. He works for a tabloid up in London, or he used to. That's his car up there on the hill. Well, not his car. He borrowed it from an ex and didn't tell her he was taking it. He took it five days ago and she hasn't seen him since.'

'Does she know what he was doing out here?'

'No. They split up ages ago and she hasn't seen him for over a month. But he still had the keys to her flat. He went to her flat when she was out at work, left a note and said he'd be back that night. He took the car keys and drove straight out here by the looks of it and

23

never came back. He was asking questions all day about the owner of this house. A fella called Lee Miller.'

'The other victim?'

'Yes. Finn,' he said motioning to the kitchen, 'was on suspension from the paper – indefinitely. He'd spent his whole time here asking about Miller. They won't say why he was suspended. But it sounds serious, so I've asked the Super to look into it for us. The editor says he can't tell us anything about it until he's spoken to the paper's lawyers, so hopefully the Super can speed things up. She probably will, knowing her.'

'So the paper didn't send him out here?'

'No, it's the first the editor has heard of it. He'd never even heard of Miller or this village. And Finn never said who he actually worked for, but he arrived around mid-day and started to knock on doors and ask questions. He gave his card to just one villager, because the old dear told him a juicy story about Miller being a scary kind of guy. Her words. He actually wrote that down. She regretted it afterwards and phoned the tabloid in a flap, using the card he'd given her, but they didn't know what she was talking about. And when someone else did ask which paper, he said it would be in all of them.'

'All of them?' I said, surprised.

'That's what he said.'

'Pretty sure of himself, wasn't he?'

Irwin nodded. 'Cocky type of guy. That's the impression we're getting of him, sir. And slick. Took the whole place by surprise. Well, you know what these guys are like.

Sounds like he was on to something, though. Comes all the way out here to knock on doors in the rain. Most of them let him in because of the weather.'

'First time he'd been here?'

'Yes, by the sounds of it. The editor reckons that if he had found something, he would have tried to sell it somewhere else. Anywhere but where he used to work.'

'So he was angry about the suspension?'

'Livid.'

'And what was the story?'

'No one seems to know. He was being very, very cagey. Was interested in Miller but never said what it was about. Just that he was after background stuff. He hit the pub. Seemed a bit edgy in there. The barman talked to him but no one else: they didn't like the idea of Miller waking up and reading that they'd been gossiping about him behind his back in the Sunday papers. So he left the pub at around seven.'

'And walked in on something.'

'That's what it looks like. Maybe tried the front door. Could have headed towards the living room, seen Miller tied to that chair in front of the fire. Maybe Miller was still alive at that point. We don't know. Tried to leg it. Ran into that table in the hall. But they caught up with him in the kitchen. Then, when they'd finished with him, they went through his stuff.'

'It's all gone?'

'Yes. A few villagers saw him with a laptop, a camera and a tape recorder. Disappeared, along with his wallet and mobile. Some kids broke the window because they were bored, but they swear that there was nothing in the car and they didn't take anything.'

'So this journalist comes along and asks about Miller all afternoon. He didn't seem interested in anything else?'

'Nope. Seemed to know all about him too.'

'But who is Miller?' I said.

'Half the village seemed to have been scared shitless of him. He'd just been released from prison.'

'Prison,' I said, surprised.

'Yes. Armed robbery. He got out in August after a twelve year stretch. He'd been inside before for the same offence. Anyway, this farm used to belong to Miller's old man. But he died and the place has been abandoned for years. Miller had been living in London since he was a teenager, but for some reason decided to come back here when he was released. But, sir, there's nothing here for a top London journalist to get all worked up about. I mean, as far as I can tell, Miller was just a criminal.'

'So Finn could have been here because of something to do with Miller's past. His criminal past, I mean.'

Irwin nodded. 'That's what it looks like. But no one knows exactly what it is.' Irwin moved towards the back door. He walked quickly as always and stepped neatly into the kitchen. His eyes surveyed the chaos before straying towards the body on the floor. He remained silent for a moment longer. He looked cold and tired and disappointed, as if he had hoped to warm up inside the house but it was freezing.

'And there's something else,' he said over his shoulder. He stopped and turned around. 'Sorry, sir, but we missed it to begin with. With all the mess in here, it was hard to tell, and it's been a bit chaotic trying to get the SOCO team organized outside. Well, it looks like Miller had someone staying with him, and he's done a runner. There's a spare room and someone has been sleeping in it. At first we thought it might have been a squatter who was here while Miller was inside. And maybe Miller kicked him out on his arse when he got back from jail. But I had another look and the clothes he left behind don't fit that: they look new. And some of the villagers are saying that Miller had someone staying with him over Christmas.'

Irwin motioned towards the hallway and I followed him up the stairs. We had to step around broken books, clothing and sheets. On the next floor, the chaos continued all the way along the corridor.

'Christ,' Irwin said, covering his nose, 'that smell is just as bad up here, isn't it?'

'What about the attic? They searched up there as well?'

Irwin nodded. 'Tore the whole place apart. They must have made a hell of a racket, but no one would have heard anything because the house is so isolated. And they really took their time, by the looks of it. I mean, it might have taken hours. What do you think they were after?'

I shrugged. 'Any strangers apart from this Finn asking about Miller?'

'No.'

'And we're sure they didn't take anything of value?'

'Not as far as we can tell, sir.'

'Any relatives for Miller?'

'Just an aunt, we think. Lives over in Shipston.'

Irwin weaved around a broken vase and some shoes lying in the middle of the landing. He led me to a small cupboard-sized room. An old mattress had been hurled against a wall. A sleeping bag had been turned inside out, and a brand-new-looking suitcase, its contents piled in a heap, lay on the floor. The clothes too looked new, though inexpensive.

'So this isn't Miller's room? We're sure about that, are we?'

'We don't think so. We thought it might be just some kind of box room used for storage. Miller's room is further up the corridor, on the other side of the house.'

'You been through all of this?'

'Yes. No wallet, no ID. Just these clothes.'

I walked across the room and looked through the small dusty window.

'What about Graves?' Irwin said finally. 'You want me to phone him? I know he's got tomorrow off but we could use him.'

I paused, thinking. 'All right, call him,' I said a little reluctantly. 'Tell him what's happening and that we'll need him first thing tomorrow, so he'll have to drop whatever he's doing and get back here tonight.'

'He's not going to be too happy about it,' Irwin said half to himself.

'Why not?' I said sharply.

'Sorry, sir.' Irwin suddenly looked sheepish. 'He's got a date,' Irwin said, embarrassed. 'Been going on about her for days.'

'That was fast,' I said, genuinely impressed. 'He's only been out here a few weeks. Who is she?'

'She's not local, sir. An ex, I think. Left him high and dry years ago,' Irwin said, looking around.

'Well, you'd better call him anyway.'

Through the window, I watched Irwin leave, thinking that it was strange to talk of dates and girlfriends in a place like this. The police constables were marching across the yard to the waiting vans, where a constable was already uncapping a huge thermos flask ready for their arrival. The search would be more systematic tomorrow when it was light. I shoved my chin deep inside my collar and looked down at the falling rain.

Bright lights shone from all the windows and spread out into the yard. I realized that I hadn't thought about Powell for hours, and I was almost grateful for the double murder.

A squad car pulled up, and I stared for a little while at the rain captured in the headlights of the car. I stripped away all the sounds around me and imagined the men coming in here. The chaos as they searched the house. Plates breaking. The noise of books tearing. They were looking for something small, then, if they were looking inside books. A letter? Money? Something that would fit. Feet thundering along the hallway. What kind of men were they? Men from the outside? Or local? What were we up against? What was

29

there in Miller's past which had sealed his fate? And why hadn't he been ready for them?

Up in the village, the policemen would be banging on every door amongst the worried, peering faces. Like an occupying army under my command, the uniformed mobs had swept in. I was glad of them. Glad of the power I could control. I suddenly felt another low feeling of apprehension: I was on the trail of men who were no strangers to violence, men who seemed at ease with it, which meant that there was a fundamental flaw in their personalities. It did not sicken them as it sickened me.

I looked outside a little longer. Only hours ago it had looked like half the village had walked down the hill and gathered at the other side of the road, staring at the house in a kind of subdued awe. Now it was just a mournful-faced man standing with his dog tied to a lead. He turned away and went back up the road. He seemed disappointed, as if he'd hoped to see someone pulling out a body bag.

# 4

By the time Graves got back to Moreton, it was almost twelve. Tired and frustrated, he left his car in the station car park and wandered through the town towards his hotel. He had been looking forward to his time off for days and had even in a moment of wild optimism booked a double room at a guest house in Cheltenham. But the evening had ended in unmitigated disaster, thanks to Downes. Somehow he had known it would right from the start. As always, Amanda put him on the back foot at dinner, so he had struggled for things to say and been nervous. It had been so bad that it had almost been a relief when the phone began to ring from his pocket. By the time he had got off the phone with Irwin, who had insisted on telling him every single detail of the case and seemed perfectly happy to ruin his evening, Amanda was fuming. She told him straight away, and in no uncertain terms, that she would be taking the next train to London and wouldn't be staying any longer. So the whole thing had been a bust. But Amanda was like that. She had been like that when he had met her. She wasn't used to being ignored.

Well, it would probably do her some good, Graves thought bitterly. She had been getting her own way since she was born, which made her spoilt and . . . He walked under the shadow of a tree and gazed at the closed curtains of the houses. What was he doing out here anyway? He suddenly felt trapped. What if he really did get permanently stuck out here in the middle of nowhere?

He continued on past a small supermarket and the bank. His stomach growled beneath his shirt. He put his hands deep inside his pockets and found himself thinking of Downes. Ever since Graves had arrived here, he'd had the feeling that Downes had secretly been examining him; from time to time, he'd noticed Downes staring at him from the corner of his eye, as if he had forgotten who he was or as if he still had half a mind to get rid of him. He looked around at the desolate town. Wondered again how it had all happened. It had been fine to begin with, because they had been so busy, but now . . . it was just so damned quiet. The idea that anything could happen out here seemed absurd somehow. The houses were too orderly. The gardens too neat. There were just so many old people around, he thought unkindly. They were all tucked up in bed snoring their heads off by now.

At his hotel, he picked a bag of laundry they had ready for him at reception, climbed the thick, heavy carpet to his room, put the bag on the bed and then raided the mini bar for snacks and a beer.

He toyed with the idea of not phoning Amanda, but ended up phoning her almost as soon as he was through the door. She didn't answer, so he left another message of apologies and hung up.

She had looked incredible, as always, when he had picked her up from the station. Even more gorgeous than he remembered her. She had dropped him years ago at university, just before his finals, without a care in the world; he had assumed at the time that she had never looked back. But she had spotted him half asleep on a packed train to London on the way home to his parents' house on Christmas Eve and things had moved on again from there. Or at least he thought they had. Now he wasn't quite sure what was going on.

Over the years he had envisaged the moment when he saw her again for the very first time. He would be arresting a dangerous-looking felon or leaving a swanky restaurant arm in arm with some amazing blonde; and he would have given her a cold stare, as if he could not quite remember who she was, and then coolly saunter off.

But, as it turned out, he had been having a nightmare on the train, a remnant of his first few days with Downes. He had been dreaming of a big empty house in the Cotswolds and a body buried deep beneath it, pulling itself from the earth like in a film, dragging its way towards him on skeletal hands. And when Amanda shook him by the arm and woke him up, the first thing he did was to knock a cup of cold coffee all over the table and on to the lap of an old man who howled with rage and harangued him almost constantly on the way back to London. She had found the whole thing highly amusing.

Now it was as if they were behaving like two old friends who had by some great stroke of luck got back in touch after many years. But there was something else afoot. He could feel it. Well, there had been until tonight.

Rather like his mother, Amanda, deep down, disapproved of his career. When he returned home for Christmas, his mother had at first seemed quite interested when he spoke about the weeks he had spent on a murder case in the Cotswolds. He'd been hopeful, but realized very quickly from her strained expression that she had found the whole affair rather sordid, which, of course, it was if you really stopped to think about it, and his father had sat there grimacing, bewildered, as if he had stopped listening exactly at the point Graves told him about Downes's nationality.

'An Argy,' he had said, sitting up in his chair and rustling his newspaper. 'What on earth is an Argy doing all the way out there in the middle of the Cotswolds?' he said, looking over his paper and helping himself to yet another Christmas chocolate. 'I mean why *there*? Of all the places some fellow from Argentina could end up, why there? In the middle of nowhere.'

'He's half English,' Graves ended up saying, justifying himself as usual to his parents, which ultimately he knew was useless. 'Actually, he was here. Here in London for a while. But he got . . .'

'What?' his father said, interested all of a sudden. 'Canned, you mean. So something happened over here in London as well? Same as you in Oxford. Well, well.' His father had seemed immensely pleased with himself.

'But I –'

'So they sent him packing. It sounds like he probably deserved it, after all you've been telling us. My God, jumping into wells and burning buildings. Whatever was the man thinking? That's no way to behave.'

Graves shook his head. He watched television for a while, unable to sleep in the uncomfortable hotel bed, wondering if perhaps his parents had been right and maybe Amanda too. After all, he was still young and his career wasn't exactly taking off, was it? He suddenly remembered feeling as if he had been placed on a production line that went straight from public school to university and then to a job in the City, his whole life seemingly laid out for him up until that point. As if he had been meant to follow a plan. But something had definitely happened to him when Amanda dumped him, and he had never really been able to figure out exactly why.

He grinned ruefully. Joining the police was, he supposed, his version of joining the Foreign Legion. Something rather old-fashioned and therefore very much like him in that regard. But had he really done a good job of it? Did he even like it? Was he even driven, like Downes? Seeing Amanda had reminded him just how cut off from everyone he had become. And then there had been that incident back in Oxford. He still felt a cold sharp feeling of anger in the bottom of his stomach when he thought of it. This wasn't at all what he had expected: to end up exiled.

He opened another beer, hoping to get some sleep eventually. But it was no use. He couldn't stop thinking about Amanda or about what he was going to do. He thought back to his transfer out here to the Cotswolds and his superintendent telling him that he would be working with a senior officer. Of course he had known it was coming, but for some reason the news had surprised him, because it had all happened so quickly. There had been a ghost of a smile on the Super's lips but his eyes had remained hard. Graves started to walk up and down in his room as he remembered.

For Graves, who had been hoping at the time for London, or Birmingham at a pinch, the Cotswolds might as well have been Mars. Disappointment and anger clawed at him so that even now, over a month later, he felt a hollow feeling at the base of his gut when he thought about it.

'But doesn't he already have a sergeant?' he'd asked the Super.

'His sergeant is ill. Actually, he's dying.' The Superintendent's features softened, as if he were searching for just the right amount of sympathy in his expression but no more. But he seemed to give up half-way through. 'Anyway, this fella has been out there for some time. So it's quite an opportunity for you, Graves. Look: big fish; small pond. When we saw his name, we immediately thought of you. He's pretty well known in the force up there.'

'But you don't know him?'

'No, not personally. More know *of* him actually. He was pointed out to me once – at a rugger match years ago.'

'Pointed out to you, sir – but why?'

'I can't remember now. Their lads versus our lot. Almost ended up in a full-scale brawl as usual. He got sent off, if I remember. Argued with the ref or punched someone in the face – or kicked them.' The Super frowned. 'Can't remember now. Good player, though.'

'But has he been informed?' Graves asked warily. 'Does he know that he's going to be . . . working with someone else?'

'Yes. He's agreed to it, although I must warn you that he was extremely reluctant at first. But he's a strange kind of fella – and very, very curious. He's foreign. A chief inspector. Named Downes.' The Super waved his hand with a flourish as he said, 'Guillermo.' His pronunciation made the name sound French. 'Guillermo Downes.'

But the name didn't sound French to Graves.

He had been aware that the Super was staring at him very intensely across the desk. He looked vaguely troubled. Worried even, as if the name would be enough to scare him off or put him on his guard.

'Big tall fella. He's a got a scar right here,' the Super said, pointing to his skull. 'So you can't miss him. He's extremely experienced, so you're going to learn from him. But you're going to have to learn fast. And he's not everyone's . . .' The Super paused and then said, 'Well, he's not everyone's cup of tea, to be perfectly honest. Started off in the Cotswolds, I believe, and then got sent to London a long time ago – in Brixton. Quickly made a name for himself but left abruptly. Better you hear that from me first.' He raised his hand, warding off the question that he knew was coming. 'Don't ask me why, because I don't know the ins and outs of it. It's probably all been blown out of proportion by now anyway. These things usually are. But it all got a bit nasty. And it looks like he's got his own way of doing things. Maybe you can talk some sense into him when you get to know him.' The Super added, with false joviality, 'Use some of that famous charm of yours, Graves.'

Graves, looking at him, had said, 'So that's it, then?'

'I beg your pardon?' the Super said.

'That's it,' Graves said, unable to stop himself, as usual. 'I'm going to get sent out there. That's the thanks I get.'

The Super looked at him without saying anything and wiped his forehead in exasperation. But what he said next surprised Graves.

'Surely you didn't expect anything else?' he said. 'Don't tell me you didn't know that this was coming.'

'Not this fast.'

'You know, Graves, it wouldn't be a bad idea to stop feeling sorry for yourself. You were lucky. Very, very lucky. There were people – people who have been here a long time – who wanted you gone. And gone for good. They might have had their way eventually if it hadn't been for Downes.'

'Sir?'

The Super's face suddenly went blank, as if he had already said more than enough.

'They figure that if they stick you two together in the same room for long enough you'll either drive each other mad or Downes'll do something to get you sacked. They want you forgotten. They want you buried for what you've done.'

Graves nodded. Yes. He understood that now.

'So if I were you, I'd tread very lightly indeed when you're out there. And if he steps out of line – if he does anything wrong, you let someone know – you let the right person know this time. You don't go over anyone's head. Otherwise you'll be stuck out there forever, just like him.'

Graves finished his beer, chucked it in the bin and got up from the bed. He didn't want to think about it any more. God, what was he going to do? Amanda had thrown everything into doubt and he didn't know why. He suddenly wished he'd never seen her again. He ran himself a bath and was just slipping into it when the phone by his bed began to ring. He padded across the carpet, hoping that it was Amanda in spite of everything. But of course it wasn't her. Not her style to ring at two thirty in the morning. He listened to the receptionist, hung up and quickly grabbed his clothes from the floor.

## 5

Graves changed in less than two minutes flat, shut the door and sprinted downstairs, still putting a jumper over his head. His hair was wet from his two-minute bath, and got wetter as he rushed out into the rain. Downes was waiting for him in his car at the front of the hotel.

Without a word Downes took off as soon as Graves was inside and fastening his seatbelt. Despite his fear of being in the backseat – hence the nickname Shotgun – Downes could be an absolute maniac when he was in a hurry. He floored it as they left the village behind and the car plunged away from the few lights of the town.

'What's going on?' Graves said.

'How was your night off?' Downes said.

'Wonderful. Where are we going?'

'To the house.'

'Miller's house?'

'Yes.'

'Why?'

'One of the locals just called the station. A squad car's been sent ahead. But they're not to do anything until we get there.'

'Why? What's happened?'

Downes glanced in the rear-view mirror with a bland look in his eye. 'Miller had someone staying with him. A man called Stanley.'

'Yes, I know all that,' Graves said irritably. 'Irwin told me you didn't have a name.'

'We do now. By the sounds of it,' Downes said and changed gear, 'this Stanley fella left the village as soon as he saw what had happened to Miller. Just turned around and left. But now it looks like he's come back,' he said, pleased.

'Come back? But why would he come back? And why wait this long? I don't get it.'

Downes smiled. 'Well, hopefully we're going to find out. The men who were after Miller were after something in that house of his. And he might lead us straight to it if we're clever about it and don't make a mess of it. He was with Miller for around a month. Was out the afternoon Miller was killed. One of the old women in the village saw him waiting outside the bus stop and getting on the bus to Cheltenham. It looks like he returned, went to the house and then headed straight to the pub. One of the villagers gave us a name, but she wasn't sure, and we weren't able to confirm it until the pub opened up and we were able to talk to the locals. A lot of the people were at work this afternoon when we carried out the door-to-door as well. This Stanley seemed to leave the farm only to go to the pub. He was in there quite a bit and they remember that night. He was as white as a sheet when he walked in. Asked for a lift to Oxford.'

'Oxford?'

'Yes. So he could get the bus to London.'

'No trains from Moreton at that time.'

'No one would give him a lift. So he had a big tantrum about it in the middle of the pub and left. It's the last they saw of him. Didn't have any of his bags. So they just assumed he'd had some kind of argument with Miller. And, knowing Miller, they didn't want to get involved.'

'So he might have come back to look for something?'

Downes didn't say anything. Instead he motioned to a blue file on the backseat.

Graves reached around and picked it up. Through the blue plastic sheeting he could see Miller's ethnical appearance, sex and date of birth all written in bold – and underneath what looked like the beginning of a very long list.

'The villagers weren't exaggerating for once,' Downes said with genuine surprise. 'In fact, it's even worse than most of them think.'

Graves began to read. 'Aggravated assault outside a nightclub in Cheltenham,' Graves said, turning the page. 'Miller was only fifteen. Then he went to London. Still very young. There are a few more incidents locally. After that it becomes serious' – he flipped the page – 'and even more serious when he goes back to London. Then he was here again and interviewed again, when he was –'

'Seventeen.'

'But it doesn't say why. Then for a few years nothing, until' – Graves drew his finger down the page – 'he's

convicted for the first time, as an accessory in London.'
Graves whistled. 'Armed robbery.'

'A high street jeweller in London,' Downes said. 'They
think he was involved in a number of similar robberies
with a gang. Same MO. Altogether, perhaps conspiracy to
commit twenty criminal acts.'

'And the gang members?'

'Never identified. They used to go in with crowbars
and swords and attack jewellers during busy trading hours.
They used balaclavas to disguise themselves and stolen
cars to get away. They got Miller as he was fleeing the
scene. He was only twenty. They gave him ten years but he
served eight. Then they got him again. Only three years
later. Jewellery again. Smaller firms. Some of them outside of London. One of them as far off as Yorkshire. In
all, they made off with more than £100,000 worth of stuff.
They had a good run for a while but it didn't last forever.'

'What happened?'

'There was a struggle in a jeweller's up in Naisborough
just as they were closing up shop. Someone heard the disturbance, became suspicious and called it in. Two other
gang members got away in a car and they left him behind.'

'And he didn't say a single word while he was inside?'

'No. Not as far as we know.'

'We offered him a deal?'

'Yes. Twice. He didn't take it. He wouldn't say who the
other men were. They gave him fifteen years the second
time around but he served twelve. He was released six
months ago and moved straight back into that farmhouse.'

Graves stared at the file for a while longer. It started to rain harder but Downes didn't slow down. Graves pushed his hand through his hair and looked across at Downes. His nose had been broken more than once and there was a menacing kind of air to him of which he seemed quite aware. He was happy to use it to get what he wanted.

The scar that began at the very top of his forehead etched a long, dark line beneath his hair. Graves wondered, for what must have been the thousandth time, how Downes got it, before looking away. Rumours were rife in the station, with some saying he had got it during his childhood in Argentina; others said it was the result of an arrest a long time ago. There was even a story that it had happened in a pub fight over a woman, which Graves thought was a bit rich and almost certainly untrue. Downes's skin looked browner in the soft lights of the car, and as the trees flickered outside the window Graves wondered if anyone had ever asked him outright about the scar and how he had got it. Powell had, probably. But Powell was dead.

'So whoever came for Miller was looking for something in this house – and they didn't find it. Is that what you're thinking, sir?' Graves said.

'Could be,' Downes said as they turned a corner. He looked eager now as they approached the village. 'Buried treasure,' Downes said and smiled. 'This is what this could all be about. Miller is released from jail. He comes back here. Then they come here to get whatever it is they're looking for. Only Miller won't tell them where it is. It can't be a grudge: he never snitched on anyone. He just did his time and went home.'

'But he hadn't actually lived in the farmhouse for a while,' Graves said. 'He'd been in London for years.'

'Yes, but what if he made off with something they didn't know about until only recently? Maybe he went back to his old man's place to hide it long ago.'

'So he stored it?'

'Exactly. Perhaps it's only recently developed some value. We won't know until we find it. The place is pretty big – you'll see for yourself in a minute. Could be anywhere.' He paused for a moment, thinking. 'Maybe they got wind of it somehow. Maybe this other fella told them.'

'This Stanley?'

'Yes. Miller lets this Stanley stay on his farm. But this doesn't really fit with the picture we've got of him so far. They don't seem to have even got along that well, from what the villagers are saying. But it could be Miller owes him, so he lets him crash in his house. Stanley may well have been there for a very specific reason; he may even have been sent there to spy on Miller. Spots something of interest in his house. And makes sure he's not around when they come calling for Miller. But I could be wrong.' Downes shrugged. 'Don't forget, Graves,' he said, glancing across at him, 'it might not have anything to do with what Miller got up to in London. I think it would be a big mistake to assume that. All right, it looks like that right now. But there are plenty of people quite capable of doing that kind of thing much nearer to home. You'll find out if you stick around here long enough.' Downes looked at him shrewdly before turning his attention back to the road.

'But if this Stanley is involved somehow?'

'He makes sure he's in Cheltenham and out of the way. He's been living with Miller. Been there for around a month and so chances are he saw something. Makes the call to someone. He comes back. Sees Miller tied to that chair and the journalist lying there on the floor. Stanley couldn't have known things had gone that far; otherwise I don't think he would ever have come back. It must have been one hell of a shock. They really did a number on Miller. It's a torture murder,' Downes said in a matter-of-fact way. 'So Stanley gets out of there as fast as he can. Too scared to get his stuff from upstairs. And now, when he thinks the coast might be clear, he comes back for it.'

'He wouldn't have read about it in any of the papers,' Graves said thoughtfully. 'There might be a few paragraphs on it online but he probably doesn't have access. The nationals probably won't run anything on it until tomorrow. So it could be he assumed that the bodies still hadn't been found; or, if he does know, he's willing to chance it before we find whatever it is,' Graves said quietly.

Downes nodded.

The police car was waiting with its lights off at the top of the rise. Varley and Russell, huddled under umbrellas, were craning their heads towards the house. Downes got out and very gently shut the door.

'Still there?'

'Yes, sir,' Varley said, before nodding quickly to Graves. 'There was a light on upstairs. A torch, I think. And then it went out again. But I haven't seen it for a good while now.'

'How long?'

'About half an hour.'

'You got the other side blocked?'

'Yes, sir. Cleaver's there now.'

'Cleaver,' Graves said. 'Oh, Christ, not bloody Cleaver. Let's hope he's still awake,' he said, remembering Cleaver's tendency to fall asleep on duty. Standing a little way off was a man around Graves's age. He looked down at his arms, seemed to manage by some huge effort of will not to flex them, and then looked up. He was wearing a coat which looked too small for his shoulders. He rolled them as Graves stared at him and the leather creaked.

'You sure it's Stanley?' Downes asked the man.

'It's him. I'd just finished cleaning downstairs' – he motioned behind him, towards the pub – 'and was about to go to bed. We'd had a busy night. People were coming from all over to talk about the murder. It was fucking packed. When I saw him, I phoned you lot. He was heading straight down there and towards the house.'

'On his own, was he?'

The man nodded. 'Stanley has changed his hair.'

'What?'

'It's not blond any more. It's black.'

47

'All right,' Downes said, turning away from him and looking at Varley and Russell. 'We're going in there. If he comes out running this way grab him, all right?'

Downes motioned towards Graves and they both began to walk quickly down the hill.

# 6

'Forensics finished this evening, so there's nothing for him to tamper with. I never thought he'd come back – he was in such a hurry to get out of here.'

Graves shivered in the rain. They had left the umbrellas in the car to make themselves less noticeable. 'But Stanley must know by now that the bodies have been found: he must have seen the police tape.'

'And it hasn't stopped him, so whatever he's after must be important.'

They both slowed down when they approached the gate. Running all the way across the yard at the front of the house, the tape fluttered in the wind. They moved crouching down beside a hedgerow to keep out of view. Then they slipped under the tape and through the yard. They trotted around the back and then towards the garden. They paused, listening. For a moment everything was very quiet and still. Then there was a noise as something landed near their shoes. Graves stared up at the curving roof of the house and shifted on the balls of his feet, looking for the cause.

Almost immediately a stone came bouncing from somewhere on the roof and fell through the darkness, landing on the patio near the back door. And then another larger one fell, this one missing an old, forgotten birdbath by inches. Graves looked up, confused. But he could see nothing. He took a few steps back on to the grass, staring at the roof as another stone came skittering along the tiles and hit the guttering. Downes was already standing beside him, his eyes concentrating as he stared up.

'What the hell's going on?' Graves said. He craned his head upwards. 'If he's on the roof, I can't see him. I don't get it. And what would he be doing on the roof? What about the back door?'

'Back door's locked,' Downes said. 'He must have got in this way and then locked the door behind him.'

A brick encased in jagged pieces of cement whizzed past and detonated, cracking into chunks on the concrete path. And then another.

Both of them moved quickly until they were standing halfway into the garden.

'You still can't see him, sir?'

Downes shook his head and ran to the back door. He opened it with a key which he took out of his pocket.

They rushed upstairs and stopped on the landing. They stood listening.

'Stanley!' Downes yelled.

They sprinted up another staircase and into the attic.

Graves spun round in all directions. 'Where is he?' he said.

Downes put his finger to his lips. 'Stanley. Come on out of there.' He smiled for some reason Graves couldn't fathom.

Downes gestured towards the carpet and pointed to the wall at the far side of the room. On the floor was a spattering of dust and a few flakes of old paint. Downes took out the torch from his pocket and shone it on the wallpaper, holding it very steady and fixed on one point. Then Graves saw it. Just below waist height, on the chimney breast, a rectangle had been cut through the wallpaper and into the plaster. It was around the size and shape of the end of a coffin. The hole was just about big enough for someone to squeeze through.

Downes hurried past him. His feet thudded on the old carpet. The beam of his torch fell on a piece of plaster lying on the floor that was the exact shape and size of the shape that had been cut in the wall.

'I think we've found Miller's hiding place,' Downes said, satisfied. He pushed his head inside the brick chimney flue, twisted round and looked up. There was silence for a while. His broad back shifted slightly as he said something, but Graves could not hear him. There was a muffled panicky response from above. Downes pulled himself out of the space in the wall.

Looking at Graves, Downes shook his head, as if now he'd seen everything and was content. He was already reaching for his radio. He motioned to the hole with his thumb and passed the torch to Graves.

Graves put his hands on both sides of the wall and peered in, shining the torch upwards. Stanley's eyes bulged wide in their sockets as he stared down at him. He was covered from head to toe in soot.

'Stanley?' he said.

'If you say anything about Santa Claus and being too late for Christmas, I swear to God that I'll come down there and fucking strangle you,' Stanley said.

Graves, who had been about to say something very much along those lines, smiled. 'Come down from there,' he said, like a mother to a reckless child.

'I can't,' Stanley said.

'You're stuck.'

'No, I am not stuck,' Stanley said, drawing the words out. 'But this whole thing's going to collapse any fucking second.'

'Don't move,' Graves said.

Stanley exhaled deeply. He stared down at Graves and looked like he wanted to murder him. Instead he said in a furious hissing whisper, 'I'll try not to.'

'What are you doing up there anyway?'

Downes was talking into the radio, when suddenly Stanley moved his arm – and just as suddenly stopped.

The chimney flue had moved with him. The bricks wobbled and shifted. The grating sound of the bricks as they scraped against each other was truly dreadful. Stanley's mouth wrenched open in anticipation. Then he closed his eyes.

The bricks shifted again and the flue started to move in a see-saw-like motion. Outside, a brick fell from the chimney stack and careened across the roof. Graves quickly pulled himself out of the hole and turned around.

'Rescue team is on the way,' Downes said.

'How long?'

'Half an hour.'

'What on earth is he doing up there?'

'He's holding something. He doesn't want us to see it. Did you see it?'

'No. What is it?'

'I don't know.'

Graves stuck his head back in the hole and shone his torch upwards. Downes was right: Stanley was holding something. Clutched beneath his shirt.

'What have you got there?' Graves asked.

Instinctively Stanley moved it out of the band of light and into shadow. A brown envelope. Immediately something fell out of it and went spiralling downwards. Graves tried to catch hold of it. But he missed. A . . . what was it? A photograph, Graves realized with surprise. A person in the photo. Yes. A boy or a girl? A boy. How old? Around seventeen maybe. Standing in a room. Behind him a kind of stretcher. And tiles. White tiles. The face had been looking at the camera. It was gone now, though, and was somewhere at the bottom of the chimney flue. More photos floated down the chimney.

Graves looked up and then heard himself let out a muffled sound of warning. 'Stanley,' he shouted. 'Don't!'

But Stanley's shoulder drew back and touched the side of the chimney as he tried to hide the envelope under his coat. It was a barely perceptible nudge but it was enough. Then came a moment – a very long moment – when both of them knew that the chimney was about to collapse.

Stanley frantically began to move in the other direction, as if he could somehow counterbalance the force of the bricks. But the whole edifice suddenly gained an awful momentum. A huge chunk of it almost directly above his head and to his right cracked and toppled over. Stanley's right arm flew up in the air, his hand still clutching the envelope, and its contents spilt out. Immediately the wind took some of the photos and ruffled Stanley's hair as a section of the chimney stack fell on to the roof. Graves ducked out of the way just in time as Stanley and a few tons of brick went sliding downwards with a great roar. Above, the rest of the chimney stack landed on the tiles of the roof with an enormous bang, as if a giant fist had smashed the top of the house. The whole building shook and the air was filled with the smell of ancient entombed stone being suddenly thrust out into the crisp night air.

Without thinking Graves rushed forward through the dust towards the chimney breast. He ducked back in and reached downwards, his arms groping blindly in the dark. Stanley had somehow managed to gain purchase. Immediately he felt Stanley's hand reach out and grab his arm, his fingers digging desperately into Graves's flesh. Just as Graves felt himself being drawn into the hole, there was another shifting sound and Stanley slipped again. Graves could feel Downes behind him, reaching for him, but it was too late.

Graves lost his balance. He found his own forehead pressed hard against the other side of the chimney flue. The wall in front of his legs gave way, but Stanley would not let go. His grip tightened. Graves tilted further forward and yelled out as he was pitched into the widening hole. And then Stanley was falling and so was he.

# 7

It wasn't until around ten the next morning that I left the hospital and began the drive to the station. It had taken almost an hour to get them out of there. When the firemen finally broke through the chimney breast in the living room and brought out Stanley and Graves to the waiting ambulance, it seemed that Stanley had suffered a terrible, almost mortal wound.

Graves had been treated in the ambulance. He had actually walked out of there. Dazed, filthy-looking and bewildered but in one piece. Stanley, who had suffered a head wound, was being kept in under observation.

I picked up speed, thinking. I had expected jewellery. A stash that Miller had hidden in the chimney possibly many years ago. But Stanley had nearly died for some photos in an envelope. But not just any photos.

I parked my car and straightened my tie in the mirror, getting ready to face Collinson. I knew she was going to be furious about Graves, but Douglas stood up and motioned me over to his desk when I walked in. As I approached, Douglas put a sausage roll in its wrapper in his pocket. Douglas never seemed to stop eating, although he never gained any weight. He had smooth features and a full head of bristly black hair and hadn't shaved. He and Irwin had both been up all night and there were a few Styrofoam cups standing in a row on their desks.

'So what have you got on Stanley?' I said, impatiently standing over them. 'Come on, you must have something by now.'

'The police are looking for him back in London,' Irwin said.

'Looking for him,' I said quickly. 'Is that all?'

'Full name Stanley Dalton,' Irwin announced. 'Been in and out of jail since he was fifteen. Minor stuff mostly. Shoplifting. Petty theft. Breaking and entering. Never served time with Miller, though,' he said, frowning. 'So we still don't know how they knew each other and we don't know what he was doing out there. But London could be the connection. That, and their criminal records. We're having a closer look at that now.'

'What about Graves, sir?' Douglas said, sounding amused. 'I heard he went head first down the chimney flue after this Stanley fella.'

I looked nervously towards Collinson's office.

'She's upstairs,' Douglas said.

'Graves is fine.'

'Bit Inspector Clouseau, isn't it?' Douglas said, grinning. 'You know, falling down a chimney like that.'

I sat down heavily on my chair. 'Graves saved Stanley's life, so if I hear anyone calling him Clouseau behind his back they'll be for it.'

'Yes, sir,' Douglas said, and raised his eyebrows in Irwin's direction.

'So, Stanley. We've been on it all night, sir, and all morning. We tried the neighbours again first thing before they went to work.'

'Stanley isn't from around here,' Douglas said. 'The villagers didn't really take to him. But he seems to have created quite an impression.'

'What kind of impression?'

'Well, not a very good one. Looks like he got drunk in that shit pub most nights and Miller would have to come and drag him out of there. We think that he might have been lying low to avoid the London police. The phone's been ringing since six this morning: they want to know as soon as we find out anything.'

'The police?' I said, surprised. 'And they won't say why?'

'He was on probation,' Irwin said. 'He was supposed to meet with his parole officer a few weeks ago. Stanley had a job interview and never showed up.'

'So they want to talk to him about breaching his parole conditions?'

'No,' Irwin said firmly. 'It sounds a lot more serious than skipping an appointment with his parole officer. A detective sergeant called Vine wants to talk to him once he comes around. He's being cagey about it. A mate of Stanley's has gone missing. That's all he'll say about it.'

'He won't say who it is?'

'No. He's given us a first name. That's it. Robert.'

'Nothing else?'

'No. Says he can't say any more than that. According to this Vine bloke, Stanley rents a bedsit in Streatham. Paid the rent until the end of the month. Bags are all packed and he hasn't been back there for weeks.'

'How did this Vine sound when he talked to you?'

'Hard to tell, really,' Douglas said, thinking. 'Polite, like I say. Hands tied and all the rest of it. You know the drill, sir.'

'So this Robert disappears, Stanley packs up his bedsit and goes to Miller's straight away? Is that it?'

'We don't know how long this Robert has been missing. But it looks like that could be it,' Irwin said. 'So Stanley must be involved somehow.'

'And he hasn't been back there? Back to London in all that time?'

'No. After what happened to Miller, Stanley got a lift into Oxford. A car showed up on the High Street and Stanley got out.'

'CCTV?'

'Yes.'

'Good. This was when? The same night Miller and Finn were killed?'

'The morning,' Irwin said. 'About 3 a.m. We knew he was heading for Oxford, so I asked Thames Valley to check the High Street for us. Pretty straightforward. The guy dropped him off near the Martyrs' Memorial. So if he was going to get the bus, chances were he was going to go past the Randolph and cut through Gloucester Green. That's where we found him.'

'You traced the car?'

'Yep.' Irwin looked pleased. 'The driver picked him up just outside of Stratford. A salesman on his way home to Bicester. He says that Stanley was soaking wet and freezing his nuts off and he felt so sorry for him he decided to go out of his way and take him to Oxford.'

'He'd walked all the way?'

'Yes. He said he needed to get to Oxford and asked to be driven there.'

'And when was this?'

'Around 2 a.m. Stanley hardly said a single word all the way there and looked really upset. And scared. Couldn't seem to warm up in the car either. He was shivering nonstop.'

'He didn't mention Miller or what he was doing out there?' I said hopefully.

'No, and he didn't have anything with him either. No bag. Nothing. He got a bus from Gloucester Green and the driver thinks he got out at Marble Arch. It was around 4.30 a.m. by then, and there weren't many passengers on the bus. That's where he thinks he dropped off a funny-looking bloke. He's a bit of a . . . well, he's a bit effeminate, that's the way the driver described him. And that's where we lose him until he decides to come all the way back here and break into Miller's house in the middle of the night.'

'So he was up there in London for five days in all?'

'Looks like it.'

I sat back in my chair and didn't say anything for a while. Then I said, 'So Stanley is in some kind of trouble. Something to do with this other fella, Robert. He gets out of London and goes straight to Miller's. So Miller is someone he knew. Must be. And Miller lets him hide out there on his property. So what was Stanley hiding from, that's what we need to know.'

'Could be he was the real target all along and not Miller,' Irwin said. 'Could be the men tortured Miller because they wanted to know where Stanley was and he wouldn't tell them.'

'But that doesn't make any sense. Think about it, Ed,' Douglas said irritably, looking at Irwin. 'Why didn't they just wait for him to come back, if it was Stanley they were after? That would have been easy enough.'

'What was their relationship like? Stanley and Miller. Anyone see those two together?' I said.

Irwin scratched his chin. 'They seem to have made an odd kind of pair, don't they?'

Douglas nodded. 'They don't even seem to have liked each other all that much. Seemed to kind of put up with each other more than anything else. Stanley seemed to be a kind of ... well, a liability, really. I was talking to one of the villagers this morning. She works in a hotel over in Bidford and she said that Stanley was completely pissed on Christmas Eve.'

'So is half of England,' I said. 'So what?'

'No, there's more to it than that,' Douglas said firmly. 'She was driving back home from Midnight Mass with her mother and saw Stanley heading towards the pub. They have a lock-in on Christmas Eve and this Stanley fella wanted to get in there. Kind of hell bent on getting in there, if you see what I mean. But Miller wouldn't let him. Just grabbed him and tried to pull him away. She parked her car and went inside, but she heard them arguing.'

'Heard them? So she was listening.'

'Yes, she said she could hear Miller giving Stanley a real earful. About how he'd told him that he wasn't to go to the pub any more and that he'd had plenty to drink already. But, according to her, Stanley gave as good as he got.'

'What did he say?'

'He told Miller to go fuck himself. And more than once. She'd seen them together before and the impression she got was that they didn't seem to like each other at all. But there was a kind of . . . I don't know. Respect or something. Hard to know what it was.'

'Respect. That's the word she used, is it?'

'Yes. She's been living here forever and she says that had it been anyone else Miller would've happily kicked his teeth in for him. No one ever talked to Miller that way. I mean this Miller: everyone seems glad to see the back of him. He's been away for ages but he moves back into his old man's house and would spend most nights in the pub on his own before Stanley came. He'd sit there with his big dirty boots on the table, according to the barman.

Liked winding people up. Most people couldn't stand him. But the woman says on Christmas Eve Stanley really went for him. Insulted him. Called him a pig. But she said it was odd because Miller just stood there and took it and then Stanley just seemed to start crying. And then it gets really strange, because Miller brought him back down the hill and led him towards the house. Was pretty gentle with him.'

'There was no talk of those two being together.'

'No. Nothing like that at all.' Irwin said. 'Apparently Miller was less than enlightened about that kind of thing. His dad was even worse, apparently. That's what they said in the pub when I asked about it.'

'And it wasn't the first time,' Douglas said. 'When Stanley got drunk, Miller would just stand there and take it and then bring him home. And Stanley didn't like being out here; he couldn't wait to get back to London. He talked about it all the time.'

'In the pub?'

'Yes.'

'So what was keeping him here?' I said.

'He didn't say.'

'And he never said how he knew Miller?'

'No, he never really talked about Miller. Got pretty friendly with the pub barman. He talked about Miller's house more than anything else. Said what a dump it was and how he had him sleeping in this small little room and how cold he was at night and how Miller was too tight to put on the heating. The barman asked him once why he didn't just go home and he said he couldn't, not yet.'

'Not yet,' I said quickly.

'That's what he said.'

'The argument this woman heard on Christmas Eve. Did she hear what Stanley was upset about?'

'No. He just kind of broke down suddenly.'

'So do you think that Stanley knew what was in that house and came back to get it?' Douglas said.

'Maybe,' I said. 'Stanley might have been there for another reason, though. Could be Miller owed him one. Or they were up to something else. We'll know as soon as the doctors let me talk to him.'

'But something to do with those photos?' Irwin said.

'You've seen them?'

'They're upstairs with Collinson.'

'Anything else?'

'The newspapers,' Douglas said. 'I had a good look through all of them, like you asked me to last night. Well, the two papers that the pub gets anyway. Mr Muscle out there, the barman, says that Finn went through them when he was in there, before he went to see Miller. Didn't seem interested in anything in particular. There's nothing with a London connection. Nothing to get a top London journo interested. It's jumble sales and locals getting their knickers in a twist over planning permission.'

'So we still don't know what Finn was doing out here either,' I said quietly. 'Only an idea that he was on to some story about Miller.'

'Yes.'

'He was interested in Miller. Never mentioned this Stanley as far as we know, did he?'

'No.'

'All right,' I said. 'You'd better show me these photos.'

# 8

Irwin motioned to the door and I followed him upstairs to the first floor. Collinson was standing over a long table in the middle of a large, thoroughly modernized incident room. She turned around when she saw me. She had her hair tied in a ponytail and she wasn't wearing any make-up and it gave her a stern, puritanical look that was even more intimidating than usual. She was around five years younger than me. Elegant and detached always. She had red hair which had recently been styled into an almost mannish but very chic cut, pale skin and narrow green eyes. A twitching, impatient quality added to her scholarly air, as if everyone around her couldn't quite keep up. It made her seem slightly older.

Although I had been working with her for almost ten years, all I knew about her was that she was married and had a dog but no children. There was a photo of her dog on a beach in her office. The dog looked subdued, like she had just told it off.

As always when I was with her, I felt on the back foot and wished I was somewhere else. She looked at me, shook her head in disapproval and let out a long sigh. She crossed her arms. She seemed agitated, as if she couldn't decide whether she should be angry or upset. The photos were on the table in front of her: laid out in a long row, they seemed to be eyeing us silently, waiting. She stood above them and let out a hiss through her teeth.

'God, Downes, I don't like the look of these. What do you make of them?'

'I don't know. Not yet. I haven't had time to go through them.'

'You were at the hospital?'

I nodded.

'How's Stanley?' she said.

'Out cold.'

She looked at me very seriously and with a great deal of patience said, 'Why didn't you just wait until he came down from the chimney?'

'Wait for him?'

'Yes, yes,' she said, her patience coming abruptly to an end. 'You could have just waited outside and he would have come out with these photos eventually, probably tucked neatly under his arm in an envelope. It would have been the simplest thing in the world. I bet you didn't even consider that, did you? In you go without even thinking, as usual. And we don't even know if we've got all of them yet. Stanley's in hospital and the Met want to talk to him – you know that?'

I nodded.

'He's involved in something,' she said, folding her arms, 'but of course they won't tell us what it is, as usual. A disappearance.'

She went back to the photos as if she could not look away. 'I hope these aren't what I think they might be,' she said.

'And what is that?'

'Mementos maybe. I don't know,' she said irritably. 'They could well be that. How long do you think they've been out there on Miller's property?'

'There's no way of knowing for now. But Miller had them stashed in an old hiding place of his.'

'Well, we've had to send out a search team to find the ones that didn't fall down the chimney,' Collinson said. 'God knows where they could be by now. Scattered half-way across the Cotswolds probably. And they tell me that Stanley smashed through almost three floors – all the way from the attic – and Graves went straight after him.'

'Well. It wasn't that bad. The bricks slowed him down a little bit,' I said weakly, 'and Stanley softened his landing.'

'Softened his landing!' She suddenly looked furious and then with considerable effort managed to calm down again. She seemed to weigh this up with other things I had done in the past to annoy her; then she closed her eyes and breathed in deeply, as if she had been practising for just such a moment as this. From the corner of my eye I could see Irwin looking at her nervously before glancing sympathetically in my direction.

'When will you be able to speak to him? Do we at least know that?'

'Tonight or tomorrow. They're going to move him to a private ward later. We better send someone to keep a watch over him when he wakes up,' I said, trying to change the subject.

'All right.' She sighed. 'I'll get Varley on it. And Graves?' she said, looking at me.

'He's fine,' I said.

'Are you sure?'

'Yes, I'm sure. Although he probably won't be too keen on small spaces for a while.'

'Try not to get him killed if you can help it, Downes. You know how difficult it was to get a replacement for Powell.' She stopped and suddenly looked embarrassed. 'I'm sorry. That came out . . . well, it came out wrong. But, Downes, we've had a double murder and now this. I talked to Brewin last night and it looks like the men who came for Miller knew exactly what they were doing. And now we know what they were looking for: these photos. But why? And what does Stanley have to do with any of it? You sure he was looking for them and not for something else?'

'I think he must have been. He knew exactly where they were.'

'But I don't understand them at all,' Collinson said help-lessly. 'Where were they taken? Who are they? And what on earth were they doing in Miller's property? And what is their value to Stanley or to anyone else for that matter? Why go to the risk of coming back for them so soon?'

'I don't know. Whatever they mean, it was enough for someone to torture Miller to death in order to get them, but Miller wouldn't give them up.'

'But why?'

'He might have been too far gone because of the head wound. Or maybe he knew that he was a dead man as soon as he saw who had come for him.' I walked across the room and began to unbutton my coat. I stood over the table and looked down. The photos provoked an immediate reaction: a kind of instant desire to look the other way. 'Miller had these stashed in a place where he knew they would never find them,' I said quietly. 'And he died for them. How many of them are there?'

'Eight so far,' Irwin said, taking a step forward. 'The search team has been brought back in to search the grounds. We had to get in some officers from Oxford. But they could have been blown for miles. This is all we've got so far.'

'And the original Polaroids?'

'Ashbury is having them transferred to the lab right now.'

'Where to?'

'Priory House,' Irwin said straight away. 'They're on their way to Birmingham. But there's a problem with the roads. The quickest route is the M40 but that's blocked. It's chaos. Apparently a lot of people are trying to get out in case the whole place floods, and a lorry's blown over and blocked the road. They're trying to get off and on to the M5.'

'And are we going to get flooding?'

'Looks like it,' Collinson said wearily. 'Miller's fields could flood at any minute: they're on a flood plain.'

'And there might be more photos and we still can't find the envelope,' Irwin said.

I stared down at the photos.

'If they are what I think they are,' Collinson said, 'they were probably handled many, many times. And definitely at least once at the edge, where the film was pulled out.'

'And we're going to have to look into dating the pictures,' Irwin said, moving forward. 'You can tell the model of camera by the type of film. Ashbury's got some of his team on that now.'

'But eight of them so far?'

'Yes.'

'And eight different boys?'

'Young men or boys in their mid-to-late teens,' Irwin said.

'There's nothing like that in Miller's record, is there?' Collinson said. 'Nothing to do with Miller and underage boys?'

I shook my head. 'And we have no idea who they are or what happened to them?' I said, looking at Irwin.

'No, sir. Not yet. We only know that the photos are old. So we think they've been on Miller's property for a long time.'

I looked from left to right. 'Where are they?'

'We don't know. It looks like a hospital or an institution . . . but it looks all wrong,' Collinson said quietly.

'It's always the same place is it?'

'Looks like it,' Collinson said.

The room in the pictures seemed sparse and functional yet its exact function was not clear. It seemed to serve no practical purpose at all. A hose was wrapped in a tight coil beneath a sink, and there were a number of white towels on a small table. Something – maybe a tripod or a medical device – was leaning slightly out of view. Some of the photos showed a black stretcher with two metal loops tied to leather straps on either side. Stirrups, I realized with growing horror. I took a deep breath and kept looking.

On the right side of the stretcher, around halfway down, was a metal tray on a green table. In another picture the tray was gone. In one picture there was a large lamp on a stand, and in another the light was angled in a slightly different position, so that the shadow gave way, revealing more tiles at the back of the room beyond the stretcher. Light in some of the photos flooded on to the floor from an open door behind the camera.

In all the pictures the ceiling was very high. Yet the angles were wrong somehow, and the floor seemed to slope downwards towards the far end. There were no windows.

Time had passed in that room. Long fronds of vegetation reached across the floor and moss grew in the cracks along the walls in some of the photos, while in others the vegetation grew less thickly. The room, which had looked old and abandoned to begin with, aged considerably over the time the pictures had been taken. The equipment, however, always looked new and well cared for and the chrome frame of the stretcher had been polished to a gleaming shine.

Only one element was constant: the boys. All without exception were bare-chested and each sat perched on the edge of the stretcher and every one of them was looking straight at the camera. They did not look particularly afraid, and somehow that was the worst part.

From left to right. A thin blond teenager. His hair in a crew cut. Around sixteen, squinting, as if getting used to the brightness in the room. Next to him a boy around thirteen or fourteen with thin features and a frail delicate body. His blue eyes are fixed on some point over the photographer's left shoulder. In the next photo, a hint of a nervous smile playing on his lips, is perhaps the oldest boy. Eighteen or nineteen. Unlike the others, his photo has been taken from above, so that the lens is looking down on him as he looks up. He strikes an effeminate, well-practised pose, his head to one side, his lips upturned.

Next is a boy around seventeen. Tall and thin with a sensitive mouth and black hair. He is very pale with green eyes. Then there's a teenager with red hair and a black stud in his left ear and what looks like the remains of a burn scar on his arm.

I took a step, moving right. Three more photos. I paused and then took another step.

A tall, muscular boy with blond curly hair. Sixteen perhaps. Beside him in the next photo and sitting very straight is a boy with black hair and the faint beginnings of

73

a moustache. And finally the last photo. He's plump and wearing a light shade of lipstick; he's folding his arms, trying to cover his belly. He's the youngest. Maybe thirteen.

I took a step away from them and folded my arms and looked down. Then, realizing that I was imitating the pose in the last of the photos, quickly held my hands behind my back.

Did they know where they were? Were they playing a game? Did they feel safe in there? It was impossible to tell. The room behind them seemed to stretch out like a long arm reaching for them. The light above gave their naked flesh a yellowish tint. I peered more closely at the first picture and saw a warped reflection of a head in the curved chrome of a sink tap. The camera was covering his face. He looked very far away in the picture and very small.

'Any way we can get this enlarged?'

'We can try,' Irwin said. 'You can just about make him out in some of the other pictures too. Obviously the reflection is really, really small. But we may be able to get some idea as to who he was. Height for sure. Maybe hair, maybe age and gender, though of course for now we're assuming it's a man.'

'Any local kids run away or gone missing lately?' I said nervously.

'Kid called Conrad,' Irwin said. 'But I checked. He's not in any of the photos and I called his parents. His dad is fairly sure he's in London. He's done it before. Always comes back, though. He's seventeen, so there's not much his dad can do. But I talked to him and he's never heard of Miller. And he never spoke to a journalist from London about it. There was just a small piece on it in one of the local papers, that's it. Anyway, those photos look really old, don't they?'

'All right,' I said finally, turning away. 'So we've got a Polaroid camera. We've got some kind of room. And these boys. We don't know who they are or where they are. Or what happened to them.'

'And I don't think we should assume anything just yet,' Collinson said. 'It could be that these boys are perfectly well and are wandering around someplace. Some of these have started to turn yellow, so they were probably taken quite a long time ago.

'The first thing we need to do obviously is somehow find out who they are,' she continued. 'What have they got in common? How did they meet the person taking the photos? Are there any buildings on Miller's farm that could have a room like this? It's a huge place, isn't it?'

I nodded. 'If Miller wasn't involved directly, he may well have stolen these photos when he was in London and then come back here to hide them. We know those men were looking for something on his property. And we know Stanley was willing to take a big risk to come back for them.'

'All right, so if he stole them, why keep them?' Collinson said. 'Unless they have some kind of value to him or to

75

somebody else. It looks like they could well have got him killed in the end. And not just him. George Finn too.'

I shoved my hands in my pockets and turned around. 'What about Finn?' I said. 'We know anything else about him?'

Collinson nodded. 'Yes, I've been on the phone to his editor.'

'He didn't want to talk to us last night. He was in some kind of trouble.'

'I had another word with him first thing this morning and he came around eventually,' Collinson said. 'But it wasn't easy. Finn was going to be their first one; he wasn't the only one doing it, but they were going to make an example of him. Their first arrest.'

'Arrest?'

'Yes. Finn was probably going to jail. He was out on bail. He'd been paying someone for information.'

'For what? Stories?'

'Yes.'

'But surely that happens all the time. Don't papers pay for stories? Tip-offs, that kind of thing.'

'Well, yes, they do. That's perfectly normal. But there're rules. The person who was providing Finn with information was always . . . well, almost always right on the money. The stories didn't always make the paper but it was good information. So that's unusual.'

'So an insider, a public official?'

'Yes. And it's serious because the person he was paying was a policeman.'

'A policeman,' I said.

'Apparently so. He'd retired years ago. They don't know exactly how long it went on for, or how it all started, but they threw the book at the officer and gave him two years. He worked for the Met.'

'And Finn?'

'The Met are running a special operation and investigating.'

'So he would pay this police officer. But for what?'

'Using his contacts to have car number plates checked or phone records accessed. Usually to get gossip on Z-list celebrities,' Collinson said, unable to keep the disdain out of her voice. 'I mean, really low stuff. It's been going on for years and years.'

'And we still don't know what Finn was doing out here, do we?'

'No. It's a hard call for the editor. Finn was one of their own, even if he did leave in disgrace. They're going to cover the story themselves: it'll be in the paper tomorrow.'

'What's the angle on Miller?'

'There is none. They never ran anything on Miller. Of course they've been looking into Finn's old stories, but he never made any mention of Miller or even the Cotswolds.'

I turned back to look again at the pictures. There was something about the composition. It was so exact. Each boy had been told exactly where to sit and where to look. I had a terrible feeling about those boys in the photos. As if I should reach across somehow and warn them of the danger. Yet each one gazed at the camera with a face that was almost expressionless. Suddenly I was sure that, once the photo session was over, anything could have happened in that room. Anything at all.

# 9

I spoke to Collinson for a little longer, then drove to Miller's house, half listening to the weather warnings on the radio as I went. I left the car at the top of the hill near the pub and then marched down under my umbrella. The area was being searched again, but this time the area of investigation was expanded. The photos could be caught in a hedgerow. Be plastered at the side of the road or lying at the bottom of a ditch.

Two police search advisers were now peering over the fields, having a look at what they were up against. One, a small dark man, shook his head and looked worried before reaching into the window of his vehicle and pulling out a map. The entire farm and the land beyond had already been divided into manageable sections, and all across the fields I could see men and women moving their way across in a steady line.

It suddenly started to rain harder, and the two men got in their car and slammed the doors. There was a pack of journalists outside the house. Russell was keeping them at bay and had blocked off the lane. Some of them I recognized from the local papers, but there were a few others who, I supposed, were from the papers in London. They shouted at me from under a mass of umbrellas. I ignored them and

79

walked past Russell, picking up speed when I saw Graves emerging from the front door carrying an umbrella.

Douglas had been right. It *had* been a bit of an Inspector Clouseau moment when he had fallen into the chimney flue, although it hadn't been at all funny at the time. They had treated him badly at his old station but he seemed to have shaken it off pretty quickly. Knowing him a little better now, I was not all that surprised. His resilience seemed to go hand in hand with a cold authoritarian streak which seemed to come naturally to him and which I could use if he was planning on staying.

Graves held up the police tape for me with his usual good manners and then led me back through the front of the house. He looked tired and slightly panicky. There was a long cut along his cheek which was covered in gauze. Beneath his shirt was the outline of a bandage wrapped around his ribcage.

'I thought you'd be taking the day off,' I said. 'How are you feeling?'

'Better. Though my ribs hurt like hell.'

'Not broken?'

'No, but they feel like it. They've found two more of those photos.'

'More of them? Where?'

'One of them got caught in the guttering at the back of the house. I got a glimpse of some of the photos when I was in the chimney. Before it collapsed,' Graves said, looking pointedly at me.

'You didn't try and grab one of them, then?' I said.

'No, I didn't. I was too busy trying to get out of there alive. Jesus. Anyway, it was hard to see.'

We started walking quickly through the hall and towards the kitchen.

'The other one was found in the village this morning by the postman. He handed it straight to us. You'll know why when you see it.'

Ashbury, the crime scene manager, had set up his stall at the far side of the house, in the unused dining room. He had erected a blue modular screen across the width of the room, cleared the floor inside so that it was completely clean and covered the carpet with plastic sheeting. He had then placed a tent inside it so the photos had no chance of getting contaminated.

Ashbury's lips were down-turned slightly and a frown had formed on his face. He stood brooding as he stared at the Polaroid. Ashbury was snappish, a lot smaller than me but around my age, with short black hair with traces of grey and a pale face. His thin jaw was unshaven and his blue eyes were set hollowly in his skull.

He had covered the dining table in plastic sheeting and laid the two photos in the middle of it. As I watched, a photographer leant in close, paused and then took a number of photos with a digital camera in quick succession. The camera was connected to a laptop.

Ashbury looked briefly outside at the rain now pelting down on the trees. 'All right, Downes,' he said, 'two so far. Both of them are different. Probably safer if you look at the image on the computer for now. And keep your mitts off them. You too, Graves. I'm going to get them taken to the lab right away.'

'What do you know about Polaroid photos?' I said.

'I knew quite a lot naturally, but I've learnt a lot more since I was woken up at five this morning,' Ashbury said irritably. 'It's not all that complicated, which is bad news for us, because it means we can't narrow things down as much as we'd like to.' Ashbury paused and leant down, looking more closely at the pictures. 'Each category of Polaroid uses its own type of film. It doesn't make a difference what model it is: as long as you're using the same category of camera, then you would be using the same type of film. For now it seems like all of them bar one were taken either with a Polaroid SX-70 or a Polaroid 600.'

'How do you know?'

'Because both of them used integral film. The film doesn't require the user to separate the negative from the positive. It simply ejects the film out of the camera and you wait for it to develop. Simple as that. Both films are identical in size as well. They both produce square prints just like these, with borders of the same size. The only difference between the SX-70 and the 600 is the speed of the film. By that I mean how quickly the film reacts to light. But the quality of the image is identical.

'The Spectra – another model – has the same chemistry in the film as the 600 but the image is different. It's rectangular, as opposed to square. So we know that these photos were taken with either a SX-70 or a 600 model.'

'Is there any way that we can narrow down the dates they were taken?'

'Only slightly. The SX-70 models were made from 1972 until 1981 and the 600 models were made first in 1978 but there have been a good number of other 600 models released since then. They're still making them now in fact. A huge variety of models were offered, though they all share the same basic design, and millions of both models were produced.'

'Great,' I said. 'And the one that wasn't?'

He motioned to the screen. 'Bear with me, Downes. Right, here's the first one,' he said. The laptop hummed softly. Running along the top corner was a thin tear. I stared at the enlarged version on the screen. It was the same room. A sink and a stretcher. A hose snaked its way along the tiled floor towards the figure sitting at its edge. I could feel my heart start to beat faster, and I leant in closer.

'A man,' Graves said quietly over my shoulder.

He was in his early fifties, handsome, with short hair. He was wide-shouldered and looked in good shape for his age, although the skin, an inevitable result of age, sagged slightly beneath his arms and around his waist. He was naked. His hair was blond and slightly yellowish and stood in complete disarray. He had a wide mouth which was set in a sullen grimace, so that you could see his straight teeth behind his lips. He was wearing a large signet ring on the little finger of his right hand.

The light in the room shone very brightly. Everything – the strange pieces of chrome equipment, the stretcher, the lamp arching above the stretcher – was the same.

He was covered from head to toe in mud, which mixed with the blood coming from a wound that must have been at the back of his skull. His left eye was half closed and swollen. There was a jagged cut above his jaw, and defensive bruises and cuts all over his arms, and blood dripping from the soles of both of his feet. The contrast between the filth covering his entire body and the neatness of the room made him look more pitiful somehow and more exposed.

I leant forward and could sense Graves standing very still beside me. There were blades of grass stuck to the man's legs and arms, as well as plastered along his inner thigh. His hands and forearms were black with freshly upturned earth. For a moment it was almost as if I could smell rotting vegetation and black mud and something sweet and overripe coming from the dark core of the photograph. He was staring at the camera, and beneath his fear you could sense the anger filling the room, that and a wild disbelief that he was there at all. But he was there, all right. Right there in the middle of hell, it looked like to me.

'My God,' Graves said. 'Who in the world is he?'

I shook my head. 'Can you zoom in on that?' I said. 'There, near that sink.'

Ashbury moved the mouse and focused on the chrome taps, which shone dully under the stark lights of the room. I crouched down and peered in as closely as I could.

Graves peered in as well. 'Two of them,' he said quietly.

I nodded and leant in closer. It was impossible to make out any detail in the reflections. But there were two figures. One holding the camera and the other standing slightly behind him in an open doorway.

'What's going on?' Graves said, straightening up. 'What the hell was Miller doing with these photos?'

'How well do you know London, Graves?'

'Extremely well. My parents keep a flat there actually.'

From behind him Ashbury rolled his eyes.

'Why? Do you need me to go to the paper?'

I paused, thinking. 'I'll finish up here. You get going. Talk to Finn's mates there. Try his flat. The Met have been there already but it's worth having another go. We need to find out what he was looking into.'

'You two finished?' Ashbury didn't give me time to answer. Instead he clicked the top-right-hand corner of the computer screen and the picture was immediately replaced with another photo, so I had no time to prepare myself for the sudden change.

'Christ,' Graves said.

This photo was in black and white, and brown with age at the edges. The same place again. A boy of around twelve or thirteen stood perched on the edge of the stretcher, staring obediently at the camera. Same stretcher, same room. His hair was cut neatly at the sides in an old-fashioned style. He was not wearing a shirt and he stared at the camera with studied concentration. He looked serious and solemn.

In the other pictures, although the equipment was well maintained, the room had looked old and derelict. Yet here there was no moss on the walls or any other sign of age and neglect. The tiled walls and floor were without a scratch and looked as if they had just been mopped clean. The medical room, as I had already begun to think of it, looked new.

## 10

When I finally got home, I found Powell's son, Alex, sitting in his car in my driveway. He switched his headlights on and got out when he saw me and waved. He was tall and good-looking, but the strain of the last months had taken its toll. Now he seemed to be relieved to be outside, and he stood for a moment in the rain, which fell and was caught in the glow of his headlamps, before fetching an umbrella from the boot of his car and opening it.

'You're up late,' I said, surprised to see him.

'It's all right, Guillermo. I just needed some air. Been sitting here thinking about Dad. I really can't stay long. I just wanted to give you this.' He handed me a manila envelope which reminded me uncomfortably of the photos I'd been looking at all day.

'What's in it?'

'I have no idea at all. It was locked up with his things in his study,' Alex said. 'He just said that I was to give it to you in person. And then make sure I wasn't here when you opened it. That's all.'

'All right,' I said, still looking at it. 'A bit mysterious, isn't it? You have no idea what it is, then?' I shook it. 'Maybe it's your inheritance,' I said, and Alex laughed. I put it under my coat, so it wouldn't get wet. 'How are you anyway?'

Alex shrugged. 'I don't really know how I am. Not yet. Well, you saw how bad things got. It will probably hit me later. Anyway,' he said, brightening slightly and turning away, 'I better get going. It's late. I'll see you Friday.' He looked up at the sky. 'That's if we don't have to change the day or the church.'

I waved and watched his car disappear. I put the envelope on the kitchen table and looked at it. I didn't want to open it straight away. I had a shower and got changed and had a drink, then put the fire on in the kitchen, thinking about my old partner and friend Powell.

He had made it through one last Christmas, just like he said he would. I took my mobile with me and the copies of the photos, grabbed my umbrella and walked through the village to the pub. I decided to have one last silent toast in one of Powell's favourite places.

It was pretty quiet because of the rain. I sat in a corner and took out the photos and looked at them. I tried to envisage the men who had come for Miller. For now, they were faceless killers defined only by what they had left in their wake. I thought of Miller staring up from that chair and maybe telling them to go to hell. I've dealt with men like Miller almost my entire life. Death is something they get ready for. They plan for it and they expect it. He must have known the moment he saw them that he was through. Had he died for those photos? Or had he died because he'd known he was through either way and just wouldn't tell them where they were?

I thought of Miller slipping upstairs alone to that attic. Had he held those pictures at night? Were they something he had treasured? Had he stared down at the faces in that room with fondness, perhaps grinning in the darkness and tracing the silhouette of their shoulders with a finger, touching the curve of their mouths? I didn't think so. It just didn't go with what we knew of him so far.

I tried to imagine Miller behind the camera, smiling at the boys, putting them at their ease. No, it just didn't fit. If only I could phone Powell and talk it through with him. But Powell was gone. *Gone.* Almost impossible to believe that I would never see him again. He was lying in a funeral home somewhere and in a few days' time we would bury him. Christ. I still couldn't believe it. How was I going to manage without him?

I took a deep pull on my pint and stared longer at the photos. The expression on their faces was strangely neutral. Hard to tell what was going on behind their eyes. A defence mechanism perhaps. They seemed to sit there as if unaware of what lay behind them. But there was an awful kind of surrender to them and a terrible kind of self-awareness too. Each one of them was playing a role, it seemed. It was the kind of room that could be scrubbed clean once it was all over with. The tiles could simply be hosed down. The stretcher in the middle could be folded away and removed or covered up. The men could emerge from that place somehow intact. There was an awful practicality to it. That was the worst part, but, at the same time, from my point of view, the most hopeful. The function of the room reflected a vital need in the men, but it also reflected who they were. It gave them away.

I drank my pint and then had another. I wondered if Graves was really going to stick around. He was still young. And if there was a woman involved, well that of course could change everything.

I knew how he must feel. I had felt the same way when I had ended up here myself and been stuck with Powell. Would Graves in twenty or thirty years mourn me the same way I was mourning Powell? I smiled to myself. I didn't think so somehow. More than once I had caught him desolately scanning his phone for messages. So an ex. I couldn't see any mileage in that myself. I wasn't on speaking terms with any of my exes, and there had been a fair few of them over the years. They got fed up with me fairly quickly and I couldn't say I blamed them for it. Most of them left hurt and wounded, unsure of where they had gone wrong. None of it was their fault.

I stared a while longer at the photos and then suddenly gave up. Ten years ago I would have lit a cigarette. In this very pub Powell had asked me a very difficult question and I had tried to answer it. It had to do with murder and mayhem and all the things that go along with them.

I put the photos away and remembered Powell reaching for his glass and taking a long gulp and looking momentarily like he wished he hadn't started. Lean, wolfish and wily, that had been Len Powell. And stubborn too – and with his characteristic stubbornness he had seemed to rally.

'You're like a dog after a damned bone sometimes and you know it too,' he'd said to me. 'And I don't understand it. I've never really understood it. I'm not saying you get it right all the time, mind you,' Powell said, and touched his head lightly. 'Christ, far from it. Actually most of the time you get it wrong. Well, to begin with anyway and then you go and get it wrong again.' He laughed. 'And the times we've gone off on a wild goose chase, well . . . listen, I don't mind about that and I don't care about Collinson either way. She doesn't scare me, you know. Not like she scares you.' Powell laughed. 'But I've seen you do it,' he said. 'And . . . you must know you do it as well, don't you?'

I hadn't said anything to begin with, as I wasn't really sure if my reply could be put into words. And I did not want to say it out loud, in case I jinxed it somehow. But Powell had looked at me straight in the eye, and I knew then that I was going to have to try.

'Tell me to shut up if I'm out of order here, mate. But . . . do you think it might be because of what happened to you? I know you don't like talking about it' – Powell put his hands up – 'but do you think it's because of what happened to you in Argentina? And what happened to . . . that girl you were with? Pilar. Something you saw maybe a long time ago when you were with her and those bastards that were after you? Do you think . . . ?' He trailed off. 'Oh, bugger. I don't know,' he said. 'It sounds stupid when you say it out loud. Forget it.' He smiled and then the smile disappeared. 'Forget it. I shouldn't have brought it up.'

'No,' I'd said, 'its fine, Len.' I had meant it too. Powell, if anyone, had had a right to know. Now, sitting in the pub, I was glad I had told him, even though it's something I try very hard not to think about unless I have to.

I had tried to explain to him the best way I could. I had told him that it was perhaps something to do with living in a place where murder was carried out on a daily basis, governed and sanctioned by the state. It was knowing what normal everyday people were capable of in the right circumstances, if they felt they didn't have a choice. It was about seeing how bad things could get once that line had been crossed. I told him that perhaps I was more attuned to it because I'd seen people turn on each other and live with it literally for years. Because back home in Buenos Aires we had looked the other way as people we knew were made to disappear, and as it got worse the more natural and the more normal it had seemed.

Powell had sat very still, listening to all of it. He did not seem surprised. He nodded to himself as if he had been expecting to hear something like this, and his hand moved restlessly for the glass. 'And when you saw it really up close,' he said. 'Back then. When those men came for you in that big old car after they took Pilar away. After what they did to her. I know you don't really know what happened to her after that, but you did something about it. I mean you reacted straight away, didn't you?'

I had reacted all right. Powell was the only other person in the world apart from my brother who knew what I'd done back home. Now he had taken my secret with him to his grave.

I snapped out of it. Even now I realized I was still clinging to the past. Somewhere halfway across the world another life had been laid out before me. But Pilar was gone. Gone for over twenty years. Yet even now she was always staring at me from the dark corners of my mind. Judging me all the time with that look of hers. I was in love with a phantom; she had sucked the years from me. Taken them away and now I could never get them back. Even now, with Powell dead, it was her I was thinking of and not him.

I couldn't sleep, so I phoned Varley and told him I was coming over to see Stanley. I'm not keen on hospitals, and the whole place made me jumpy, but it was better than rattling around in my big old house and thinking about Powell.

I drew in a long breath and rubbed the back of my neck when I got there and wiped the rain from my face. The hospital had that late-night feel to it. The lights had been dimmed along the corridors. Without the constant stream of activity it seemed deserted, apart from small, very busy pockets of activity here and there.

I scanned the room numbers on the second floor and then headed left, expecting to see Varley at any minute. I phoned Varley again but this time there was no reply. I could hear his phone ringing from a long way away up the corridor. I blinked and kept walking. It wasn't like Varley not to answer. I strolled along the corridor and then hung up and the phone stopped ringing.

I stopped and listened. Already fading into nothing, the sound of something shifting, perhaps of material sliding against the wall, was breaking the silence. Then came the screech of something being moved along the floor. Most likely a chair. My head moved quickly to one side.

I started to run when I heard a much louder sound, as if someone had dropped something heavy. There it was again, louder this time. Then I heard something breaking with a tinkling bang.

From the far end of the corridor came a panicked reverberating shout. I stared ahead. Doors were opening and closing. Patients were filling the corridor, muttering and talking in excited whispers, while a few others started to mill around in their slippers and hospital dressing gowns. I rushed past a nurses' station near some stairs where a number of corridors met. Varley was lying on the floor straight ahead. His breathing was harsh and uneven. His whole body suddenly convulsed, as if he were in the grip of a nightmare, and I took a step back. I noticed with rising horror a vicious looping arc of blood spray on the wall behind his chair. Around the chair legs lay a can of Coke on its side, hissing its contents on to the floor. A doctor was already pushing his way through the crowd towards Varley.

The door to the room behind him was still open. I moved quickly inside and then put on the light. The broken remains of a vase were strewn all over the floor. The sheets and blankets on the bed were piled in a tangled mass. A blue screen had been knocked over and lay crumpled, as if it had been hurled across the room.

I felt a sudden chill. My heart was pounding. To begin with, I had thought that Stanley was responsible for Varley. But the mess in here ... Without a backwards glance, I pushed my way through the small crowd and sprinted to the nurses' station. A nurse was standing near it, staring down the hall, but she stepped back startled when I loomed in front of her.

'A patient. He went running? Someone was after him.'

She looked undecided and licked her lips.

I smashed the edge of my fist on the desk so hard that the windows rattled and a pen jumped and fell off the edge. 'Where? Which way did they go?'

She pointed to a door behind her.

'What's down there?'

'X-ray. Day surgery. Physiotherapy. Pathology,' she listed off automatically. 'But they're all locked for the night.'

'Lifts? Stairs?'

'Stairs. Unless you take the fire exit. But then there's the alarm,' she said, as if suddenly remembering. 'The alarm would go off.'

But I was already running.

I surged forward, flung myself through some double doors and headed straight out into the corridor. I checked all the doors as I ran, just in case. They were all locked. I ran half slipping and then went plunging down the stairs. Then I sprinted past some chairs in rows and towards the darkened windows of a canteen. Then I headed quickly towards the end of the corridor.

I looked round in all directions, poking my head around doors and into unoccupied dark corners. No sign of them anywhere.

The warmth of the hospital hit me suddenly. I felt as if the air were being sucked out of my body; I took off my coat and clutched it under my arm. A hard jab of fear hit me right in my gut. I didn't know where I was any more. Somewhere at the front of the hospital perhaps.

I pushed through some double doors. The A & E department. Activity suddenly everywhere. I slowed down to a jog and scanned either side. Doctors and nurses were moving quickly along the corridor, too busy to stare at me as I moved past them.

Two soaking wet ambulance men brought in a man on a stretcher. I slowed down to a fast trot, staring into a cubicle where a blood-spattered drunk sat perched unsteadily on an examination table. Cubicle curtains closed and opened. But I was close. I could see it in their faces as I went by.

'Where?' I shouted.

'Over there,' said the drunk, wincing when he moved.

I was near the exit.

And then suddenly, ahead of me, I saw Stanley flash by as he darted across a corridor. He was making his way towards the exit. I was amazed he had got this far. His bandage was still on his head. He was wearing a hospital dressing gown that flapped around his ankles. He ran past the rows of chairs in the waiting room, and the small crowd gathered there stared as he smashed against the door and pushed it open. A few moments later a lean, wiry-looking man appeared, staring wildly in all directions, and then went straight after him, pushing the door so hard that it rattled on its hinges as it hit the wall.

I took a few steps. The drunk man in the cubicle opened his mouth in warning. But it was too late and as I moved I thought, *Two. Two of them.* Just like before, in Miller's house. One of them had stayed behind just in case.

He appeared to my left, behind a curtain. The curtain zipped along the railing. He took a sideways step and then his elbow moved straight and hard, cracking me above my left eye. I lifted my right arm to cover my face, but in an instant he had my forearm. He squeezed hard and pulled it towards him, at the same time grabbing my shirt with such force that the seams at the collar broke. He delicately lifted me into the air and hurled me sideways, so that I landed sprawling in a tangled heap. The curtain behind me fell. A woman screamed. Within seconds he was standing over me. He landed a vicious chop right in my face. And then another, which sent my head whipping to one side. I lashed out, kicking, and almost immediately felt another hammer blow as the back of his elbow came down on the back of my head.

He started to walk away. I managed to get to my feet. He was already pushing open the door. I flung open the door and followed him out into the rain, half staggering the whole time. I held my hands to my side, breathing hard in and out. I wiped the blood from my eyes and spat blood on to the ground. Far ahead I could just see Stanley heading towards some stairs that led to the car park.

From the top of the rise behind me, a car came hurtling along, churning up water in its wake and grinding to a halt near the entrance to an underpass. The passenger door swung open. The wiry-looking man emerged from the darkness of the tunnel and slipped inside. The door slammed shut and the car went tearing through the underpass.

I moved myself up the short flight of stairs to the car park. There was no one around. I took a few seconds to catch my breath, but I knew I didn't have long.

'Stanley!' I yelled. 'Stanley!' I paused, scanning the walls and peering over the roofs of the cars. The sounds of police sirens came from somewhere. Already I could hear a car moving up the ramp from the exit down below and the roar of another car as it came racing through the underpass.

'Stanley, they've gone. You've got to come out. It's me from last night. From Lee Miller's house. You remember? DCI Guillermo Downes.'

I took a few blundering steps. The car park stretched out before me. There were deep puddles here and there, and a lot of cars, even at this time of night.

'There's no way out of here. They will find you again. You knew they were coming, didn't you? You know what they did to Miller? They did it half for fun, Stanley. They wanted to know what he had hidden in his house. But Miller wouldn't tell them. He kept his mouth shut and maybe saved your life. They pulled out his tongue for him and then made him watch it burn. Come on, Stanley. I can help you.'

99

I remained motionless. I looked up and down the car park. It was empty. I searched a little longer, and then when I saw a police car heading up the ramp I wearily motioned it over. Stanley was gone.

Graves had left for London straight away once he had spoken to Downes. He took the 1.49 train to Paddington, arriving in London at three thirty. By the time he finished at the paper it was gone ten. He tried Downes but there was no reply. Then he phoned Amanda on the off chance that she might want to see him, and to his surprise she told him to meet her at a bar not too far from the very large house her parents had bought her in Notting Hill.

Graves took the Tube. He pushed through the turnstile and waited for the train, managed to get a seat and then almost immediately gave it up to a woman, who looked surprised at the courtesy.

The Tube suddenly drew to a stop between stations. It must have happened to him a million times before. But for the first time he felt a sense of claustrophobia. The thought came to him that he was buried deep underground. He stared straight ahead and tried not to think about it. But he could feel the heat and the sweat crawling along his back. He stared hard out of the window at the black dirty bricks.

He breathed long and deep, with his eyes fixed on an invisible point, willing the train to start. Why couldn't they tell them why they had become stuck here? Buried again.

Oh, Christ. He was suddenly back in the collapsing chimney. The bricks were just inches from his face. He tried to steady his breathing. He placed his bag down at his feet with slippery hands. Then he picked up his bag and pushed his way through the people standing in the aisle and stopped at the end of the carriage.

The train had still not moved. He breathed in deeply, really starting to panic. The air in the chimney had been suffocating. Even though he had been able to hear them breaking through the chimney breast and coming for him, he had felt as if he would be stuck down there forever. Oh, thank God. He looked up. The train was moving at last.

He told himself that he had been panicking over nothing, but he was very pleased to get off at Notting Hill Gate all the same, and he emerged gratefully into the night air. His shirt was still clinging to his body. He didn't want to think about last night. Never wanted to think about it again actually. If he had expected any sympathy from Downes, he had got none.

He tried to calm down as he headed towards the bar. Why had he risked his neck for a total stranger? What he had seen with Downes only weeks before was still enough to give him nightmares – and now this. Was it something you could ever get used to? He remembered the outline of the stain near the chair in the living room, and the smell in there. The crime scene routes of access laid out in the dark. The sound of the rain beating on the roof. The squalor of death. The ordinariness of it all, which gave death its awful, lingering power. His mother had been right. It *was* sordid. Why wade through it every day, when he didn't have to?

He forgot about all of it the moment he saw Amanda. She was sitting at the bar. She had brown skin and blonde hair which reached her shoulders, a dainty curl of it hanging with apparent carelessness above her left eye. Her lips were compressed in concentration as she read a paperback. Her other hand hovered above her glass. Her long slender legs were crossed. There was a certain chill to her which had scared him off to begin with, and it was keeping the wolves at bay even now. Her eyes were deep blue. He could quite happily just watch her for hours.

Graves tried to pull himself together and wished he'd had time to get changed. When he marched up to the bar and she saw his face, he found himself having to fend off a million of her questions. She finished her drink, and they had a late dinner in the restaurant over the road. Then they went to another bar for a nightcap.

The last thing he wanted to talk about was work, but Amanda seemed to waver between huge interest in his job and almost total amused indifference, as if Graves had engaged on some absurd enterprise which he would one day give up. Something he was beginning to think himself but he didn't say it.

'So,' Amanda said, 'you were going to tell me more about this Shotgun of yours the last time we were together. Before the phone rang and you left me in the lurch.'

Graves looked up at the ceiling. 'Was I?'

'Yes, you were. You still haven't told me why you left Oxford either. Did they kick you out or something?'

'Something like that,' Graves said vaguely.

'You're not going to tell me, are you?' She shook her head. 'God, you haven't changed. All right, so tell me about Shotgun, then.'

'I'm not sure it's even true. Could be someone else.'

'Come on,' Amanda said. 'Really? Out with it.'

'Oh, I don't know. Only that Downes nearly killed someone when he was in London,' Graves said breezily. 'That's what I heard anyway.'

'Killed someone?' Amanda said.

'Actually there's no way of knowing if it's true or not. And it's certainly not the kind of story you tell in a place like this and definitely not to someone like you.'

'Like me?'

'Somebody with your background,' Graves said.

'Ha, you can talk,' she said.

'Havelock was the man's name. Anyway, an old case. Forgotten now.' His expression was suddenly bleak.

'So what happened?' she said impatiently. 'I want to know. You can't just leave it at that.'

Graves sighed. 'All right, you asked for it.' Graves took a long pull on his gin and tonic. 'You sure?'

She nodded.

'Downes wasn't always in the Cotswolds. He was sent to London, and was sent back to the Cotswolds when he was around my age. Don't ask me what he was doing in

England, because no one seems to know and he never talks about it.'

'What was this Havelock case?'

Graves nodded. 'Havelock killed four men one winter. Late eighties. He'd just been diagnosed as HIV positive. It was a death sentence back then and so he decided to get his own back.'

'What do you mean? His own back. I don't understand?'

'It was revenge,' Graves said. 'I know it sounds bonkers. But there you go. Revenge on those who'd given him the virus. He blamed the whole gay community for it. So he went after them. One by one. Even though he was gay himself.' Graves turned around. He paused and then lowered his voice. Amanda had to lean forward to hear him. 'He picked them in bars and clubs. There was an accountant, a librarian and a factory worker.' He paused. 'Well, I think it was a factory worker after the first one. The first one was a florist. He picked them up, took them home and killed them. Sometimes he didn't even wait that long.' He didn't mention that Havelock had torn the florist's tongue out with his teeth, strangled him and then mutilated the corpse with a razor. He'd done pretty much the same to the others. But worse.

'But what's that got to do with –'

Graves impatiently put up his hand. 'You asked me to tell you and so I'm telling you, Amanda. The team assigned to the case were making very little progress. It wasn't like it is now, you know. Attitudes were totally different. They said the Met were dragging their heels, and there was a lot of bad feeling on both sides. Said they weren't taking it seriously enough. But it must have been difficult, because nobody could remember seeing anyone or anything out of the ordinary.'

'He must have been known,' Amanda said. 'Known in the community.'

'In theory. But of course in those days no one really wanted to come forward, even if they did know something.' Graves stared hard across the bar. 'Could ruin you. So they were drawing a complete blank. But they knew it would only be a matter of time before he attacked someone else.'

'So they just *waited*?' Amanda said angrily.

'Yes. But the rumour at the time – and this was long after it had all blown over, mind you – was that a young police officer, a sergeant, had taken an interest in the case. A personal interest. It was all hushed up afterwards, because he had no right to get involved in the first place. But he made it his business to find out what was happening. Turns out he was extremely unhappy with the way the case was being handled. He got so fed up with them that . . . he started to look into it himself. In his spare time, when he wasn't working.

'They think that he got hold of the files, made copies and went back to all the bars and places where the victims had last been seen and double-checked. He became quite friendly with some of the locals, and for some reason they seemed to take to him.'

'Oh,' Amanda said, quite surprised. 'So is he . . . is he –'

'Christ, no,' Graves said quickly. 'Well, I don't think so. But he can be pretty charming when he feels like it. And he's a little bit different. Anyway, word got around that he could be trusted. It takes a while but eventually he gets something. It turned out that some years before Havelock had attacked another man in a car park, but it had never been reported. The victim didn't want anyone to know. He'd just managed to get away by the skin of his teeth. Said this guy had tried to strangle him. But now word gets back to our young sergeant.'

'Who goes straight to his superiors and tells them, right?'

'Of course. But instead of a pat on the back, he nearly gets sacked right there and then, and they tell him to keep his nose out and his trap shut. They don't even follow up on it.' Graves sipped his drink, imagining a younger and furious Guillermo Downes and not liking the image very much.

'And?'

'And so he ignores them. Goes straight back and persuades this fellow to come along with him and watch some of the bars in the area where the other attacks took place. But from the outside, though. So it's safe. They do this for weeks and weeks. Then one night this fella recognizes him. Havelock's leaving with a man. There was no time to call anyone – this was before mobiles, remember. So Shotgun followed him. Followed him on his own.'

'Followed them.'

Graves nodded. 'Havelock, it seems, was an ex-army commando. He'd done two tours in Northern Ireland. Got in some trouble over there and been discharged. Anyway, what happened afterwards is all hush hush, so no one really knows exactly what went on. Only that Downes followed the two men down an alley, Havelock was carrying a razor, and Downes took it from him. Havelock ended up in hospital. Nearly died – they kept all that quiet too. The case officers of course got all the credit for it in the end,' Graves said. 'And Downes didn't last long in London after that. They wanted to be rid of him, so he got sent back to the Cotswolds, where he'd first started out.'

'Back to the Cotswolds.'

'That's what I heard.'

Amanda looked at him. 'And that's where he stayed. And you? You'll stay there too now, I suppose.'

'I don't know,' Graves said. 'What difference does it make?'

'Well, it might make quite a lot of difference,' she said.

'To whom?'

'To me, of course.'

'Right,' Graves said, and looked at her. Yes, she was definitely going to leave him high and dry again. Yet here he was. All he had to do was stand up and leave.

'A policeman,' she said. 'Dealing with all *that* . . . all that awful stuff day in, day out. And in the middle of nowhere, when you could be here,' she said, looking around at the warm glow of the bar.

'I told you that you shouldn't have asked,' Graves said.

'I knew it when I met you,' she said. 'I knew you wouldn't . . . you wouldn't . . . I don't know. When we were going out I knew you were a –'

'Bad prospect?'

'Well, yes,' she said, 'if you want to put it like that, yes. Remember you're the one who said it, not me. A bad prospect, and that's exactly what you've become,' she said and actually waved her finger at him. 'Everyone had such high hopes for you. You could have done anything you wanted. My parents thought the world of you when I introduced you. You remember them, I suppose. You were quite happy to ignore them of course.'

Graves hardly remembered them. What did he care what her parents thought of him? What did that matter? What was it with rich girls and meeting their parents?

'But I knew it. I knew you wouldn't –'

'Knuckle down?' Graves suggested.

'Will you please stop doing that?'

'Doing what? Putting words in –'

'Will you please shut up. And what do you do? You end up in the back of beyond in some awful-sounding town, cleaning up after other people.'

'What would you have me do? Be a merchant banker?' Graves said. 'Work in the City?'

'Well,' she said, 'what's wrong with that?'

Graves looked at her and thought, *Oh, just about everything*, but said nothing.

Amanda was still looking at him. He shifted on his seat, feeling like a sullen teenager.

'Are you all right?' she said. 'Something's happened, hasn't it? You don't seem as sure about everything as you usually do.'

'What do you mean?'

'I don't know . . . What about that big old cut along your cheek? Why won't you tell me what happened?'

'There was an accident. I had to help someone out.'

She kept on staring at him, and then finished by saying something entirely predictable. 'It's not too late you know,' she said. 'It's not too late to change your mind.'

# PART TWO

## 13

I'd made such a mess at the hospital that the nurse patched me up with great reluctance. Douglas and Irwin came in and helped to arrange the search for Stanley, but when there was still no sign of him by 5 a.m. I went home.

I set my alarm for eight, but slept right through it until ten. I crawled out of bed feeling like I was a hundred years old and crept downstairs. It was still raining. I cupped three aspirins into my palm, swallowed them and looked at myself in the mirror in the bathroom. It was an alarming sight. My face was a mass of cuts and bruises. I forced myself to grin. Still, no broken teeth, which was something, I supposed.

I managed to drink a coffee and the aspirins made me feel better almost immediately. I ran through the rain to my car. I felt as if things were already spiralling out of control. The way they had come for Stanley so fast took my breath away. How had they known where to find him? Who had told them? They worked in tandem, which meant something: either they had worked together in the past or they had been trained to work in the same way. And if they had been trained . . . A deep stab of solid fear twisted in the bottom of my stomach. I knew only too well what trained men were capable of. I'd experienced that back home. I felt around the corners of my mouth, thinking.

The sound of the rain beat down on the roof of the car. I turned on the ignition, switched on the heating and began to drive slowly to the station. I phoned Graves on the way, wondering what we were up against and hoping I was wrong.

'Any luck at Finn's paper?' I said, when Graves answered.

'Yes, I was there for a good while yesterday and again this morning.' Graves sounded slightly breathless. 'I've been trying to reach you. What's going on?'

I told him.

'Christ. So they were already there? In the hospital? They were just waiting for the right moment?' Graves said in rising disbelief. 'But how the hell did they know he was in that room?'

'We don't know. But they'd probably been searching for a good while. Maybe for hours.'

'But Stanley got away, right?'

'Not a trace of him. And no trace of the men either,' I said. 'Look, tell me what they said at Finn's paper about him.'

'Finn had been getting on everyone's nerves. He wanted to know why the police were suddenly after him, as he'd stopped paying this retired officer a long time ago.'

'So he hadn't done it for a long time? How many years?'

'At least ten. So Finn was confused about that. If it was all so long ago, why was it suddenly coming back to haunt him? Apparently these two had been very careful about it. They met only when they absolutely had to and only small stuff was handed over – traced number plates, phone records, that sort of stuff. I think what really bothered Finn was the timing. He wanted to know why now, after all these years. The whole thing seemed very suspicious to him.'

'Do they know how the Met got wind of it?'

'No, sir. No idea. The investigating officers won't tell me a thing. They say I'll have to talk to their superiors first and get permission.'

'All right. But he was doing some digging of his own?'

'Yes. His friends tried to make him see reason. There was no cover-up. It wasn't some conspiracy of people out to get to him, and they tried to make him just accept it. He'd broken the rules and now he had to pay. He phoned up a few of his friends late at night. Drunk. And he started going on and on about it. How everyone had it in for him but he would never say who they were or why.' Graves sniffed. 'But then they didn't hear from him for a while, so they thought . . . well, they thought that he must have finally let it go and was simply getting his defence in order before his trial. But then he suddenly returned to it a few weeks ago and was really worked up this time, more than ever before, it seems.'

I slowed down. 'So when they heard from him again, did he say anything new?'

'He said that it was something to do with a story he'd written.'

'An old story?'

'Yes.'

'How old? Anything to do with Miller?' I said quickly.

'No. No connection at all. But he did say that the police only started to get interested in him soon after this story had run and that he wished he'd never written it. It was about a council worker.'

'A council worker? Where? In London?'

'Yes. He was found dead in his flat years ago. In Southwark. So nowhere near the Cotswolds at all, and it was almost twenty years ago,' Graves said before sighing deeply at the other end. 'And I can't see how it can all be connected. So it doesn't make any sense and it's probably a wild goose chase.'

'Yes, but Finn thought that the police were out to discredit him. Because of this story. How sure was he?'

'Pretty convinced, by the sounds of it. No one seemed to care about it any more, apart from the victim's son, and it's been doing the rounds forever.'

'So it's a well-known story.'

'Well, it *was*, decades ago. But Finn seemed to get interested in it all of a sudden and, totally out of the blue, practically begged the editor to run it. So that's a bit odd as well. Wasn't really like him to go on a crusade. Especially not for something so old. But he got quite worked up about it, and the editor said they would run it but only if things were slow. Finn was a top reporter, so the editor went out of his way to oblige him.

'After the story appeared, the Met was forced to reopen the case. A few of the other papers picked up on it in a small way. I phoned the victim's son. He lives on a council estate in Southwark and has agreed to see me. I'm nearly there now. And he says that Finn visited him with another reporter, but I haven't been able to find out who yet. I'll probably have to go back to the paper to find out.'

'All right, Graves. There must be link to Miller. See if you can find it. Keep at it and call me when you've got something,' I said and hung up.

# 14

I parked the car and headed quickly inside through the rain, ignoring the stunned looks as I walked in. Collinson ushered me straight into her office. She grimaced when she saw my face and her mouth opened as if of its own accord in appalled shock.

'Are you all right, Downes?'

I nodded. 'How's Varley doing?'

'Not too good actually,' she said, looking worried. 'He's still in the hospital.'

Sitting next to her was a tall man in a rumpled suit who appeared not to have slept for a week. His hair and shoulders were wet. He was around thirty-five, tall and thin with cropped brown hair and blue eyes. His overnight bag was standing outside the office; another suit in a bag was lying sprawling on an unused desk. He reached for a plastic coffee cup on the edge of Collinson's desk and took a big gulp as I sat down. Collinson looked at him drinking his coffee with growing irritation, but he didn't seem to notice or care. He had an open, friendly kind of face and a self-depreciating manner; on first impression, he seemed bemused. Combined, it somehow gave him an air of confidence, and he nodded in my direction and grinned as if he knew me before replacing the coffee precariously on the edge of Collinson's desk.

'Still no sign of Stanley?' I said, looking at Collinson.

'None. Somehow he managed to get away. He's a wily bugger. God knows how he did it. But we can't find him anywhere. You sure you didn't get the number plate?'

'It was too dark. Just the car. An Audi. Looked new. What about the men? Still nothing? Anything at all?' I said hopefully.

She shook her head. 'No sign of them. We've got your description of the man who attacked you and several others saw the other assailant racing after Stanley in the hospital. But they were in and out of there pretty quick. There was CCTV in the hospital, which was meant to cover the main access areas, A & E and the car park. But the cameras were disabled moments before the attack on Stanley. A security guard had noticed and was heading downstairs. Pretty low-tech approach, as they just cut the wires, but good enough for their purposes.'

I looked sideways. 'So you're from the Met, I suppose.'

'Vine,' he said, and put out his hand and I shook it.

I noticed that beneath his apparently relaxed manner his eyes were watchful and intent. There were hard lines around his thin lips and his eyes were slightly bloodshot. He reached for his coffee and took another gulp.

'So no one noticed where Stanley went. Pretty hard to imagine, with his arse hanging around his ankles in a hospital dressing gown, isn't it?' Vine said and smiled.

Collinson glared at him. 'We checked all the roads leading in and out of the hospital,' she said, feeling the need to justify herself, which was unusual for her. 'We set up roadblocks all the way around the town. There's been no sign of him and no sighting of him *anywhere*. He must have got some clothes from somewhere and now he's lying low. Or he's managed to get out somehow. He could be halfway to London by now.'

'I thought you were supposed to be keeping an eye on him,' Vine said, looking at me. 'The officer you posted out there doesn't seem to have been much use, does he?'

'We didn't know what we were up against,' I said as evenly as I could manage. 'Stanley was waiting for them: he somehow knew they were coming. Or guessed that they would be. It's the only explanation for why he got out of there in one piece. It looks like he's pretty resourceful – we didn't know just how resourceful until now. The Met are looking for him and the Flying Squad by now as well, I imagine.'

'So who are they? Do you know?' Collinson said with growing anger.

'I don't have the slightest idea,' Vine said, and stretched out his legs languorously in front of him. He turned to me. 'And you only managed to get a quick look at them, is that right?'

I nodded. 'I was pretty close up to one of them for a little while. But I was on my back most of the time.'

'Or flying through the air, by the sound of it,' Collinson said drily. 'But it was a good job you were there, Downes. If we'd known how determined they were, we would have done things a lot differently. But of course your office didn't feel fit to tell us and you won't tell us even now what it's all about, will you, Vine?'

'I wish I could but –'

'Oh, come on. Why all the secrecy? What's Stanley done and what's the connection between him and Lee Miller?' I said, suddenly feeling very tired of it all. 'Why don't you just level with us instead of playing silly buggers and save us all some time? Is this the first time Miller's come up in connection with Stanley?'

'Yes, as far as we know,' Vine said, slightly taken aback.

'And what about Finn?'

'The journalist? It's the first we've heard of him too.'

'Are you sure about that, Vine?'

Vine made a pretence of looking offended. 'What do you mean, am I sure?'

I sighed. 'So no connection has been made in London between the case you're looking at and Finn and Miller?'

He shook his head. 'No. None.'

'But you're here because of someone else, right? A friend of Stanley's whose gone missing. This Robert –'

'Robert Wilson.'

'You still don't know where he is?'

'No.'

'So Wilson's still missing and Stanley is still on the run. And they know each other.'

'Yes, we think so.'

'Know each other how?'

'We're not exactly sure.' Vine frowned. 'Friends, we think. Or they used to be. There's some connection between them. But we haven't been able to figure out what it is. If they were friends, we think it was a long time ago but we don't know that for sure.'

'So this goes back a long time?' Collinson said, leaning forward.

'We think so. Yes.'

'And now the only person who might help you find him is gone,' I said. 'Stanley seems to know what he's doing, so it might not be so easy to find him again.'

'You sound like you're almost happy about that,' Vine said.

'Maybe I am. He's a survivor and a lot tougher than he looks. That's the impression I'm getting of him, anyway. He knows how to lay low for a while, which might buy us some time. But it won't be long before those men catch up with him again. And God knows what they'll do to him if they do. Did you know that they tortured Miller to death?'

'I was aware of the details,' Vine said. 'The intruders were looking for something, obviously, but you don't know what it is.'

I watched him closely for a moment longer, wondering. 'Actually, we do.'

'Now look, Downes,' Collinson warned. 'Don't you think you should –'

I put up my hand and she stopped, taken by surprise midsentence.

Vine's eyes glimmered as he waited for me to go on. 'Well, what?'

'They were looking for some photos.'

'Photos?'

'Polaroids of a room,' I said, looking very carefully for a reaction. In front of me Collinson tensed but I motioned for her to wait.

'What room?' Vine said quietly.

'We don't know where it is. The odd light suggests it's underground. I'm not sure. It's full of equipment – hospital equipment – that's out of context for that place, and it seems to have been moved over time. Does any of that sound familiar?'

Vine shook his head and brushed away an imaginary piece of lint from his trousers.

'Everything in the photos looks wrong somehow. And one boy is in each picture. They appear to be there of their own volition – that's what it looks like, anyway.'

For a fraction of a second Vine didn't move a muscle. His eyes attained that watchful quality again before once more softening into seeming unconcern.

'Doesn't ring any bells? Are you sure?' Collinson said.

'Why should it? I'm just here because of Wilson. Why are you suddenly talking about a . . . a medical facility? What's that got to do with anything?'

'I was hoping you were going to tell us,' I said.

Collinson hunched forward, pressed the palms of her hands together and stared at Vine, wondering, I knew, if she could trust him. 'Downes?'

I nodded, stood up and motioned for Vine to follow me. He stood up and all three of us headed upstairs. He took his plastic cup of coffee with him.

# 15

There was an electric feel in the incident room and a sense of rising urgency. All of us could sense it the moment we walked in. A handful of constables manned the phones and computers. Another constable, a balding overweight man called French, was glaring at a fax which had come through. He tore it off, walked quickly to the other side of the room and handed it to Douglas, who took it without saying a word.

No one even looked up as we entered and walked towards the middle of the room, where Irwin was standing still and very straight near the whiteboard, tapping a pen against his teeth. He had just written a number of guidelines which were often used for Long-term Missing Person Review cases and would help us to see any connections if there were any. Copies of the photos had been pinned to the board.

Irwin moved away, looked doubtfully towards Vine, and I nodded, giving him my approval, and all three of us looked at the photos. Vine put his hands in his pockets with apparent nonchalance and leant forward. He was doing his best to hide it but he wasn't the greatest actor in the world, and I could sense the rising excitement as he stared at the photos. I took a step closer as well. For some reason I suddenly had the impression that I was looking at photos of exhibits of animals in a museum, because of the way the boys were captured in that strange, unreal light.

'Three so far,' Irwin said over my shoulder. 'They faxed them through this morning. There're a good number of years between the time they disappeared. Five years between the first and the last.'

'Five years,' I said, shocked.

'So those boys *did* disappear?' Collinson said. 'Something did happen to them in that room?'

'We don't know that for sure,' Irwin said uneasily. 'All we know is that they went missing. And only three so far. The age of each boy in the photos matches the age at which he went missing. We're trying to match the clothes they were last seen wearing and the few clothes in the photos,' he said, pointing to them. He continued: 'There's been no trace of them. No bodies. Nothing. The boys went missing a long time ago. At least twenty years.' Irwin nodded when he saw the expression on Collinson's face. 'Yes, I know. Some of them even longer. Twenty-five years is the longest, and, as I said, there's a five-year gap between the first one and the last. So whatever was happening there . . . in that place, not only happened many years ago but also over a very long period of time.'

I turned around and looked at Vine, who had been listening to this all very intently. 'You weren't expecting this? You know anything about it?'

Vine didn't say anything straight away. He moved away reluctantly, it seemed, from the photos, but his eyes still seemed to be greedily absorbing each detail. He saw me looking at him and his expression changed to one of more even curiosity 'No, I wasn't. Should I have been?'

'Do you think Stanley might know where this place is?'

He shrugged. 'I really wouldn't know,' he said.

'You're lying,' I said, suddenly fed up with him.

'I'm sorry,' he said coldly.

'I said you're lying, Vine. You know what it is. It's written all over your face. Or you've heard of it before. Come on, what did you expect to gain from coming down here? It doesn't make sense unless it all ties in with this. Stanley knows what this is and so does this man Robert.'

'Look, I didn't come here to be –'

'What did you want to speak to Stanley about?' I said, moving forward.

Vine looked uncomfortable.

'Downes,' Collinson warned.

'Is it to do with missing boys?' I said, taking another step towards him. 'A long time ago?'

Vine glanced up sharply. 'I can't tell you that. I'm sorry.'

I leant over him so closely that I could smell the coffee on his breath and Vine stumbled backwards, hitting the back of a desk and dropping his coffee to the floor. I could feel the activity around me pause. Vine pushed back against the table. His eyes got a little wider.

'Are you sure about that? Because if there's one thing I know about you stupid bastards up there in London, it's that you don't like admitting when you're wrong. Have you been wrong, Vine?' I said, poking him hard on the chest with my finger. 'Is it something you missed? Or are you here to tidy up after somebody else's mess? Is that what this is all about? Were you sent down here to see how far we've got and then report back to your superiors, so they know how badly they fucked up? Well, have a good look if you like. Go on.'

'And so what do you think it is?' Vine said quietly.

'A killing ground,' I said simply. 'It's all it can be. But you got here too late. Stanley's gone because you didn't think that it might be a good idea to warn us that there was a leak somewhere in your office. Someone tipped them off about it, Vine. It didn't come from us. It came from you. So come on. Why? What's this all about? Why did Miller have these photos? What's in that room?'

Vine pushed my hand away from his chest. 'Keep your hands off me, Downes. I don't know what you're talking about,' he said. 'Why don't you just take me into an interrogation cell and we can do this properly?' he said, looking for help from Collinson. 'Or take me out the back and beat it out of me. Jesus, they warned me about you before I came here. Did you know that?' he said, looking at Collinson. 'He's still remembered up in London for all the stupid shit he pulled when he was with the Met.'

'Good,' I said.

'Downes,' Collinson warned again.

'Why did they send you?'

128

'I told you, I can't tell you,' Vine said, losing his temper. 'How many ways do you want me to say it?'

'No. Why *you*? Why you in particular?'

Vine didn't say anything.

'Maybe it's because they want this to stay hidden,' I said, leaning in. 'Because they knew you wouldn't do your job properly.'

These last words seemed to snap him out of it and he rallied. He straightened and took a step forward. 'You don't know the first fucking thing about me or what I'm capable of, all right.'

'That's more like it,' I said, grinning at him. 'So, come on, what's happened to Robert?' I asked, more gently.

Vine put his hands up in the air and looked once more towards Collinson for reassurance. He didn't get any. For a moment longer I thought I might have pushed him too far, but his shoulders sagged and he relented quite suddenly. 'Oh, Christ,' he said helplessly. 'We don't know, all right.'

'What about Stanley? Does he know anything about this place?'

'He might do,' he said, and let his hands fall to his sides. 'I didn't know – exactly. Not until this moment. But he might. There've been rumours about it. Just rumours.'

Vine moved away from me and eyed me from a few feet away. Collinson and Irwin stepped back, giving him some room. He looked subdued and worried. He glanced towards the photos on the whiteboard and then looked away. 'God, all right. Well, it's what you say it is. It's the medical room. That's what the boys call it as well.'

'Boys?'

'Rent boys. Boys on the street. It's a place where they were taken.'

'Taken there and brutalized,' Collinson said as calmly as she could.

'Yes. We think so, well it's been a rumour. Nothing else has ever come of it. It's a place that's mentioned only amongst certain people who know of its existence. People have heard about it from someone else, who have heard about it from someone else, but we've never had anything concrete. I didn't think I would ever actually see it. I mean see proof of it.' He suddenly looked excited, like a professor talking about a rare relic or artefact; and then, perhaps realizing how he must be appearing to us, calmed himself. He swallowed. 'But we don't know where the room is or what its real purpose is. Though it seems to be designed for a very specific purpose, doesn't it?' Vine walked towards the photos and had a good look at them this time. 'It's odd, isn't it? The hose. The stretcher. The sink. It's almost arranged so that you can . . . well, so that you can clean up the equipment afterwards.'

'So it's designed. Designed for hurting them?' Irwin said.

'Yes. Some of them . . . some of them leave. They are allowed to leave. That's what we hear. But when they leave they're not quite the same. And sometimes they don't leave at all. That's how we came to know of its existence. But we haven't got wind of it for many, many years now.'

'You'd never heard of the photos? Of anyone documenting what was happening in that room?'

'No. Never. That's new.'

'You never heard of adults being taken there?'

'Adults?' Vine said, surprised.

'Yes.'

He shook his head.

'The photos, they seem to be part of it as well,' I said. 'Maybe one of the most important parts. They need to document it. To save it, so they could relive it. But . . .' I moved closer to the board. 'You notice how the boys are all sitting in exactly the same position. They all seem at ease. They don't know what's about to happen to them. So whoever is minding them up to that point has shown great control, Vine. Maybe even kindness. But I think that once the photo is taken the control ends.'

'How many boys, in total?' Collinson said.

'We don't know.'

'Where is it?'

'In the country somewhere. We don't know where,' Vine added quickly and looked at Collinson. 'They're drugged first in London, we think, before they're taken there. But we don't know who does it. It's all been so fragmented. There's never been anything definite that we could really move on.'

'But it could be around here?'

He shrugged. 'It could be. But then it could be anywhere,' he said helplessly.

'But you believe Wilson might have something to do with it and you want to talk to Stanley about him, right? Let's have it, Vine. What's really happened to him?'

Vine sighed loudly. 'Wilson was under our protection. He had come forward.'

'With information about this place?'

Vine paused, then suddenly made up his mind. 'No, about something else. He came forward to us with some other information.'

'So he was in danger?'

'Yes.'

'And he knew it. Because of something he and Stanley know. Something about this room?'

'No. Well, maybe. We didn't think so at the time. He never mentioned it. But it certainly fits. And would explain why he was being so careful. And why he was so scared. Robert knew better than anyone what the dangers were. He was happy to talk to us about certain things. Certain events. Things that he was made to experience. But he could never give us the proof we needed. As a witness, he was worse than useless.'

'Why?'

'He has a history of violent assault, for one thing. But he knew things. People. Said he knew someone who could help us. Who had proof of what'd been happening. But Robert said he wanted to talk to him first.'

'So he was playing for time and waiting to hear from Stanley?'

'Yes, that's what we think. And one afternoon Stanley called him and went to see them. Later we were able to trace them to a café near Trafalgar Square.'

'So when was that?'

'Around six weeks ago.'

'So about the time Stanley went to stay with Miller,' Collinson said quickly.

'Yes. There was some kind of argument in the café. We don't know where Robert went to after that. We thought he might have gone back to his flat but there was no sign of him anywhere. Then yesterday we heard that Stanley was wanted in connection with a double murder out here. That he'd been hiding out with Miller.'

'But you'd never connected Stanley with Miller before?'

'No, never. We know hardly anything about Stanley.' Vine took a few paces back and said, 'Look, that's all I can tell you for the moment. I'd better get on the phone before I say something else and get in even more trouble. Would that be all right? May I go now?' he added sarcastically.

Collinson nodded and we watched him leave. We waited until he had disappeared down the stairs.

'So three boys for definite so far?' I said to Irwin.

'Yes, sir,' Irwin said.

I stared at the photos. 'Miller knew about that room, and so did Stanley.'

'But he's too afraid to tell anyone,' Collinson said.

I nodded. 'And after what almost happened to him last night, I can't say I blame him.'

## 16

Graves found a somewhat confusing map of the Galton Hill Estate near the entrance, and it had taken a while to find Neil Baines's flat, located at the back of a warren of tower blocks. Baines had told him in his small neat living room all about his father's murder, and now he headed quickly down the stairs and phoned Downes from the doorway of a derelict pub across the road.

'Finn definitely went to see Baines's son, and there *is* a connection,' Graves said a little breathlessly, 'between the murder he was looking at and teenagers on the estate.'

Graves had felt a thrill of discovery when he had talked to Neil Baines, but now, saying it out loud, it all seemed less convincing. Even Neil hadn't seemed to believe half of it. It was all so long ago. Speculation and half-truth. All the same, he persisted and told Downes everything he'd learnt. 'There was no known motive for his father's death. And you know that rumours always circle unsolved murders, sir. What we know for sure now is that Finn did go to see him with this other journalist, and he was pretty worked up about it. Made a big song and dance after the editor gave him the okay for the story. After he'd interviewed him, he returned to the flat, saying he'd forgotten his wallet. But he just wanted to talk to him on his own, without the other journalist there. That's when he told him he had something else.'

'Something new on the case?'

'Yes, sir. He couldn't be sure yet but he was checking it out. He said he would be in touch but he never called him again. Neil Baines called him after the story ran. But he never contacted him again.'

'So we don't know what he had. That would have been far too easy, I suppose,' Downes said half to himself. 'But Neil Baines's father was murdered, right?'

'Yes. And Finn said he thought he knew why.'

'Go on.'

Graves could feel Downes waiting at the other end of the line. 'He didn't tell him. But he told me that there were a lot of rumours on the estate about his father. People say that his father Leo Baines was about to blow the whistle on something that was happening there.'

'And his father worked for the council, right?'

'Leo Baines was the Facilities Manager for Social Services. He didn't show up for work, which was unlike him, and they found him dead the next day. Finn was the first person to have shown any kind of interest in the case for years. Baines's son seems to think there was some kind of cover-up.' Graves peered out of the doorway at the traffic.

'And was there?'

'It sounds unlikely to me.'

'So how was his father murdered?' Downes said.

'The fire brigade were called in. Someone had lit a fire in his flat at around five in the morning. But he had already been dead for several hours by the time the police arrived. He'd been bludgeoned to death.

'One of his neighbours had seen three men coming out of his building dressed in suits on the afternoon he died. They were carrying folders. He'd never seen them before. Didn't think much of it until later. Thought they might have been estate agents or something.'

'They were never traced?'

'No, so of course that just added to all the speculation surrounding his death.'

'Any other suspects?'

'A few,' Graves said. 'Guys his father had been seen with the night before in an off-licence and a few times after the pub closed. But they were never identified, the case just went cold after that. Baines was surprised to hear from a journalist interested in it after so many years. Especially one from a top paper like Finn's. The Met were forced to reopen the case after the story ran. They went around to talk to him, but they didn't seem to have anything new. Seemed to be going through the motions more than anything else. But, according to him, his dad was frightened about something before he died. His mum told him all this: his dad phoned her in the middle of the night to say a man had come to see him. And that he'd left it too late.'

'Left it too late? Those were his words?'

'Yes. Someone Baines knew had come to see him, and Baines hadn't believed . . . whoever it was to begin with. But he told me that this guy was worried, and the rumour is that he'd seen something relating to kids at one of the buildings he was responsible for. And he told Baines about it.'

'What, a council building?' Downes said.

'Yes. He thinks so. His father looked into it. Wanted to know who had access to certain properties; asked lots of questions; collected files from the council offices. And he found something. He didn't want to believe it, but he told his ex on the phone that it must be true. And he made a big deal about it a few days before he died, when he was in the local pub. He said that he was going to tell someone, and that he didn't care what happened to him. And his friend told him that he should shut up and that he should be careful about what he was saying in public. But Baines got more and more worked up.'

'But we have no idea what he had?'

'No. And he never got the chance to tell anyone about it.'

There was a brief pause on the line. 'I don't know, Graves,' Downes said doubtfully. 'Sounds like a lot of rumour to me, and all of it a bit too neat. Seem that way to you too?'

'Yes, sir.'

'Anyway, *surely* the police must have looked into this. I mean, something this big. Involving children on a council estate. And a murder too.'

'Baines never actually reported it.'

'The theory being he never had time, I suppose,' Downes said cynically. 'And those files he collected. They disappeared too?'

'Yes, sir.'

There was a long pause on the other end of the line. 'We're going to have to follow it up. Finn was interested in it and it could be the reason why he drove all the way out here. Find out everything you can. There must be some more detail on what exactly this person had seen and why Baines was so scared before he died. You're going to have to keep looking and –'

'Call you when I've got something. Yes, I know,' Graves said, hung up and stepped back out into the cold.

Irwin had made some notes, which he now reached for as I settled down into a chair and breathed a sigh of relief. Outside the wind gusted and the branches of the trees began to creak and sway, gathering momentum. The rain fell in an ever thickening wall. All the dire predictions about floods which I had only half listened to over the last couple of days looked like they might well come true.

'So here's the first one,' Irwin said, appearing in front of me and motioning to the picture of the boy with the red hair, the black ear stud, and the burn scar on his arm. 'Howard Curran. He was fifteen. He ran away in 1977. More than twenty-five years ago. He was reported missing at 9.15 p.m. on Friday 6 May, and was last seen around 10 a.m. earlier the same day in Tooting. It wasn't the first time he had run away.

'Later there was information that he visited Havant, Leigh Park and Paulsgrove in Hampshire, sleeping rough as he went. He was believed to have been using the train to visit a number of areas after he went missing.'

'So the sightings were confirmed?'

'Yes, sir. After about three months' – Irwin paused, looking at his notes – 'he just vanished and was never seen again. Not once did he contact his relatives or any of his mates.'

'Why did he run away? Trouble at home? Drugs? What?' I said, leaning back in my chair.

'No specific reason as far as they were able to tell. Pretty tough background, though. He'd been in trouble a lot at school. Arrested twice for shoplifting. Bit of a tearaway. Lived alone with his dad. Dad on the dole.'

Irwin moved along the whiteboard and pointed to another picture. It was the tall, muscular-looking boy with curly blond hair. 'Now this one is Callum Pryor. Sixteen. He went missing two years later, in 1979,' Irwin said sombrely. 'Callum is different, as it doesn't look like he was planning on running away to begin with and he'd not gone missing before. So it looked suspicious right off the bat.' Irwin ran his hand along the back of his neck.

'He wanted to go to a party and he sneaked off after a row with his parents. They'd told him that he wasn't allowed to go, but he went anyway after they went to bed. He was reported missing by his mum the next morning. He was at the party for several hours and was seen leaving alone, and then travelling on buses in north-west London. Last known sighting is on a bus at around 4.30 a.m. in Kingsbury. He got off at a place called . . . Valley Drive.' Irwin looked up from his notes.

'According to the few passengers on the bus, he seemed disorientated and maybe under the influence of alcohol or drugs. There had been plenty of both at the party. The bus was also taking him further from home and the theory is that he must have realized this and got off. There's a park nearby. So the police thought that something might have happened to him in there. They brought in the underwater team to search the lake in the park. But they found nothing. Further searches continued throughout the week, but, again, nothing was ever found.'

'Any later sightings?'

'He had friends in Kenton and Wembley Park, and they think he may well have been living rough for a few months.'

'All right. And the third one?'

Irwin moved along the whiteboard to the photo of the boy with black hair and the beginnings of a moustache. 'This is Paul Goodwin. He was sixteen years old. He was last seen at Hull train station on the evening of Tuesday 12 October 1982, when he was due to catch a train to Selby. He told his sister that he was leaving home for good and would be staying in Selby with friends for a while. He never arrived, but he later rang his family. He told his mother that he had decided to go to London. But he did not return home, and none of his friends ever heard from him again.'

'He had links to London?'

'Hemel Hempstead and St Albans. So the Hertfordshire Constabulary liaised with the Humberside police as to his whereabouts but were not able to find him. He was last seen in Croydon, sleeping rough and speaking to someone who was trying to help him out by the looks of it, at around one in the morning. Was asking him if he was all right. He was described as around thirty years old, five nine, with an athletic build. He never came forward.' Irwin put his notepad on the table. 'That's all we've got.'

My headache was coming back; I reached for the bottle of aspirin in my pocket and unscrewed the cap. 'So all three of them spent some time on the street before they went missing.'

'Yes.'

'Were they ever in care?'

'No – that would be in the reports.'

'What about a council estate in Southwark? Any rumours about anything there?'

'No, sir.'

'Okay. Check to see if any of the boys had a connection to an estate called Galton Hill. Finn was looking into a murder of a council worker called Leo Baines who worked there and lived nearby. And there were no convictions for prostitution or anything else?'

'No, none,' Irwin said.

'And no mention of this fella who was trying to help the boy out in the other reports. You better go over that again: call the investigating officers, if they're still alive, and find out.

'So these boys are on the street,' I said, cupping three aspirins in my hand. 'And they just vanish into thin air. There's no sighting of them for over twenty years. Until these photos show up.'

Irwin looked uneasy. 'Looks like it, sir. But why would Miller keep them?'

I frowned. 'I don't know – unless he had something to do with it or they had some value. But the time frame is all wrong. Think about it. If what Vine says is true, there've been rumours about this place for years.'

'But that fits for the boys we've identified, doesn't it, sir? And we know now it's two men. Two men attacked Miller and two men came for Stanley.'

'All right, but let's say these two men were . . . I don't know, around twenty when they started to take the boys into that room. Right,' I said, standing up with some difficulty and approaching the board. 'Let's put their minimum age at twenty for argument's sake. Well, they would be in their mid-forties by now. But the person who attacked me was no more than thirty-five at most. Then there's the picture of the man they took into that room,' I said, looking at it. 'How does he fit in with the boys? Who is he? What is he doing in there?'

Irwin put his hands into his pockets and stood next to me. 'And then there's the other photo. The black and white one. I don't understand how that fits in at all.'

'That's a lot older, because the room is new. And it's not even a Polaroid, just a normal everyday roll of black-and-white film, according to Ashbury.' I swallowed the aspirins in my hand. 'All right. And what about DNA?'

'We're going to need Low Copy Number DNA. Birmingham says it will be a week at least.'

I nodded. 'And what about Miller's place?' I said.

'Nothing there either,' Irwin said, and folded his arms. 'The SOCO team haven't been able to get any good footprints from outside or inside, and there are no signs of tyre tracks on the lane or in his yard. There's no murder weapon for Finn anywhere on Miller's property or in any of the fields near it. The tongs were scrubbed clean. All the fingerprints match Miller's or Stanley's, apart from a few in the kitchen, which match Finn's. So they must have been wearing gloves. And there's nothing on the farm that resembles the medical room. And now we have to move fast, because it looks like the whole place could flood soon with this rain.'

'No more of those photos?'

'No. None.'

'Finn's flat?' I said hopefully.

'Nothing in there either. These guys really know what they're doing. According to the Met, no fingerprints which aren't Finn's are on their database. But it was searched, just as we thought. Really thoroughly. They had his driver's licence from his wallet. So they probably went straight there as soon as they finished with him and searched his flat.'

I told Irwin that he could take a ten-minute break and I ducked across the road and grabbed a sandwich. I felt slightly better but not much by the time I got back inside.

We kept at it, going back and forth. But there was nothing on the man who had apparently offered to help Goodwin, and nothing on the other boys either. The photos were all we had. I kept looking at them. It was hard not to. The answer was there somewhere. It had to be.

But, as we got busy on the phones and stared at the pictures, looking for anything that might give us a clue to the room's location, we all knew that there was one single rule in the manuals when it came to missing people.

When in doubt, think murder.

## 18

George Finn's address turned out to be an unassuming basement flat opposite a fish-and-chip shop at the end of a long terraced street in Balham. Police tape covered the front door. Graves got the number of the landlord, phoned and waited. It was almost two thirty and he hadn't eaten anything for hours: he ran across the road and got a bag of chips. He thought about Amanda for a while. Very pleased with himself. Things could not have gone any better. He had been feeling chuffed about it all day. Graves could still hardly believe his luck and couldn't wait to finish work and go see her again. But she already seemed to be making plans for him. She had been like that when he had first met her.

Of course she had a point. Was the way he had been treated in Oxford even remotely acceptable, he thought, as he helped himself to another chip? So why not just leave? It had made sense when she had brought it up this morning over breakfast. Well, why not? He was still stunned at the enormity of the decision ahead of him and couldn't quite believe that things could move so fast if he let them.

The landlord, a short, swarthy-looking man who introduced himself as Tariq, showed up, and Graves threw the half-eaten bag of chips into a bin. Graves showed Tariq his identity card, and they went down the stairs. Graves carefully replaced the police tape after Tariq unlocked the door.

The flat looked like a bomb had hit it. Drawers had been tipped out upside down. The mattress in Finn's bedroom had been overturned and lay on its side. Pots and pans in the kitchen had been thrown all over the place. Rubbish bins had been pulled out and shelves turned over. There was a small study at the far end with little in it but a computer monitor with wires hanging from it. Traces of powder where the Met had taken prints were everywhere. But nothing had been smashed or broken.

There were a few signs of the former inhabitant's presence, like an outline beneath the chaos – an alarming number of vodka bottles were standing by the sink.

Alone in the kitchen while the landlord checked for any signs of damage, Graves could hear a neighbour moving about upstairs and some music being switched on. The walls of the flat were paper thin.

'Bloody hell,' Tariq said, stepping into the room, 'they must have been really quiet or waited until the neighbours were out. And how on earth did they get in?'

'With a key,' Graves said, looking at the mess.

'A key. Where did they get a key from? They got it from George, didn't they?' Tariq said in rising horror. 'I mean they got it from him . . . what . . . while he was, what, lying there dead or something?'

Graves nodded and was about to turn around when the front doorbell rang. He was sure that the neighbour had spied the landlord through her window and was coming downstairs to corner him about some issue relating to her own flat. The landlord winced and seemed to be thinking the same thing and looked like he wanted to duck out of sight. The doorbell rang again and echoed loudly in the small hallway. Graves waited and then turned back and headed towards the bedroom, frowning when he heard a key rattling in the lock. The landlord paused and then moved back, and both of them watched the door from the bedroom.

The door was pushed open and a woman walked in. Her auburn hair was untidy, as if she had come in a hurry, and she quickly shut the door behind her. She paused, uncertain, and then, seeing the lights on in the living room, looked in. Her eyes narrowed when she saw the mess. Then she took a few faltering steps inside.

Her footsteps drew to a sudden stop. She reappeared almost immediately and then began to move up the hallway. She looked up, and when she saw the two men peering at her from the bedroom she flinched in a ducking roll against the wall. 'Oh my God, Tariq,' she said. 'You absolute stupid bloody fool. You scared me half to death.' She strode forward and rapped him on the shoulder with her umbrella. 'What,' she said, hitting him to emphasize each word, 'are you playing at just standing here? What the fuck is wrong with you?'

Tariq put his hands up. 'Sorry,' he said.

'But what are you doing? You know what's happened to George, don't you?'

'Yes, I heard.'

'I heard yesterday.' She shook her head and closed her eyes. 'I got a call from some awful-sounding village in the middle of nowhere about my car. What was he doing all the way out there anyway? I mean the Cotswolds. Do you know?'

Graves took a step forward out of the relative darkness of the bedroom and looked at her. She was in her early thirties, slender and pretty and almost as tall as he was. Her hair curled over her shoulder and she had a small cleft in her chin. A sharp angry frown creased her forehead and she regarded him with growing irritation as he looked at her.

'Who's this guy?' she said, pointing at him with the back of her thumb.

'He's with the police, Emma,' Tariq said. 'The whole place's been trashed.'

'So who did this?' she said, looking up suddenly. 'This mess in here? Is it something to do with what happened to George and that other man?'

Graves didn't answer straight away. 'Look, do you mind telling me what you're doing here and who you are?' he said finally. 'Didn't you see the police tape on the door?'

'I needed to get something,' she said and shrugged.

'Get what?'

'Some letters.'

'Letters?'

'Yes, personal things,' she said irritably. 'I used to live with George.'

She had certainly got over her initial shock very quickly, Graves thought. She seemed to burn with a restless kind of energy. She was wearing a white blouse underneath a long black coat and her hands reached for her bag and then closed it shut when she couldn't find what she was looking for, and then she was off again and halfway up the hall.

'So whoever killed George,' she said, 'they went straight to his flat afterwards, didn't they? But why would they do that?' Her eyes lit up. 'What were they after in here? It must be something. And what was George doing all the way out there? I don't suppose you know anything yet,' she said dismissively, looking him up and down.

'You two split up?' Graves said, ignoring her.

She nodded.

'When?'

'God. Months ago now.'

'But you still have the key to his flat and he still has the key to yours?'

'And?'

'So when?' Graves said with growing impatience. 'When did George take your car?'

'A week ago. I got back from work and the car wasn't there.'

'But you tried to phone him?'

'Of course I tried to phone him. I was furious with him. He had no right to take it and he knew it. As soon as I got back from work I phoned.'

'And he didn't answer?'

'No.'

'But you left a message?'

'Yes, I left a message,' she said, as if Graves had asked her something stupid. 'Of course I left him a message. I told him to give me my fucking car back.'

'No explanation. Nothing about where he was going in the note?'

'No.'

'So you waited for him to phone – and when he didn't?'

'I waited. Not much else I could do, was there?' she said, looking at Tariq and rolling her eyes.

'And it was an impersonal kind of note? The one he left you when he took the car. Do you still have it?'

'No, I chucked it away. It was just a few lines. "I've taken the car again. So sorry,"' she said, imitating her ex. 'Look, George was always sorry about something,' she said exasperated. 'He was that kind of person.' She paused, realizing that maybe she had been unkind. 'It didn't really end too well between us, if you want the truth. I dumped him before you ask. He said he'd push the car keys through the letterbox when he came back. And that he'd be back later that night. But he didn't come back. I thought maybe . . . well, that . . .'

'That he'd done a runner because he was in trouble.'

'Yes. Maybe, or that he'd wait until I was at work again and leave the car. I hoped he hadn't but . . .' She shrugged. 'Well, if he had . . . well . . . run off somewhere

I wasn't going to be the one who got you lot involved, although he probably deserved it.'

Graves folded his arms. 'But he was worried about something as well, wasn't he? Not just the police. He was sure that the whole reason he'd been charged was because of a specific story. You know all about that of course.'

'Of course. He told me.'

Graves nodded. 'But you went with him as well. You were with him when he spoke to Neil Baines. It was you, wasn't it?'

'Yes, it was me. So what?'

'Stay here,' Graves said.

He motioned her towards the living room and then led Tariq outside, telling him that he'd lock up and leave the keys with the neighbour upstairs. When he returned, Emma was already sitting perched on the edge of a sofa being very careful not to touch anything. In the small cone of light thrown out by the lamp you could almost forget that the whole flat had been turned upside down.

He sat down in an armchair in front of her. 'So you went along with him to see Neil Baines. So you must know all about how Finn got interested in that story. It was out of the blue, wasn't it? That's what your friends at the paper say.'

'I don't have any friends at George's paper. I'm a journalist. Different paper. We try to do a little bit better than the rubbish they churn out day after day. No one else would go with him; they were tied up with other stories.

So he phoned me and asked if I wanted to go along. I didn't have anything much else to do, so I thought why not and we went to see him. God knows how many times that poor man's told that story before.'

Graves nodded. He too had felt immensely sorry for Neil Baines.

'George wrote a piece saying that Baines's father had got wind of a cover-up involving council workers and maybe councillors too messing about with children on the estate – and was murdered for it.' Emma said. 'I'm surprised they ran it. It only made a few paragraphs in the end, but it was enough. The police had to reopen the case.'

'So you helped. But your name was never connected with the story?'

'No.'

'All right, so George filed the story in August. But he became interested in the story again around Christmas time, when he was arrested and charged. Did you know that? His colleagues at the paper are saying that he was sure it was all some kind of plot against him connected with the story on Baines. Did he tell you the same thing?'

'Yes, pretty much.'

'He phoned you?'

'Totally drunk.' She smiled fondly, remembering, and then suddenly looked serious. 'George drank. A lot. He told me that I must never say that I had anything to do with it if anyone asked me. I wasn't going to anyway. I'd forgotten it. I thought he was just being over-dramatic.

The next day he phoned first thing in the morning. Sounding a bit sheepish of course.'

'When was this?'

'Just before Christmas.'

'You don't know why he suddenly got interested in the Baines story, do you?'

'No' – she looked at him for a moment and then, making up her mind suddenly – 'but I'm looking into it now. I suppose you're going to find that out sooner or later so you might as well know now. Ever since I heard what happened to George.'

'What – you're looking into the murder?' Graves said, shocked.

'Yes, of course. What do you expect me to do? Just sit around and wait for you lot to sort it all out? No, thanks. When I heard about George, I thought, my God, he must have been right all along and none of us had taken him seriously. I mean, we just thought he was going crazy.'

'So you think he was right to be afraid?' Graves said, still taken aback by how cold-hearted she seemed now.

'Yes. George's death proves it,' she said cheerfully. 'If you talked to Neil Baines, you'll know that his father was scared before he died. And angry too. Whatever he'd been looking into at the council got him killed, according to him anyway.'

'Yes, I know,' Graves said. 'But it's almost twenty years ago now and it could be something his son just wanted – needed – to believe. The idea that his father died for a reason is easier to swallow than the idea that his father just died in a random assault in his home.'

She was looking at him with growing impatience. 'Yes, I know all that. But before Baines died someone told him something definite. And that's when he decided to look into it. Did he tell you that?'

'Yes.'

'Well, I know who it was,' she said, straightening up on her chair and looking at him. She waited. 'Are you going to ask me who or not? Actually it was a caretaker,' she said, before he had time to answer.

'A caretaker? How do you know?'

'It's not all that complicated. Didn't take the police long to find him; they just never bothered to tell Baines's son. He says that someone spoke to his father a few weeks before he died, right?'

'Yes.'

'And Baines regretted not listening to him. Wished he'd heard him out, taken him seriously.'

'Yes.'

'I thought that if it was on council property, chances were it was someone who had something to do with the properties Baines managed. Baines supervised a lot of people. I talked to the receptionist who used to work for him. She's head of the whole department now. Very smart woman. She told me that Leo Baines was responsible for around fifty people. Building managers. Building staff for repairs, that kind of stuff. Plumbers. Electricians. And caretakers. Each one is on a rota. So it can be office buildings, administrative buildings, libraries, anything like that. They're responsible for a lot of things. Safety. Security. Apart from the usual stuff like cleaning up and locking up. More than you'd think. She had a look at Baines's old files for me and the person we're after is a man called Brandon Quint. She remembers him coming to the office a few weeks before Baines was killed.

'His widow remarried, and she lives and works over in East Dulwich now. I tracked her down and talked to her this morning, and she says that her husband was responsible for dozens of buildings around Southwark. "A very responsible, stand-up type of guy." Her words. And he was a big favourite of Baines. There had been a lot of cuts at the council but Baines managed to keep him on. He was in charge of a library, some car parks, some of the residential tower blocks, and he even did some gardening in one of the parks in the summer for extra cash. But she said he was also responsible for something else. For another building nearby. Not too far from where he lived, and that's where he died.

'You want me to tell you how her husband died and when?' Her eyes widened in triumph. 'All right, I'll tell you. He died in a fire.'

'Where?'

'In one of his properties. A children's care home.'

'A children's home?' Graves said quickly.

She looked at Graves very closely and her eyes brightened. 'That means something to you, doesn't it?'

'Go on,' Graves said.

She looked at him a while longer and said, 'He would have to go round there if anything needed doing. Maintenance work, that kind of thing.'

'And he died there in a fire?'

She nodded.

Immediately he could feel her looking at him, gauging his reaction.

'And listen to this,' she said. 'Quint died two weeks after he went to tell Baines about his concerns. And Baines was dead less than a week later.'

Graves was very still for a moment. He could feel her waiting. He looked up and said calmly, 'So you're saying that this caretaker named Quint sees something in a council-run property, a children's care home. He tells Baines about it, and is killed in a fire at that very place. Baines starts to make a big fuss about it, and he's killed too.'

'Yes, that's exactly what I'm saying,' she said in growing excitement. She stood up. 'I looked at the court records first thing this morning and it was in the papers as well. You want to hear what happened? I seem to be doing your job for you anyway, so I might as well keep going now that I've started. You want to take notes?' she said, looking at him, and Graves realized she was serious.

'No, it's all right, I can –'

'All right, then try to keep up. The fire was caused by an electrical fault in a television on the second floor. In the recreation room. It spread through the building so quickly and so suddenly that the emergency services didn't know what they were up against, and some of the residents were trapped. Two carers who were asleep upstairs, and him. Quint.'

'What time was this?'

'Around two in the morning.'

'So what was Quint doing there at that time of the morning?'

'That's the whole point. His wife says she doesn't know. She'd been waiting up for him all night. No one knows what he'd been doing there. He'd been a bit down for a few weeks. Worried about something, but he didn't say what it was. Got quite angry about it, which wasn't really like him. And one night he said he was off out to the pub and he didn't come back. Next thing she knows the police are knocking on her door, telling her that her husband's been killed in a fire.

'The two carers – they lived there – somehow got trapped on the second floor. The boys just ran and managed to get out through a fire escape. They were on the first floor. The whole place was destroyed. But the blaze moved unusually quickly,' she said, looking down at him. 'Within half an hour of the first 999 call it had spread to several other floors. It turned out later that the home had been identified as a fire risk and was due to be shut down anyway. And when it was all over, it was discovered that the council hadn't carried out any fire checks for at least a year. The carers died of smoke inhalation and burns.'

'And the caretaker?'

'Quint was found downstairs, in a hallway. He'd succumbed to smoke inhalation. He was pronounced dead at the scene by paramedics.'

'And Baines's receptionist told the police about Quint going to see Baines before he died?'

'Yes, she told them.'

'But nothing suspicious was ever reported in relation to the fire?'

'No, the official report says it was an accident. But you can see where this might be going? Something they –'

'They?' Graves said with exaggerated disbelief. 'Who are they?'

'They . . . the . . . oh, I don't know. Someone. Whoever it was who got to Quint, and to Baines as well. Come on. It's as clear as day. There's a cover-up somewhere. Both Quint and Baines saw it and both of them were killed because of it.'

'All right, it has a certain logic to it,' Graves said, standing up. 'I'll give you that. But I don't know . . . I mean, come on. This Baines murder was looked into at the time. You already admitted that the police were on to this caretaker and talked to his widow. No doubt they looked into it just as thoroughly. There can't be anything in it. Otherwise Quint's widow would know about it; they would have told her. It's more likely that Quint could have been in the home for a good reason. There could have been an emergency which his wife didn't know about. They might have phoned him at the pub and he could have gone

159

over there last minute. And look, there isn't anything that special about Baines's murder, if you think about it. Someone got into his flat, killed him and then set fire to the place to get rid of his body. Things like that happen quite a lot, I'm sorry to say.'

She was looking at him and shaking her head, as if she should have known better than to expect anything more from someone like him.

'I'll look into it,' Graves said as cautiously as he could. 'Have you got the address for Quint's widow?'

She nodded and began to do up the buttons of her coat. 'There's something you're not telling me. Come on, I can see it in your face. It fits, doesn't it? There something else, but you don't want to tell me what it is. It doesn't matter: I'll find out, you know.'

Graves practically had to push her out of the flat. He took her keys and locked the door behind him, wondering exactly what she'd been looking for in there. He waited until she was out of sight before he reached for his phone and called Quint's widow.

## 19

Graves took the No. 185 bus all the way to the nursing home. It seemed to take forever to get there: the bus stopped every five minutes and pushed its way sluggishly through the traffic. It was almost five thirty by the time he arrived.

He got off at Dulwich Library and walked the rest of the way up a small hill. He asked for Mrs Parnham, Quint's widow. The well-maintained routine of the care home at night filtered through to him as he waited on a long wooden bench. There was the noise of cutlery being cleaned and moved about. Some low conversation from the catering staff at the other end of the corridor. A sense of activity before they were hastened up to their beds like children.

He started thinking about the fire, wondering if there really was anything in what Emma had said. Baines murdered. Quint dead. Both council workers. Yes, there had to be something. He felt a stirring of excitement, a pulse like electricity running through his body. He thought about Quint caught in the middle of the fire, his inert body prone on the floor, the smoke pouring in all around him.

Graves pushed himself off the wooden bench when Mrs Parnham, wearing the uniform of the home, appeared a few minutes later and led him without a word along a straight wide corridor to a small room at the other side of the huge dining hall. The room had an old desk, some chairs, lockers and a long row of coats hanging on hooks.

Mrs Parnham reached for her cigarettes, offered one to him and, when he refused, lit her own with a cheap plastic lighter. Then she sat down on a chair and motioned to the seat opposite. She was near retirement age but sturdy-looking, with a long, heavy face, very clear but slightly protuberant blue eyes, and hair, which was no doubt supposed to look blonde, but seemed beige in the cold light of the staff room.

'You're here because of Brandon?' She did not seem surprised or particularly put out.

'Your first husband, just before he died. Something was bothering him. What was it he was worried about? Did he ever tell you?'

'Well, I didn't want to tell that reporter too much,' she said. 'In case she got the wrong idea,' she said, looking up sharply. 'You know what that lot are like.'

'Yes, I know,' Graves said with feeling. He lapsed into a short silence, annoyed that Emma had beaten him to this particular witness. 'There seems to be a lot of specula-tion surrounding his death. I hear that he might have been worried about what was going on in one of the buildings where he was working and he went to talk to his supervisor about it. Was he really worried or is that just a rumour?'

'Oh, he was worried all right,' Mrs Parnham said firmly. 'It was a care home for boys. They were usually put there when they'd been in trouble. Been in and out of foster homes most of them.'

'How many were there at that time?'

'Oh, not many. Two or three at the most, I think, at any given time. The home was in an awful state of repair and they were gradually winding it down for closure. Most of those boys'd been through hell and back. So they weren't all that easy, as you can imagine. But Brandon always tried to be friendly with 'em and they often took to 'im after a while. He wasn't pushy or anything like that. He was just, you know, solid. He were there a lot. Cleaning after 'em for a few hours a day and fixing up the place after they'd made a right mess of it. So he'd get chatting to them and know them after a while.' She stopped suddenly and there was a short silence as she stared at her cigarette. 'But there was one kid they brought in. Kid called Miles.'

'Miles?'

'Yes. He weren't like the others. He were quiet most of the time, but he could be a real handful when he felt like it. Even worse than the others. Used to drive the care workers round the bend. Unpredictable: he could go off on one in a second. You wouldn't know it to look at him. That's what Brandon used to say. Anyway Brandon kind of made friends with him. It took a while but he made sure the other kids didn't gang up on 'im.'

'Do you remember the other children's names?'

'No.'

'But you remembered Miles's?'

'Yes. Brandon was worried about him and he asked the carers about him as well, to see how he was getting on. He were a bit younger than the others.'

'How old?'

'Around thirteen or fourteen, I think,' Mrs Parnham said, as she blew smoke up in the air. 'And then one day Brandon went into work and Miles suddenly wasn't there any more.'

'Wasn't there?' Graves said quickly. 'What do you mean, Mrs Parnham? He'd been . . . what, moved to another care home? Or to a foster home?'

'Yes, that's what they told him.'

'Where?'

'In another local authority, over in Hounslow. It wasn't that strange. Of course they came in and out all the time, and usually he didn't think twice about it, but he'd have some idea if they were going. He wished he'd had a chance to say goodbye.'

'Did they say why he'd been moved?'

'No. Nothing, really. I mean, it wasn't his place to ask why. Sad to see him go I s'pose, but that was about it. Nothing much you can do for these kids. But then he ran into one of his old mates over in Hounslow. Worked for the district council.'

'Another caretaker?'

Mrs Parnham took another long drag on her cigarette, peered at him through the smoke and crossed her arms. 'No. Social worker. Brandon'd known him a while back, as he used to work in one of the homes in Southwark but changed jobs. And Brandon asked him to say hello to Miles for him if he saw him. You know, just a friendly hello from his old mate. And the social worker said he would ask around and let him know. But then he called Brandon and said that he'd asked around but there was no Miles there. Never had been. Asked him if maybe he'd got the name wrong.' Her eyes had a faraway look as she remembered. She fell silent again.

'Go on,' Graves said.

'So Brandon went back and asked the workers in the care home. They said he must have misheard. Miles had been placed in a foster home.'

'Which he didn't think likely.'

Mrs Parnham frowned and her expression changed to one of doubt and sudden worry. 'No. This Miles, he was difficult, like I said, and he wouldn't have been easy to place. And then Brandon asked the boys in there if they knew where he'd gone and none of 'em would say. And Brandon said there was just this silence when he asked. Absolute silence,' she said, looking at Graves. 'And then when he asked them what was wrong, they wouldn't say. Usually they were a bit cheeky. Would give him some lip or a bit of banter. But not this time. And he told me later that the way they shut up like that had made his blood run cold. So he started to get worried. He didn't like it. When he asked the carers about it again, one of them said that he should spend less time talking with the boys and more time cleaning up. They'd never talked to him like that before, *ever*.

'So he started to ask around at all the care homes. But of course they're not supposed to give out that kind of information and they phoned his supervisor.'

'Leo Baines,' Graves said quickly.

'Yes. Mr Baines called him into his office. And he told him that there had been a few complaints and that if he wasn't careful he was going to get himself sacked. Well, Brandon had known Mr Baines for years. And he told Mr Baines he was worried about this boy, because it looked like he had just . . . vanished into thin air. So Mr Baines said that he would look into it for him and that he should leave it all to him – there had probably been some mix-up. And they left it at that.'

'And did Baines get back to him?'

'Oh, yes. He phoned him a few weeks later and told him that he had called some of his contacts. And he'd got word that Miles weren't in London at all but had been moved up north somewhere. That's what the mix-up was all about. Miles was perfectly all right and had a nice new family as well. He was settling in.'

'And he trusted Baines?'

'Oh, yes. But after a while it started to nag at him again.'

Graves said as evenly as he could, 'So what was your husband doing at the children's home when he died? I heard that the fire broke out pretty late at night.'

Mrs Parnham stubbed out her cigarette and a helpless expression crossed her face. 'He went out there sometimes to check on things. It wasn't the first time he'd been there at night,' she added quickly. 'He'd gone to the pub. I think it was a last-minute kind of thing, you know. Well, it could have been that,' she said doubtfully. 'As I said, the building was a mess. And they knew where he used to drink. And he'd always go when they phoned. He'd never complain; he was always happy to help out . . . But no one ever knew for sure what he'd been doing there. And he'd never been there that late before. I mean,' she said, shaking her head, 'two in the morning.'

'And did you tell all of this to the police after the accident?'

'Of course I told 'em.'

'And what did they say?'

'They said it was an accident.'

'They didn't think —'

'That was the worst part,' she said quickly and closed her eyes. 'Brandon was trying to help and, though nothing was ever actually said outright, they made out like he'd been doing something wrong. You could see them thinking it. That maybe he'd become interested in the boy because . . .' she said in rising anger. 'Well, I wasn't having that and I told them so. He just wanted to make sure the kid was safe, that's all.'

'So you told them all about this boy Miles?'

'Yes. And they checked.'

'And?'

'Miles was fine. It was just like Mr Baines had told him. Miles had been fostered by a family up north somewhere. They even showed me a picture.'

'A picture,' Graves said, surprised.

'Yes. Of Miles and his new family.'

'Can you remember what he looked like? The name of the family perhaps?'

She paused, trying to remember. 'No. Sorry.'

'Where it was?'

'Somewhere in Sheffield maybe. I think it might have been Sheffield. Not really sure now, it's all so long ago now. God, I can't remember.'

'And when you heard about Baines . . . that he had been murdered in his flat a few weeks after your husband died. Did you ever think that might have been connected somehow?'

'No, and I didn't really think about it – not until the police came to talk to me after he died.'

'So they knew Baines had seen your husband before he died?'

'Oh, yes. Someone in his office had told the police about Brandon going to see him. So they looked into it.'

Graves drummed his fingers on the side of his chair, thinking. 'Last year they reopened the case on Baines. After the story appeared in the paper in August, they came to see you?'

'Yes.'

'And the reporter?'

'I'd never even known that there had been a story on Mr Baines in the paper. But these policemen were different. One of 'em said he was from a special unit. They look at old cases, and that they were looking at what happened

168

to Brandon and Mr Baines again. The other one didn't say much – just listened.'

'Did they ask you anything new?'

'No, I don't think so. They mentioned the journalist who wrote the story. Asked if I'd talked to him.'

'And you told them that you hadn't?'

'Yes. But then the quiet one, he leans across and asks me if Brandon had noticed anything like this before.'

'What do you mean?' Graves said quickly.

'He wanted to know if the reason Brandon had become suspicious about Miles was because it wasn't the first time a child had disappeared.'

'And was it?'

'That was the only time, as far as I know.'

'So you told them exactly what you've just told me?'

'Yes. Word for word.'

## 20

This time Graves called Downes from the doorway of a busy restaurant, and he stared at the traffic as he waited. He thought about Quint: a reliable type of person and friendly too, it seemed. There had been men like that at his school. Groundsmen and cleaners who had lived locally and worked at his public school during the day and had a good rapport with the lads. Something happens that he doesn't like. And then he's dead and the one person he tells about it is dead too. A sudden feeling of dread filled him when he thought about it.

'So what does Miller have to do with a murder in London almost twenty years ago, which everyone apart from the victim's son seems to have forgotten about, and a fire in a children's home?' Graves said.

'Well, that's what we need to find out,' Downes said.

Graves could hear cooking in the background. Downes had probably gone home for the night. 'Obviously that's what we need to find out,' Graves said curtly. 'But it could all be linked to this missing boy, Miles.'

'Maybe. What about the other boys in the home? What happened to them? They survived the fire.'

'I'm not sure.'

'Find out,' Downes said, 'and get names for them if you can. We'll get the warrant sorted out for you. You'll need a court order to look at the records of the home.

'The only way forward is the archive. We have to make sure. So you've got a long day ahead of you tomorrow. Anyway, you're probably best up in London for now, out of this rain,' Downes said moodily. 'It's making things difficult for us. Miller's property is flooded and the house is covered in half a foot of water, according to Ashbury, and we can't get anywhere near it.'

'And the court order?'

'You'll get it somehow. Sometime tomorrow. I'll have Collinson arrange it at this end and I'll phone as soon as it comes through. You'd better go to talk to the cold case officers while you're waiting for it, and see what they know about this Baines murder.'

Graves saw his bus coming down the hill, looked in both directions and then ran across the road. 'There was someone with the cold case detective when he spoke to Quint's widow. He wanted to know if Quint had noticed anything like this before. He didn't say anything else. Just that.'

'And had he?' Downes said.

'No. It was the first she'd heard of it.'

There was a long pause on the other end of the line. 'And this other detective – who was he?'

'She doesn't remember. He didn't give a name. Sat there listening, mostly.'

'Vine,' Downes said thoughtfully. 'It could be Vine. There's a lot he's not telling us. Yes,' Downes said, sounding surer of himself and anger edging into his voice, 'I bet it was Vine. He seems to be ahead of us on this whole thing. All right, you keep looking and I'll try to talk to Vine. But look, we don't know if this Miles even existed. If he did, and then went missing, Quint and Baines and Finn could all have been killed for the same reason. But what we really need to find out is how Miller fits into all of this and what tipped off Finn to Miller in the first place. Finn made the connection. It's now up to us to make it too.'

# 21

I hung up the phone. The whole house was damp from the constant rain. The only news on the radio was about the weather. They brought on a few old timers who could still remember when it had happened last time. Homes and businesses ruined. Whole towns and villages swept under water. Three people dead. I half listened as I cooked and stared outside and read through some of the files and got nowhere. I wondered about Baines and how he had been killed. There was a connection, there had to be, and I was sure Vine knew what it was. I wolfed down a steak and grabbed my coat and headed back into the rain and to the station.

But Vine wasn't there and hadn't checked in to the hotel or the guest house in the town. I made the rounds of all the pubs but he wasn't to be found. Then I checked the train station, in case he was heading back to London. But no sign of him.

I pushed open the doors to the station and shook the rain out of my hair. Irwin motioned me urgently towards his desk.

'Another one's just come in,' he said breathlessly. 'A kid called Freddie Bowman. And this one's different. London sent us the details. They managed to get an ID from the photo and the details we faxed through this morning.'

'Different. Different how?'

'He's local. And we know what happened to him. He died from an overdose in May 1983. They found him in a squat in London. He was a runaway, like the others.'

I snatched the file from his hand and went through it quickly at my desk. Then I told him to call Freddie Bowman's mother and say that I would be straight over.

It took me a good hour to get to Freddie Bowman's house, by which time it was gone eleven. I tried to remember the exact moment it had first started to rain, and found that I could not. I stopped, stunned, when I saw the house rising above me in the dark. I paused for a while longer. The lights were on. It didn't look like it was once the home of a runaway. In fact, it looked like a cottage on a picture postcard, and maybe it actually was on one somewhere.

The front door was opened before I even had time to knock, and I found myself looking at a neat, sturdy man in his mid-sixties. He was wearing a white shirt which looked like it had just been ironed. He was balding, had blue eyes and smooth features and a fastidious but very direct manner. He wasn't that tall, but he still had to stoop when he stepped through the old doorway and on to the gravel.

'About time you showed up,' he said gruffly. 'We've been waiting for you for ages. Mrs Bowman's upstairs.'

He stared at me for a moment longer and then turned on his heel and trudged upstairs. I sighed and looked at the ceiling, then walked along the long hallway and peered into the living room. I wiped the rain from my face and took off my coat.

The size of the house from the outside was deceptive. I had imagined low ceilings and small rooms but the whole house had been modernized. It also had extensions that went some distance towards the hills, and a very large, rain-swept garden at the back.

I gingerly shook hands with Mrs Bowman while the man introduced himself curtly as Charles Shaw. Then he leant against the window-sill, looking across the room and down at me as I lowered myself into a seat.

Mrs Bowman stopped in her tracks when she saw how slowly I was moving. She closely inspected my face. 'Are you all right?' she said.

'Yes, I'm fine. It's not as bad as it seems.'

'Shouldn't you be in hospital or something? I'm sorry but you look terrible.'

'Honestly . . .' I waved it away.

I was genuinely touched by her concern, especially after the shock Irwin must have just given her on the phone. She was thin and her hair, which had once been blonde, was straight and grey and tied back in a ponytail with a blue and slightly frayed ribbon. She had a high forehead, a wide generous mouth and green eyes just like her son's in the picture, but hers were now slightly red around the edges. You could tell straight away that she was what Powell would have called Old Money, and you would have known it in a second even without the house. She looked brown, as if she had just got back from holiday. Skiing probably, I thought as I looked at her. There was a certain coolness about her style even now. A measured aloofness and control. The ribbon gave the impression that she had randomly picked it up, yet it just happened to match perfectly with the eyes of a thin and angular lizard bangle coiled around her wrist.

She suddenly looked stricken. She turned the bangle and then let her hands fall into her lap. 'So there's been some news. Some news about Freddie. After all this time.'

'Possibly. Although I'm afraid I won't be able to tell you all that much right now. I just want to go over a few things with you, if that's all right, and ask you a few questions. I'm sorry about the time but it's important.'

'All right,' she said uncertainly. 'What do you want to know?'

'I need to talk to you about your son and how he ran away and . . . and how he died.' I leant forward in the chair. 'Have you ever heard of someone called Lee Miller?' I said.

'Lee Miller? No. Why?'

'Did you know him or know of him maybe? He lived in a farmhouse in Newbold on Stour.'

'No. I've never even been there. Drove by a few times.'

'But the name?' I said gently. 'Lee Miller.'

'I never heard the name before. Should I have?'

'Are you absolutely sure about that?'

'She's already told you that, Downes.'

'What about you?' I said, looking at Shaw. 'Who are you anyway?'

'I'm a friend.'

'You live here?'

'No, I certainly do not.'

'I asked him to come,' Mrs Bowman said quickly. 'When I got the call from your station.'

'How about a journalist called George Finn?'

'George Finn. No.'

'Have you had any other journalists come knocking on your door recently, asking about your son?'

She shook her head. 'No. Not for years. I mean, there was some interest after what happened to Freddie. But it all died down years ago. Why would a journalist want to talk to me about Freddie? It doesn't make any sense at all.'

'Come on. What is all this? What's going on?' Shaw snapped. 'Why all the sudden interest in Freddie after so long? What's so important that you have to worry Mrs Bowman like this? She gets a call right out of the blue and –'

'Believe me, I wouldn't be here if it wasn't necessary,' I said, interrupting him and looking once more at Freddie's mother. 'Could you please just go over again what happened to your son.'

'Freddie ran away when he was sixteen. He was having trouble at school. Drugs, we found out later.'

'There was a wider problem at the school, wasn't there? Private school?'

'Yes. He was a boarder. He came home for the holidays. We knew he was in trouble. His grades were slipping and he'd had a few disciplinary problems as well. He'd tried to hide it from us, but Daniel had spoken with some of his teachers and found out.'

'Your husband?'

'Yes. Daniel had suspected it for some time, but he searched Freddie's room and found some cannabis stuffed into a jeans pocket. He was furious. He confronted Freddie, there was an argument, and the next thing we knew our son had packed his bags and gone.'

'Missing teenagers don't qualify as news,' Shaw said. 'You must know the statistics, Downes. We tried to get the police interested, but there was only so much we could do.'

I nodded. 'So what exactly happened to him?'

'Freddie bought a train ticket to London,' Mrs Bowman said. 'He only bought a single ticket, not a return. In fact he refused to accept the return ticket, even though a return is the same price as a single. He'd taken the bus to the station. Daniel used all his contacts and so did Charles,' she said, looking at Shaw. 'Everyone we knew tried to help. We called in a lot of favours. But we just weren't able to find him. In this day and age, with mobile phones, it's easier. Back then there was no system in place for runaways. A handful of charities would help out. A few call centres. That's all there was. Well, we thought he would come to his senses and that we'd hear from him, but he never called. And then a month after . . . I'm sorry,' she said. 'I didn't really think I was going to have to go through this again. Not so long after . . . Freddie was found dead. He'd –'

'He overdosed, Downes,' Shaw said bluntly, 'as you well know if you've read his file. He'd been sleeping in an abandoned house, which was being used as a squat. He was in the sleeping bag he'd taken with him from home.'

Shaw couldn't seem to help his direct manner, but he had cause to regret it. He reached into his pocket and handed Mrs Bowman a tissue from a packet and touched her tenderly on the shoulder.

'It was just such a shock after all this time,' Mrs Bowman said.

'I know. I'm sorry. It's all right, Mrs Bowman.'

I nodded towards Shaw and watched as very gently he led her away and back upstairs. I waited until he came back again.

He looked tired and the fierceness that had been in his eyes was gone. He sat down and sighed heavily. 'Christ, what a mess. What's this all really about?' he said.

'I'm going to need a picture of him.'

'Of course.' He stood up, walked to the other end of the house and then came back a few moments later. He was holding a picture of the boy in a silver frame. Very gently he took out the photo and handed it to me. It showed a boy in his mid to late teens. He was standing in front of a long stretch of garden in the summer. I peered out of the window. The same garden. He was tall and thin with sharp features but with a sensitive mouth. Around sixteen or seventeen years old. There was a slightly detached look about him. It was him, all right. He matched the fourth Polaroid photo I had seen.

'Mrs Bowman will want that back of course,' he said.

'I'll make sure she gets it.'

'Look, Downes, before you go. Freddie's father. The whole thing was a total mess. Mary's been on her own ever since it happened. Her husband, Daniel – when he found out about the drugs, he just flew off the handle. Mary tried to calm things down, but it was no good. Freddie left and didn't come back. Daniel had a hell of a temper, and he was petrified the press would get wind of it. He was in politics – did you know that?'

I shook my head.

'He was a very big deal around here for many, many years. The press would have had a field day had they known about the drugs. So we tried to keep it quiet. We thought that sooner or later Freddie'd run out of money and come home. If we'd gone public, I think we could have found him. I know that's what Daniel thought in the end.'

'What was Freddie doing for money?'

'He took £10 out of his bank account, which he'd been saving. He had another £20 which Mary put into his account after he left. She shouldn't have done that, but she was worried about him, naturally. Maybe it kept him off the streets for a few days longer; we just don't know. Or it could have been the reason he was killed.'

'They think it was drug-related. That's what it said in his report.'

'Yes,' Shaw said, leaning forward. 'There were a few sightings that might have been Freddie. He was seen a few times with another boy around his own age. Apart from that there was nothing we could follow up on. But Freddie was sixteen. Almost an adult. In two months he would have been seventeen and the police have got more important things to look into. You know that.'

I nodded. I was afraid it was true. 'No brothers or sisters.'

'None. A month later . . . they got the call. When Daniel got the news, he blamed himself for all that had happened. Daniel was like that.' Shaw fell silent suddenly.

'Go on.'

'He killed himself.' He was silent for a moment longer. He moved his head forward slightly. He leant back in the chair and ran his hand through what remained of his hair. He looked forlorn and suddenly a lot older. 'They told her right here in this very room. So she lost both of them in the same day.' Seeing my expression, Shaw said, 'Quite. So you can imagine what it was like. The police contacted his office in London and I phoned him here and told him. Then I came straight here. But he wasn't at the house and Mary didn't even know where to look for him. We found out later that he'd made the decision almost as soon as he got the news.'

'Where did they find him?'

'He jumped off Broadway Tower.'

'Christ,' I said.

Shaw shuddered visibly at the memory. 'When it was all over, we found out that Freddie had been in London for the entire time. The pathologist report found evidence of drug abuse, specifically heroin.'

'Where did they find him?'

'In an old abandoned building in Wandsworth. A squatter found him. Saw someone lying in a sleeping bag near a fire which had burned out. He tried to wake him up and then saw that Freddie wasn't moving. He went and got a policeman. The family got the call soon after that. We don't know what kind of people Freddie had fallen in with. They were probably after his money and he was a bit . . . naive for his age. Eager to please and extremely sensitive. So the theory at the time was someone knew he had money.'

'Befriended him?'

'Yes. Maybe waited until he was unconscious and then left him there. But not before they had taken everything he had.'

I thanked him and left. They were doing some road maintenance works further along the street, but they had been abandoned because of the weather. I watched the house for a moment. There was a smell of tar and heavy upturned earth when I cracked open the window. A sudden gust of wind blew against the car and the rain fell harder. I closed the window and put on the windscreen wipers. I hadn't wanted to take the copy of the Polaroid into the house with me, but I had brought the file with me in the car. Now I turned over the Polaroid and compared the photos. There was a look in Freddie Bowman's eyes not of fear but of loathing, which set it slightly apart from the others when he was in that room. A look of defiance as well, perhaps masking his fear. But the fear was there all right. I hadn't seen it straight away.

Despite everything, Freddie fitted the pattern. A runaway on the streets. He too could have turned to prostitution – which is how he may have ended up in that room. I put on the ignition and began driving slowly back home and watched the road through the smeared glass and listened to the rhythmic sweep of the wipers, wondering how a boy like Freddie Bowman had finished his life in such a place. And how, one day very soon, I was going to have to return to that house and break it to his mother.

## 22

After spending the next morning speaking to the cold case detectives in charge of Baines's case, Graves got a curt message from Downes saying that the warrant had come through. And so he spent the rest of the day buried in the archive in Southwark; and then Hounslow; and then he phoned Downes on the way back to Finn's paper for the third time. He took the bus again, even though the Tube would have been quicker.

'We got lucky,' he said, sitting down at the front of the upper deck. 'The local authorities kept everything. I think they're obliged to, in fact, in child protection cases.'

'Even so,' Downes said, 'I still thought you'd be there all day.'

'No, they led me straight to the files,' Graves said.

'Vine,' Downes said quickly.

'Yes. It was definitely him. Vine had been there before us. He had to sign to get access and his signature is there. Only a few weeks ago too. The archivist told me exactly what he told Vine. So it saved me a lot of time. If Miles had been in a children's home in Southwark, there would be a record of him.'

'And there wasn't?'

'No,' Graves said, remembering the look of very real worry that had crossed the face of the archivist, a slightly overweight man who had led him through endless shelves. 'There are extensive records, as you might imagine. For a boy in care a lot of records have to be kept. The carers have to follow a very strict set of guidelines. I mean really strict. So it's all in the archive. The home had been operational for almost thirty years before the fire. And the records are complete all the way up to the fire. And there's not a trace of a child called Miles. The fellow in archives had been wondering about it since Vine went to see him. He even looked again on his own, but there is nothing, absolutely nothing at all. I mean, every single trace of this boy has been systematically removed. And I can't see any reason why Quint's widow would make up something like that.'

'You mean why invent a boy who never existed?'

'Yes. And after the fire there's no record of the two boys who lived there being moved to another home, which I really don't understand either. So then I checked with the local authority in Hounslow.'

'Vine had been there as well, I suppose?'

'Yes. There's no mention of a Miles ever being in the system. They ran five children's homes back then and there's never been a Miles.' Graves stared at the traffic down below. The bus drew to a stop, and a gang of school children got on and started thundering up the stairs. 'The only person who seems to have ever noticed that this boy was alive was the caretaker Quint. If there really was a Miles, someone somehow managed to get to the records in both districts and erase all of it. And they did it in such a way that their alterations would be invisible. And there's something else,' Graves said. 'You asked me to get the names of the other boys who were there when the fire broke out. I suppose you had an idea who they might be.'

'Stanley Dalton and Robert Wilson,' Downes said straight away.

'Right,' Graves said. 'Stanley was fourteen and Robert was fifteen. Stanley had been taken into care from his father's house in Brighton; Robert had been in a home in Reading and was transferred to Southwark.'

'All right, that's good stuff, Graves. But what about the cold case investigation of Baines? Vine was the other detective who visited Mrs Parnham, wasn't he?'

Graves sighed. 'Yes. But that's where the whole thing falls apart, sir. The cold case detective seems to think the whole thing's a dead end. He told Vine the same thing. The officers in charge of Baines's case did look into it very thoroughly indeed at the time. They had to open up the case again because of Finn's story and they weren't happy about it. Vine asked the cold case unit if he could tag along, and they didn't see any reason why not.'

'And there's really nothing in it?'

'Chances are it was just a botched burglary. The area where he lived was pretty rough then and it's not all that great now. There had been a number of really violent burglaries around there, and they never caught the person who was doing it. Someone could have easily followed him back from the pub, seen that he was a bit the worse for wear, and steamed in. And at least three witnesses say that he got involved in an argument with two big-looking lads as he came out of a burger joint the night before he was killed. No one knows what it was all about, but it was probably drunken stuff by the sounds of it.

'The men in suits who were seen leaving his building, carrying files. There are two estate agents' offices up the road and plenty of office buildings were being rented out at that time. Not to mention a recruitment agency around the corner.'

'So nobody actually saw them leaving his flat?'

'No. Whoever it was could have just been walking past or hanging around for a smoke. No files were missing at all. And the local man who said he'd seen the men later retracted his statement anyway. He said he'd got the day wrong.'

'And the paper?'

'If this damned bus ever gets there, it'll be my next stop.'

## 23

Graves spent what was left of the day at George Finn's paper, talking to as many of Finn's colleagues as he could. It was the same story everywhere. No one knew what Finn had been doing out in the middle of nowhere.

Just as he was about to give up and leave, a friend of Finn called Platt, who had not been there the day before, stopped in his tracks in the middle of the newsroom when Graves told him who he was and without a word led him down to the archive.

Amongst the stacks, everything was quiet and far removed from the nonstop frantic energy of the rooms above, and Graves felt that he could finally catch his breath. Platt was in his thirties, youthful-looking for his age and wiry, with reddish hair and a slightly pink face.

'So George *did* come here?' Graves said.

'I wasn't supposed to let him in, because he was suspended, but . . .' Platt shrugged. 'I've known George for years.' He picked up speed and turned on the strip lights that illuminated the archive.

'Did he say what he wanted to look at?'

Platt put his hands in his pockets and stopped walking. 'He wanted to see if there was an angle that someone might have missed. Something he might be able to sell or work on in his free time. An all-rounder or a Sunday for Monday.'

'All-rounder?'

Platt grinned. 'It means he could have sold it to the competition – everyone welcome for a fixed price.' Platt kept on walking and Graves followed him. 'I shouldn't have let him in of course. If they,' he said, looking up, 'find out, I'm done for. Who told you about me anyway?' Platt asked with sudden suspicion.

'No one directly. Some people said you two were friends, that's all.'

'You know he wasn't even supposed to talk to any of us.'

'How many times did he come here?' Graves said, catching up with him.

'Just the once. A few nights before Christmas. Stayed a couple of hours, got fed up and then buggered off. I met him around the corner for a few pints.'

'George was the first to be suspended, wasn't he?'

'George was the first to be *charged*,' Platt said meaningfully. 'A load more have been suspended. They're hoping to bag others as well. George felt like he'd been thrown to the wolves. Can't really blame him, can you? And,' Platt said, staring around the archive room, 'George had hit rock bottom. Said he couldn't stand another second on his own in that flat doing nothing. So he was going to look at stuff he might be able to use. He didn't get anywhere down here, though.' Platt stopped quite suddenly in front of a bulky-looking microform reader.

'But if he *was* on to something,' Graves said carefully, 'who else might know? Any close friends? Anyone at all?'

'No, he was on his own. They all turned their backs on him, apart from me.'

'What did you two talk about in the pub?'

'Apart from getting the sack, getting dumped and going to prison, you mean?'

Graves paused. 'All right, but let's say he came down here for a reason. Let's say he was on to something. If he was looking for something specific, would he have told you about it?'

'No, I don't think so,' Platt said without feeling.

'He would have kept it to himself?'

'Yes.'

'So he could have been lying to you?'

'Oh, yes.'

'Where was he sitting when he was down here?'

'At the microform reader. He'd got bored and was sitting there, drinking on his own. He had a flask with him.'

'So there's a chance whatever he was looking at might still be in the machine?'

'Well, I suppose so. People don't really use microfilm or microfiche much these days.' He walked over to the reader. 'Yes. There's a roll of microfilm still in it,' Platt said, surprised. He turned on the machine, which slowly whirred into life and made a surprisingly loud noise. An image came up sideways on the screen, and Platt pressed some buttons to rotate the film.

Graves peered over his shoulder. 'Can you zoom in on that for me?'

'Sure. On what?'

'The picture there.'

Platt twisted a dial and the photo got bigger. The photo showed a man in his fifties standing in front of a Jaguar E-Type. He was ruggedly handsome. He was wearing jeans, a shirt that was open at the neck, a worn pair of hiking boots, and he held a sweater under his arm. He was grinning at the camera. He looked very self-aware and composed and healthy. A dog was sniffing around some shrubs in the background.

Graves looked more closely and took a long deep breath. The awful stench of Miller's farmhouse suddenly came back to him and he instinctively took a step back.

Platt was gazing at the photo in stark amazement. 'So George was looking into this,' he said in awe. 'And he really was on to something. Christ. No fucking way.'

For a moment Graves felt like giving Platt a big hug, but the thrill of elation subsided almost as quickly as it had come. There was a strangely desolate air to the photo, despite the sun shining overhead.

'You don't know who that is, do you?' Platt said.

To gain time, Graves straightened up and looked around the stacks of shelves. From upstairs, phones rang shrilly in the newsroom.

'No, I don't,' Graves said, looking at the screen again. 'But I've seen his picture before.'

# 24

I got home around nine. It had been a busy day, chasing down leads, talking to the villagers again and trying to find out as much as we could about Miller as well as about Freddie and the other boys. We tried all the national papers as well to see if Finn had attempted to sell his story, but he had not been in touch with any of the editors of the major papers. We talked to the police in Warwickshire and Gloucester, and we double-checked our own records to see if we could identify any of the other boys in the photos.

Missing persons cases are reviewed every twenty-eight days for the first three months in the jurisdiction where they are first reported. Then every six months. Then every year, once a year, after that and usually by a high-ranking officer. So if someone had gone missing locally there would still be a record of their disappearance, along with all of the latest information on where they could be. And we waited in vain for more word on any of the other boys from the National Missing Persons Bureau in the Met. But it had been a long and frustrating day, and I was glad to get home.

For a while I sat with a drink and watched the rain pouring outside. Powell's funeral was in two days' time but it could well be postponed if it kept on raining like this. Powell's envelope was in my room. Part of me wanted to wait until the funeral was over before opening it. But Alex was bound to ask me what had been in it when I saw him at the church, so I went upstairs to fetch it and then opened it in the kitchen. I wished almost immediately that I had not.

Half an hour later, I was pacing up and down in a wild desperate panic, the photos we had found in Miller's house and Stanley and Baines and all of it forgotten, and I was trying Carlos on the phone for around the tenth time. I slammed the phone down and half ran back into the kitchen, staring at the file and the contents spilling out on to the floor. I walked away from it and started roaming through my house again. Pacing from one room to the next. I poured myself a Fernet-Branca and drank it fast before pouring another and then phoning Carlos again. But there was no answer.

I went back into the kitchen and forced myself to go through the contents again. This time I read it slowly. There was no letter from Powell at the beginning. Powell had not left any kind of note or any explanation; nor, knowing that it was useless, had he offered any kind of apology. His findings had been carefully laid out in chronological order so I could figure it out for myself.

On the first page was a letter from my brother. Seeing my brother's handwriting was still so unexpected that in a way I had to let the reality of it creep up on me before it sank in. My brother and Len had never met, and lived on opposite sides of the world. Yet here in this folder was almost a year of correspondence between them. It made absolutely no sense at all. What had Powell been doing writing to my brother? My mind reeled away from it as I turned back to the first pages. But there it was. My brother's handwriting was unmistakable. Block capital letters, and the same old-fashioned English our father had drummed into us when we were kids in Buenos Aires.

I tried to focus but the words seemed to blur and lose all meaning. I tried to make sense of them, but to begin with there was still just the sensation that there was something going on. Something going on behind my back.

There were names and dates – whole lists of them – and then a number of old documents, which Carlos had got translated for Len's benefit. I forced myself to slow down. I put down the file. Turned around, stared out of the window and took a deep breath. Then I picked up the file and started going through the pages.

I could feel Powell's will behind it all. His professional interest was cold and detached but insistent all the same. I started from the beginning and read all the way through. My brother had told Powell straight away that it was hopeless. There was no way that we were going to find out what had happened to Pilar. *Los Militares* had abducted her during the military dictatorship many years ago and, like countless others, she had never been seen again. Too many years had passed. It had all been forgotten and was best left that way.

But of course Len, with that easy manner of his, had whittled away at Carlos. My brother had sent him a picture of a cemetery and along with it an anthropologist's report outlining the details of a mass grave discovered on the outskirts of Córdoba. But I already knew that Pilar wasn't there. I had read the witness reports and seen the photographs many times before. This was just another false trail which had long since gone cold. Again, my brother had underlined that it was hopeless. Len had urged him not to give up. Relentlessly he argued that, now that time had passed, something might emerge into the light. It often did with cold case files like these. After all, he should know. He'd looked into enough of them over the years with me.

This had been followed by yet more letters, as Carlos had alternately lost his temper with him and calmed down, and then finally but very reluctantly agreed. And, after several months, Carlos told him again, and firmly this time, that there was still no trace of the man we had been looking for and that there never would be.

But Len had kept on pushing. So Carlos once again reluctantly embarked upon a search. Throughout the letters you could sense his enthusiasm for it slowly returning. But, to begin with, it was just more dead ends and confirmation of what we already knew. I kept turning the pages.

Around two thirds of the way into the file was a letter with a tone that suggested Carlos had needed to write it down, so he could actually believe it himself. He was full of almost awed disbelief. Finally a break. A break after all these years.

I stood up suddenly and walked away from it. Everything was happening much too fast. My head began to pound and the muscles in the back of my neck to tighten. I spun round on my heel and marched back to the table and made myself go through it.

Carlos was talking about a witness. I breathed in. A witness.

I read the letter twice before I could actually figure out what it all meant. A man called Antonio Burdisso had come forward. He had been in a police station in the province of Buenos Aires. A routine matter. He had simply gone in to report his car stolen and come face to face with someone whom he recognized almost straight away – *El Comisaría,* the police commissionaire – as he walked out. The police commissionaire had not recognized him. Not even blinked when he had walked in. Burdisso had filed the report on his car. Then not uttered a single word about it for three months. He had been too afraid and he hadn't wanted to rake it all up again. Then finally he told his wife. And she told him straight away that he had no choice but to report it to the authorities and then the press.

And suddenly a name. Pablo Castellani.

No time now. No time to prepare myself. A picture of a face taken outside a petrol station as Castellani filled up his car. Older now, and angry-looking in a hot Buenos Aires afternoon. His moustache was gone but it was him all right. Much heavier-looking. A face I recognized from a long time ago. A member of the abduction squad who had come for Pilar and later for me all those years ago.

I turned the page. Stuck to a plain piece of paper with my brother's habitual neatness, the same neatness with which he sent me articles about my football team, River Plate, was an article. I read through it very carefully.

After Burdisso had made his report to the authorities, and the investigation was just beginning into Castellani and his alleged role in the Dirty War, Castellani was abducted from his home and found several days later, abandoned in a slum, beaten and naked. Above the article there was a picture of Castellani. He would not say who his abductors had been.

Next was an angry letter from Len, rebuking Carlos for it. Of course Len did not know what my brother was capable of. I had perhaps painted a picture of my brother as a lovable rogue, and he could play that part when it suited him. But Carlos was a lot more than that. In fact Castellani was lucky he was still alive, because my brother had loved Pilar in his own way. No response from Carlos for a while. They must have talked on the phone. An agreement was reached. I ran my hand through my hair. I felt the fear and panic tunnelling their way through my insides. I felt as if I were twenty again and running. If Castellani had been found, it had to mean . . .

Images of Pilar came crowding in on me as I went quickly through the pages. I forced myself to go on. The barriers I had erected for self-defence – all of them crumbled in an instant. I wanted to throw the file in the fire and watch it burn. I stared at the pages lying now on the table. Castellani had been found and now they were working backwards and discovering how El Rubio had made himself disappear all those years ago, how he had slipped back into the flow of normal everyday life and become just like everybody else. Because Castellani would have given Carlos a name.

I looked at the date on the first page. They had been looking for him for an entire year. Ever since I had sat in the pub in the village and told Powell about Pilar and the men who had tracked and abducted us. I wondered if Powell had known then, when he'd asked me about what had happened to Pilar a year ago, that he was dying.

The manila envelope stood empty now, next to the sheets of paper which lay gathered in a heap on my table. Within minutes I had gone through the entire contents of the file again. But finally I could make sense of the contents. Now all that was left was a single written page and beneath it a photo. Carlos asked Len whether they should let me know or if he should take care of it himself immediately. Len had never answered, because the sickness had taken hold of him.

I went into my bedroom. I fished out the key from my desk drawer and before I could change my mind opened the lock of the box room. I flicked on the light. I hadn't been in there for a very long time so there was a musty smell. Stacks of newspapers and books, along with several files stuffed with photocopied clippings, covered the floor. I had ordered them from news agencies and libraries ages ago. I had arranged them in chronological sequence, hoping that this might put a lead to Pilar into relief. That maybe there was some mention of her in the camps, or someone perhaps had remembered her or knew what had happened to her after she had been taken away.

I surveyed the mess of the room, ashamed of myself. I had kicked a chair halfway across the room and it had left a big nasty dent in the plaster in the wall; the back of the chair was splintered and broken. An old bulletin board was lying half wedged against the door. I crouched down and reached for it and then put it back up again, so that it stood on the wall next to the window. All the pages which I had stuck up on it many years ago I now removed very carefully, one by one. I took the photo that Carlos had sent and placed it right in the middle. And I stared at it. *El Rubio*. The blond man.

My hands were shaking. He looked older of course, but it was him all right. The photo had been taken recently, by the looks of it, as he stepped out of a car and was heading to an apartment building. He was wearing a suit. He had just been playing tennis and was holding a gym bag and a tennis racket. He had a suntan and looked very fit and well. Around five years older than me, but he had seemed much older back then. But he was still in good shape. His blond hair was slightly yellowish now. The photo had been taken from across the street, through the slightly smeared window of a bar.

It was him. The blue eyes. The slight pout which gave his face an overripe, almost feminine quality. I stood looking at it for a long time. I ran my hand through my hair, feeling the scar again.

Powell had asked me only once about Pilar and what had happened to her, and I'd told him. I knew now that this was his parting gift to me.

I stood looking at the photo for a long time. Some part of me had hoped that he would still be alive. Both my fists were gripped into tight balls. We were just kids when he had hunted us down. We had never stood a chance against him or the other members of his unit. All these years, I'd dreamt about finally getting my hands on him, and now here he was. I was glad that he wasn't some decrepit old man. Glad that he'd been able to keep in shape, so he would be ready for me when I came for him. Actually he hadn't really changed all that much.

But I had.

## 25

The phone woke me. I'd an idea that it might have been ringing for some time. I answered it bleary-eyed, hoping it was Carlos ringing me back. But it wasn't him.

'Sorry, sir. I know it's really, really late. But I have been trying to reach you for ages,' Graves said.

'What time is it?'

'Two. I'm in Oxford. I managed to get the last train from Paddington but it only gets as far as Oxford and the next train to Moreton isn't until five thirty. I'm going to call a cab. I was wondering if I could come to see you when I get in.'

'Here in my house?'

'Well –'

'No, it's all right,' I said quickly. 'I'll meet you at your hotel. So what is it?'

'Finn had been to the paper's archives. A mate of his called Platt let him in. Platt thought Finn was losing it. You'll see why when I show you. I couldn't believe it myself to begin with. It's probably better if we meet, though.' Graves sounded slightly breathless. 'It will sound a bit . . . far-fetched, when I tell you, sir, to say the least. But the man in the photo . . . it looks like Finn had found out who he is. He's been missing for almost thirty years. He was quite well known. Well, the story's well known. It's going to seem a bit odd to begin with,' Graves warned again. 'So I'd really like to take you through it, if that's all right.'

'Okay, I'll be there at your hotel,' I said.

I headed outside and into my car, and tried to concentrate on my driving and not think about what Powell had found out about *El Rubio*. I focused on the rain and the road and the engine roaring down the narrow lanes and drove as fast as I dared. But as I drove it was *El Rubio* I thought of. He was out there still. All these years and that son of a bitch had been walking around like nothing in the world had happened. Playing tennis, for Christ's sake.

The car pushed through the rain. The villages whipped past me and then were enveloped in shadow. Pinpricks of light on the horizon were swallowed up. Across the ocean Buenos Aires moved to its own rhythm. Amongst the high-rise tenements and the sweltering heat *El Rubio* was out there, living his life.

The car pounced forward and I took a curve and the car screeched around a corner. The headlights of a lorry came towards me too fast and I caught a glance of surprise on the driver's face. I swerved out of the way at the last second. The lorry's horn blared after me.

I kept driving. I felt a black rage building up inside me. It used to be the only thing I had been able to feel and the only way to get rid of it had been work. Non-stop work. Now it was back again, just as badly as before. I breathed in deeply and slowly eased my foot off the accelerator. Remembering him. Remembering the Ford

Falcon when it had come for me, being thrown into the back seat.

The Falcon smashing straight into that food cart and then shooting at an angle through the railings and into the river delta, as if the metal bars had been made of wood.

I slowed down and then stopped when I came to a verge. I turned off the engine and slowly began to calm down. I had a responsibility to the boys in the photos. I stopped thinking about myself and concentrated on the very complicated task ahead of me. Then I drove to the hotel and asked for Graves at the front desk. But he hadn't showed up. So I went back to my car and managed to doze off again. Someone tapping on my car window woke me.

Graves looked tired but triumphant, and a little bit dazed after having spent so long buried deep in various archives.

He threw his bag into the back and I drove him to an all-night café for lorry drivers on the Fosse Way. Its lights shone like a beacon through the falling rain.

'Are you all right? You look terrible, you know that, sir?' he said as we walked in and shook the rain off. 'If you don't mind my saying.'

I looked around. The café was deserted apart from a lorry-driver staring forlornly into his tea and wearing wellingtons. The owner had put on the heater to try to dry out the place, so it was stuffy and the windows were misted over.

'Yes. I'm all right.'

'I'm sorry, but you don't look it. Is it about Powell? I don't mean to pry. I only heard about it the other day. Of course I knew he was very ill. I wasn't there when Collinson made the announcement at the station. I never had the pleasure of meeting him,' Graves said, which was polite even for him.

'No, it's not about Powell.' I realized suddenly that it couldn't be easy for Graves having to step in and replace him. 'Actually it is but . . . well, he left me something. Something I'm not sure I really want. Anyway, thank you, Graves, it's very kind of you to be concerned,' I said, doing my best to match his good manners. 'I used to come here with him sometimes. He had a hell of an appetite and couldn't get going without a full breakfast most days. Never got used to it myself. So what have you got there?' I said, leaning forward.

'It's kind of thrown me for a loop. I still can't believe it. But you're going to have to bear with me. Finn wasn't at the paper because of Baines. I thought he might have been in the archive, because he was looking at the fire in the kids' home. But it was something else entirely and it fits. And I still can't believe it.'

Graves ordered tea and toast and I ordered a coffee from the waitress, a plump woman in her thirties who recognized me when she came to our table.

'I've been trying to get my head around it on my way here,' Graves said when she was gone. 'George wasn't after just some story. He was after *the* story. There were a few library books at George's flat, all on the same subject, and I hadn't thought much of them at the time. But I went back and checked after I visited the paper's archive. This is one of the books. I didn't recognize him straight away, but of course I know the story. When the other journalists get wind of it, it's going to be absolute chaos.'

Graves pushed the book across the table. 'All the books he took out cover the same case. But this is the best summary. It's a bit over the top, but, well . . .'

It was a hardcover library book. The pages were a little grimy. I looked at the date stamps inside the cover. It had been taken out around once or twice a month for years. I checked the date.

'So he took this out –'

'A week before he went to Miller's house. Page 155,' Graves said, and sat back in his chair.

The book cover showed a wood. There seemed to be some stone steps in the middle of it, and then I realized quite suddenly that it was in fact an old abandoned cemetery. The name of the book was written in crimson and the author's name beneath it in black.

*Thirty-eight real-life cases of strange powers, historical mysteries and haunted locations, none of which have ever been adequately explained.*

'You're joking, right,' I said, shocked.

Graves shook his head.

I flicked through the pages. There were UFOs and monsters living in lakes, accounts of Atlantis, the Bermuda Triangle, crop circles and crystal skulls, monsters and meteors, pyramids and poltergeists, and something called the Devil's Footprints in Devon, which was a new one on me.

I looked at Graves. 'Really?'

Graves, seeing my expression of acute cynicism, said quickly, 'I know how it looks, sir. But it's serious. Finn was actually looking into a major crime committed thirty years ago. Page 155,' he said again.

I turned the page. *Strange and Mysterious Disappearances*.

I looked up again.

'Fourth one along,' Graves said impatiently.

'Which one?'

'Joe Garrett's.'

I looked down and read in a loud voice: '*While there have been many cases of strange disappearances, perhaps none has been more baffling or strange than the case of self-made millionaire and entrepreneur Joe Garrett. His disappearance led to one of the largest manhunts in police history, and to this day theories, many of them wild and outlandish, abound as to his whereabouts.*'

'What is this?' I said, looking up in disbelief. 'Finn was looking at *this*? Are you sure?'

'Yes, I'm sure. I wouldn't have come rushing back here otherwise,' Graves said indignantly. 'I know how it looks. But, please, just read it.'

'All right. All right,' I said. Graves could certainly be pushy when he felt like it.

'*Indeed, there have been numerous claimed sightings of him all over the world and dozens of theories as to how and why he vanished amongst speculation of suicide and rumours that he even faked his own death after it emerged that his business affairs were in deep trouble. Over the years it has been believed that he was living a new life as far away as Venezuela, where he was last seen raising cattle; he has been seen at an airport in Malaysia, where he was spotted in a wheelchair being pushed on to a plane by a mysterious woman; and he was even, according to one book devoted to the entire subject, tracked down to a remote village in the Pyrenees. This was later proved to be unfounded.'*

'You sure you never heard of him?' Graves said.

'No, I don't think so. A businessman?'

Graves nodded, sat back in his chair and winced, tenderly touching his ribs. 'Bit more than that. Pretty well known. Made a fortune on the stock market. Quite a flamboyant type and then made an awful lot of money in property, I think.'

I carried on reading in a loud voice. *'Yet none of these sightings has ever been confirmed nor has the reason for his sudden disappearance been adequately explained. Nor, it would seem, will this mystery ever be solved. Almost thirty years have passed since Garrett was seen for the very last time, and we are no closer now than we were when he first disappeared to finding any real clue to his whereabouts.*

*'While many believe that Garrett may well have committed suicide, perhaps because he had been forced to sell a number of his businesses to cover some of his debts, he had been in high spirits after dining with members of his staff following a business meeting in Scotland.*

*'The next morning, after breakfasting alone, he set off back to London in his car, along with his dog, an Airedale terrier. The first*

stop on his itinerary was a hotel in the Lake District – the idea being, as friends later recalled, that he would make his way slowly home to his penthouse in the Pavilion Hotel, a property he owned in London, made famous by the great number of celebrities, actors and politicians who have kept rooms there at one time or another. He continued on his journey the next day and visited his mother, who lived in a large cottage he had bought her some years ago in Lower Slaughter, a very picturesque village lying in the very heart of the Cotswolds.'

I looked up at Graves.

He was sitting back in his seat and knitting his hands behind his head. He looked very pleased with himself, as well he should. 'I told you,' he said.

I turned the page and slowed down. 'He arrived at his mother's house on schedule at lunch-time. Later that same evening he would be hosting the tenth-anniversary celebration of the theatre in Chipping Norton – a project that Garrett, a keen patron of the arts, had been involved in raising money for over many years. He unpacked, had a leisurely lunch with his mother and then went for a drive, taking his dog with him. He never returned.'

I quickly turned the page. 'That evening, Mrs Garrett and the organizers of the theatre raised the alarm. When there was still no sign of him, the police carried out a search of the nearby area and later discovered his car at the bottom of a lonely lane near the famous Rollright Stones – a complex of ancient limestone monuments located on the Oxfordshire–Warwickshire border.'

'The Rollright Stones,' I said quietly.

'You know them?'

'I've been there.'

I looked back down and started reading again. '*The Rollright Stones are of a more primitive design than Stonehenge and have been a traditional meeting place of witches since at least Tudor times and probably long before that, presumably because of the Stones' mysterious power and their pagan origins. Legend has it that it is impossible to count the King's Men – the name given to the stones which stand in a circle – and for time immemorial the monuments have been the focus for myriad tales of witchcraft. This would only add yet more mystery to Garrett's disappearance.*

'*There was no sign of a struggle. No sign of anyone else's presence and no sign of foul play. But Garrett's dog was still locked in the car and suffering the effects of dehydration; it ran off as soon as the police opened the door and was never recovered. Garrett's wallet was in the glove box and all of his other personal belongings were found at his mother's house.*

'*When Garrett failed to make an appearance the next day, a comprehensive search of the woods and surrounding area was carried out. The nearby rivers were dragged for his body, but nothing was found. The London police were alerted of his disappearance and, when there was still no sign of him, detectives obtained the keys to his penthouse at the hotel.*

'*His room had been ransacked. But there was no sign of forced entry and all personal items, as far as they were able to tell, including his clothing, were still there. Over £1,000 in cash was stashed in a tin. A number of valuable paintings and other objects had not been removed. Weeks later a number of other rooms on the same floor were also broken into, and the incidents reported to the police. A connection to Garret's disappearance, however, has never been established.*

'*The only single trace of him was this single photo, which was found some days later by a rambler, who handed it straight to the police. Standing looking relaxed and unsuspecting beside his car, it is believed that it was taken just moments before he was abducted.*'

'Next page,' Graves said, smiling.

I turned the page and looked at the picture. Joe Garratt possessed the kind of exaggerated features that would look good on a big screen or on stage. Even in the bright lights of the medical room, covered in mud and freezing cold, his looks had stood out, as they did now, here in the worn pages of this book.

Graves had brought the photocopies of the Polaroids with him to London, and now he triumphantly placed the photo from Miller's house beside the photo in the book.

'Christ, it *is* him, isn't it?' I said, genuinely shocked.

'It's him all right. I like the bit about the dog disappearing, don't you?' Graves said thoughtfully. 'Quite a nice touch, that, and the bit about the wheelchair's not bad either, and all the stuff about those stones. But if you take away the flowery tone, you've basically got an account of someone disappearing in suspicious circumstances. And guess what? Garrett has a connection to the children's home in London that burned down. He was a trustee there for many years before he went missing. And not just that home: several of them, all over London. He did a lot of other charity work as well. I researched him in the paper's archives, and it sounds like he was a pretty decent guy. Had a really good war record. But his business wasn't doing too well. He owed a lot of people a lot of money;

his business was broken up after he died. There was a lot of speculation after his death about whether it could have been one of his creditors or a business rival who'd made him disappear. But they found nothing.'

'No heir?'

Graves shook his head.

'So he was taken from that place and then straight to that room – is that what you think, Graves?' I said, still shocked to see the photos side by side.

'Yes. If you look at both pictures, obviously a lot has happened since that moment when he's standing in front of his car. But the haircut is the same. The ring on his finger is the same, and he looks exactly the same age too.

'It looks like he might have known them. He seems happy in the picture, doesn't he? Well, relaxed anyway. I think the person who took that picture was the same person who took him into that room.'

'Or people.'

Graves nodded.

'So what you're telling me, Graves, is that Finn had solved one of the' – I looked at the cover of the book, still hardly able to believe it – 'one of the most baffling and unexplained mysteries of all time, is that it?'

'That's *exactly* what I'm saying,' Graves said. 'No wonder Finn nicked his ex's car and drove straight out here. Probably didn't think twice about it. And it explains why he was being so cagey when he was asking his questions about Miller. He didn't want anyone else to get wind of the story. Had he got this story, all would have been forgiven. Sure, he would have had to serve his time if he was convicted, but he could have taken his pick of jobs once it was over.'

'Redemption,' I said quietly. 'He would have redeemed himself with this story.'

Graves nodded. 'Miller must have known something about Garrett, and Finn must have known it too. And that's the thing that still doesn't fit, sir.' Graves looked suddenly angry. 'Miller's still there in the background. We've not forgotten about him but we've been too busy chasing up all the other leads. But how the hell does he tie into all this? There's nothing that ties him to these missing boys. And now this. How can there be any connection between a millionaire who went missing thirty years ago and an ex-con like Miller? None of it makes any sense. I mean, we know what Finn was after when it comes to Baines and Quint. But none of it fits with this,' Graves said, pointing at the book.

I nodded. I could understand Graves's frustration. 'And Miller would have been just a kid when Garrett disappeared. Garrett had been missing for at least five years before the other boys went missing. But,' I added quickly, 'there *is* a connection – it's just that we can't see it yet. I know what you mean, though, Graves. Miller is the key to all this. He has to be. He's not in the photos. I thought that might have been the connection, but he's definitely not there.'

'But why would he have the pictures? Maybe he was safeguarding them for someone,' Graves said.

'I don't know. Could be he stole them and kept them. Perhaps it would have given him some sort of leverage – he might have been bribing someone. And they simply came down and killed him. That would be the simplest explanation, but somehow I think it's all a lot more complicated than that.'

'But how did Finn find out about Garrett?' Graves said irritably. 'How did he know that there was some connection between Garrett and Miller? It still doesn't make sense that Finn was able to tie it all up after decades when no one else could.'

'I know. And it's possible that Miller didn't even know who Garrett was,' I said. 'He wasn't all that famous, was he? Well known but that was a long time ago.'

Graves nodded, leant back and put his hands behind his head. 'But what do you want me to do now? You want me to focus on Garrett, or do you want me to go back to London to find out more about this missing boy Freddie?'

I watched him for a while, thinking. 'No,' I said. 'I need you here. I want you to get as much as you can on Garrett. I've the feeling that he may yet help us to unravel all of this.'

'God, it seems hopeless,' Graves said. 'Writers, journalists, police must have been searching for him for years and years and never found a damned thing. I mean, where do you want me to start?'

I sat back for a moment, thinking. 'Probably best to start in Lower Slaughter, his mother's village, and work on from there. This weather isn't going to make life much easier. But you're going to have to try Chipping Norton as well. I know it looks like an almost impossible job to find out what happened to him after so long, when so many others have tried and failed. But remember, Graves, we know something that the others who were looking for him never knew. We know what happened to Garrett now, thanks to you. Or at least we have an idea. We know he didn't go missing of his own accord. He wasn't running from anything. He didn't pull a disappearing act or kill himself or end up in a wheelchair or in such a far-flung and exotic a destination as South America,' I said, and smiled. 'He was abducted. He was taken to that room. So there're a lot of questions that need to be answered if we're going to get any further. How much time did he spend out here with his mother? Was he known around here? How important was that theatre to him? Who did he see when he was here, and is there any way at all that we can tie him to that room, wherever it is?

'My God,' I said, thinking it really did seem hopeless but didn't say it. 'But if we can find out what happened to him, we'll be closer to finding out what that place is. Where is it? It looks like it must be in some kind of formal facility.'

'You think it could be around here?' Graves said, as across the café the lorry-driver stood up and headed towards the door.

'I don't know,' I said. 'The boys went missing in London. But there are rumours that they could have been brought out to the country, according to Vine.'

'Have you talked to him?'

I shook my head. 'He's been hanging around but I can't find him. He's up to something all right. I'll deal with Vine. You deal with Garrett. Whatever you hear about Garrett, however slim it seems, you follow it. Some villages have already been cut off by the floods, but you'll have to do the best you can.'

Graves finished his tea and twisted the empty cup in his hand.

'So what do you think they did to Garrett in that room?' I said, watching him very closely.

Graves peered at the Polaroid, and then pulled the book closer, and then examined the Polaroid again, more carefully this time. 'Well, he's already dirty when they bring him in. So they've assaulted him outside somewhere,' Graves said, half to himself. 'And then they sit him down and take that photograph. And he's scared – not like the boys. Also unlike the boys . . . there's a need to humiliate him.' Graves ran his hands through his hair and leant back. 'So that was probably important to them. But it's more than that, isn't it?'

'More than that how?' I said, watching him very closely and hoping he'd make the jump. 'What happened to him after that picture was taken?'

'Well, look at all that mud.' Graves's face contorted into a sudden scowl. 'And the blood on his feet. His body was never found. So they buried him somewhere. But maybe they put him to work before they dragged him into that room and saved themselves some trouble.

He was as good as dead as soon as he stepped inside it. And maybe they wanted him to know that too.'

I lifted my coffee to my lips and took a sip and regarded him over the rim of the cup thinking, *Yes, you'll do*. 'So how? How did he know?' I said as casually as I could manage.

'Maybe his feet had been pressing on something hard and sharp. Hard and sharp enough to cut him. So it could have been the edge of a spade. If one foot was bleeding, he would switch to the other, and then the other foot would start bleeding too. I think they stripped him, beat him and brought him into that room. But I think they may have given him a spade and made him dig his own grave first.'

PART THREE

## 26

Graves went to his hotel, dropped off his overnight bag, had a shower and got changed. The hotel wasn't taking any more guests, and the restaurant had been closed off. Halfway through his shower the lights dimmed, went off and then came back on again. He put on his Hunter boots, borrowed the largest umbrella the hotel had and put on his Barbour jacket. He felt optimistic to begin with, as he headed out to his car. The police would have asked the same sorts of questions almost thirty years ago, but not precisely the ones he was going to ask. He would be giving the impression that he was following a fresh trail rather than one that had lain dormant for so long. All the same, he knew that he was probably in for a long and frustrating, not to mention extremely wet, day. It was strange to think that only he and Downes knew what had happened to Garrett.

He started at the Rollright Stones, just to get a feel for the place more than anything else. The small path threading its way through the woods was waterlogged and he had to wade through in his boots to get near it. It was a desolate spot, just as the book had said. The stones stood in a circle in the middle of a field, in half a foot of rain water. More wet fields sloped off in all directions. There was no one around at all because of the rain, and the small hut standing at its entrance looked abandoned. He splashed around the circles twice and saw no one. He counted the stones three times and got a different number each time.

He returned to his car and drove to Lower Slaughter. It took him a good hour to get there. Twice he had to turn around and find another way. The wind had picked up speed. The fields were vivid green beyond the falling rain, and the rain poured over the guttering of the houses in the village, a steady, encroaching force gathering at the edges of roads and narrow lanes. Everywhere he could hear the sound of the water rushing underground.

He parked as high up as he could. For a while he stayed in the car, staring at the picture of the man in the book and then once again at the photocopy of the Polaroid, hoping that there would be some let-up in the rain, but knowing, when he peered up through the windscreen, that there wouldn't. If you weren't actually looking for the resemblance, you probably wouldn't have been able to see it. Now, knowing it was there, it was unmistakable. He placed the book along with the photocopy in the glove box, got his umbrella, braced himself for the rain, stepped outside and shut the door.

The first cottage he tried stood in the middle of the village and faced the green. Then he tried all the other properties in the village on the vague chance that someone might remember anything at all about Garrett. There was a dim recollection of the name in the village shop, but that was it. All the newspaper headlines were about the weather and the havoc it had wrought so far. A lot of houses looked boarded up and sandbagged, the owners having fled, perhaps, to higher ground.

Suddenly the image of the medical room came to him, and he saw Garrett staring at the camera. That he had been abducted here could mean that the place where he had in all likelihood died was somewhere nearby. But there was no guarantee of that. Was it really out waiting somewhere amongst the hills?

His phone rang. He had hardly been able to hear it with the rain. He scanned the number and didn't answer it. It was Amanda. He put the phone back in his pocket, wondering what he was going to do and why he hadn't answered it. He realized that ever since he had found out about Garrett he hadn't really thought about Amanda at all. No, actually it had begun before then, when he had found out about Baines. She had been forgotten in the excitement.

He supposed he felt just as Finn had when somehow the journalist had made the connection. Whatever that connection was. Nothing else seemed to matter right now. The trail was something he and Downes could see – and only them, so it was theirs.

Seeing Amanda again had knocked him off balance and set in motion a reckless train of thought, he realized now. She had spoken about his future, or rather her vision of it. But could he really see himself working in an office day in and day out, investing other people's money and staring at spread sheets? As his feelings clarified, he knew that he couldn't imagine anything worse.

The village looked pristine in the rain. He was alone. And suddenly he had a great sense of freedom, as if he were skiving off school. The knowledge that he was glad to be back at work came to him with a jolt.

He carried on knocking on doors, getting nowhere. He had thought that the last month or so in the Cotswolds might have been an aberration. An unusually busy time in what would turn out to be an endless routine amongst muddy farms and cowpats and stately homes scattered about for the tourists. It was still hard to believe that anything could really happen in those far-off and remote hills.

He imagined Garrett in his car. That dog of his. Garrett motioning to the dog and the dog leaping into the back seat. Waving to his mother on that hot summer day. A summer haze as the car takes off down the road. The car disappears from sight. And Garrett gone. Wiped off the face of the earth at that moment. And here Graves was all these years later, looking at the house. And maybe he was closer than anyone else had ever been to finding out what really happened to him. It was as if the time which stretched out between both events was somehow being squeezed together.

Garrett had come here to visit his mother. So he must have spent some time in this village over the years. He kept on telling himself the same thing as he wandered from door to door, getting soaked. Maybe he met someone. Did something. Saw something. What had he done to deserve being dragged, terrified, into that room? Or had he simply been in the wrong place at the wrong time?

He got back in his car and looked at his map. He had decided to try the nearby villages first before taking on Chipping Norton, as Downes had suggested. He drove to the next village and left his car near an old church. He started knocking on doors and was unsurprised when he got the same response. No connection. No one even remembered him. There was a dull, almost constant ache beneath his ribs from his fall down the chimney, and it became worse as the morning wore on and the rain seeped beneath his coat. He tried all the houses along the green, then the other houses along the road and in the cul-de-sacs. The church was locked, and there was no sign of a vicar. He got in his car and drove to the next village, where the same process was repeated.

The further he went from Mrs Garrett's village, the more hopeless it all seemed. Most of the people who now seemed to inhabit these cottages had not been born here or had moved in only recently. They were the Cotswolds yuppies whom Downes held in such contempt. Some recognized the name but that was all. Others knew of Garrett's mysterious disappearance but didn't remember the name. In the intervening years since he had been abducted it had become legend. The years had stripped it of its horror, so that it was an amusing anecdote which lingered and added to the local Cotswolds charm. He stopped off for a quick lunch at a roadside pub and dried off the best he could in front of the fire. He knew he would have more joy in Chipping Norton because of the theatre. The traffic slowed to a crawl at the roundabout. There was a sense of the town being under siege. The council was out in force. Men in wellingtons were clearing out drains. A number of businesses were closed and boarded shut. The school was empty. He parked the car up in the centre of the town and tried the theatre first.

Buried in a far corner of a corridor was a picture of a grinning Garrett receiving a cheque from the Chairman of West Oxfordshire District Council and then another of him standing on the stage and cutting a cake with a dramatic flourish, laughing alongside three other men, all in honour of the theatre's fifth anniversary.

Graves read that the building had once belonged to the Salvation Army, then fallen into disrepair after being briefly used as a furniture store. It seemed that Garrett had seen its potential straight away. A lot of money had been invested – private funds as well as government grants and lottery money – in the years since Garrett had gone. Garrett, a patron of the arts, had lobbied tirelessly to get the place opened. The town was still grateful to him for it.

Graves wandered around a while and then talked to the woman in the box office, who knew the name but had never met him. She gave him a list of numbers for the trustees, which he folded and put in his pocket and she let him out and locked the door behind him. The show for that night had been cancelled.

He decided that he would phone the trustees later and focus for the time being on the town. He kept on searching. The barman in the fourth pub remembered his predecessor talking about Garrett in fond terms: a generous type of man who spent a lot of time in there. The reason for his disappearance seemed as unfathomable now as it had back then.

The more Graves asked around, the clearer his impression became. Garrett had been friendly with half the town. A lot of the older people remembered him or had known someone who had met him, and he was remembered as someone who had once been a familiar sight. A bundle of boundless energy and enthusiasm who had seemed to have become attached to the area very quickly after he had bought his mother her cottage.

He kept asking in cafés and charity shops and the few others places that were still open. He looked for motives under the rim of his umbrella and in the wet doorways of shops. Any arguments with anyone? Any problems with any of the locals? Hospitals. Medical facilities. Any connection to Garrett and hospitals? He tried another charity shop. The smell of old clothes was cloying after the rain outside. He stared at a plastic box full of old ties. The ties of dead men most likely.

He tried the shops near the war memorial and again came away with the impression of a charismatic individual who had a knack for remembering your name and was quite happy to stop and chat. He walked quickly through the town. His clothes were wet again. The wind blew the rain straight into his face and under his umbrella and on to his clothes. All the talk was about the rain. The water was rising against the doorsteps of the shops and the town hall, and here and there were signs of the damage it had caused. A street was closed off down the hill near the theatre, and a few sandbags had split and spilt out on to the ground, which gave some of the streets a grubby, dirty feel.

He headed up a small hill. It was getting dark. The day had seemed like one weary drudge from one face to the next, so that all the faces now blurred together. He tried in a small bookshop and then at a florist's. And then, un-believably, he encountered something different. By the time he heard it he was almost on automatic pilot and only half listening, so that he had to stop the woman and ask her to repeat herself.

He listened to her very carefully. He didn't call Downes immediately. It was a rumour, nothing else, and probably wouldn't lead anywhere. So he listened and then made sure. He walked out of the shop and stood on the door-step, thinking, his lean face puzzled and brooding. Then he walked back into the rain. He kept searching.

## 27

There was only one relative for Miller, the aunt who lived over in Shipston on Stour. I phoned her and talked to her briefly and was on my way downstairs when I walked into Collinson.

'Vine,' she said. 'You still haven't seen him?'

I shook my head.

'Where the hell is he?' she demanded, and looked around the corridor. 'Vine was in the Southwark archives looking for Miles, right?'

'Yes.'

'Well, that's not the only thing he's been keeping back. I'm going to kill him if I see him.' Collinson closed her eyes. 'Vine's been lying to us all along. He was over at Miller's this afternoon, and Ashbury wouldn't let him in and he couldn't get in with all this rain anyway. And apparently he was hanging around there last night as well. I called up his superiors to find out what's going on. And get this,' Collinson said in disbelief, 'they didn't even know he was here.'

'What?'

'Yes, I know. They knew all about this missing boy Miles. But they told him to forget about it. He's not even supposed to be here. He called in sick last week and he's been on leave ever since. But listen, Downes ...' She stopped mid-sentence. 'Are you all right?' she said with genuine concern.

'Yes, I'm fine.'

'If you're sure.' She went on looking at me and took a swig of bottled water. She was the only person in the station who didn't live off junk food and coffee when she was at work.

'Apparently Vine has been making a big fuss about this Robert Wilson for some time, but they can't see anything in his disappearance and are sure he's going to show up sooner or later. They've looked into it. *Thoroughly.* But Vine wouldn't take no for an answer. They thought he must have forgotten about it, because he took a few days' leave. Said he was off on holiday, but his leave ended days ago.' She suddenly looked furious. 'And listen to this. Apparently Wilson served time with Miller.'

'You're kidding. And he didn't tell us?'

'No. We've never been able to connect Miller to this in any way, but prison must be the link, and Vine didn't even have the courtesy to let us know,' she said, still furious. 'The time he could have saved us.' She took another swig of water and closed the cap. 'I'm going to make some calls to London this afternoon and try to get something else on Miller. I'll let you know, all right?' she said, already moving away. 'And if you see Vine tell him I want to see him,' she said, and turned around. 'Straight away.'

The rain fell outside, gusting against the station windows. I had found it increasingly hard to concentrate all day. I could barely be bothered to eat, and was drinking endless cups of coffee, and I knew I was showing the strain. In fact the whole day seemed to be a slow blur, and all I wanted to do was to go home and think about what I was going to do about *El Rubio*. And tomorrow, I realized with a sudden wave of exhaustion, I was going to have to watch while they put Powell in the ground.

My teeth clenched tightly together as I headed down the corridor and thought about Pilar. I had to stop half-way along and try to calm down. My hands were trembling and I shoved them deep inside my pockets. I felt a rising nausea and I rested my back against the wall and listened to the solid business-like activity of the station. I thought about the pictures of those boys. The answer was there, but I still couldn't see it.

Burton, the Duty Sergeant, was busy talking to a tall slender woman in front of him with far more courtesy than usual when I headed past the desk to get some air. He smiled, which was unusual for him as well, and gestured reluctantly in my direction over her shoulder when he saw me. For a moment I thought he might even start twirling his tie around his fingers. But, catching me looking at him, he turned around and made himself very busy.

She turned when she saw me. She had a small suitcase on wheels by the bench. She was wearing a cream-coloured turtleneck sweater under a black overcoat and a scarf. She had a high forehead and hard restless eyes.

'Who are you?' I said.

'Emma Forrester.'

'Finn's ex.'

'Yes,' she said.

'We've been trying to reach you. Why haven't you been answering your phone?'

'I've been busy,' she said vaguely.

'Yes, I know. My sergeant told me you cut through the tape on Finn's front door and used your key to get inside. What were you looking for?'

'Personal things. Some letters. I told him that. I'm not in any trouble, am I?' she said indifferently.

'I'm not sure . . .'

'Who are you?'

'Downes.'

'No first name?'

'Guillermo,' I said. 'So are you planning on running the story in that paper of yours?'

'Funny sounding name. Well, Guillermo, I wasn't planning to. Not yet anyway. So they denied it.'

'Who?'

'The Met. If you've talked to Graves, you'll know all about that.' Her face was upturned and suddenly innocently expectant. She smiled quite sweetly and ran her hand through her hair, shaking it slightly loose, and she tilted her head to one side, looking at me. I knew what that was supposed to make me do.

'The police looked into it again,' I said. 'After your ex's article. We checked it all out with them. It looks like there's nothing in it. They did a pretty thorough job, by the sounds of it. I'm sorry that I can't give you anything else.'

She narrowed her eyes. 'Mmm, are you really?' she said mildly. 'So Baines's murder could have been, what . . . a random attack? And you really expect me to believe that? What about Quint?' She took a quick step towards me. 'Oh, come on . . . come on, Guillermo,' she said, throwing her arms in the air and turning on her heel. 'You expect me to just accept that and get on the train and go all the way home. Come on . . . what's your name again? Am I saying that right? Is it Spanish or something?'

'No, I'm actually —'

'Look, George wasn't stupid. I knew him. He was insensitive, slightly immoral. But driven. He knew when something wasn't right,' she said, taking a step towards me. 'He came all the way here for a reason. And he was killed because of it. He was on to Baines,' she said. 'And Quint as well. You're honestly going to tell me that someone just went into Baines's apartment one night and beat him to death for no reason and then set the place on fire.'

'Well, it does happen,' I said, realizing how thin it sounded when said out loud.

'George comes down here in my car after he's become convinced that he's been thrown off the paper and is facing ruin.' She lapsed into a sudden silence. 'I wish I'd listened to him now. But I didn't; nor did any of his other so-called mates. So he came down here to prove all of us wrong. George had good instincts. He knew a story when he saw one. And it must have been something with legs to get him all the way out here. It says in the papers that the other man, this –'

'Miller.'

'Yes. He wasn't just killed. He was tortured to death and he was no walk in the park from what I'm hearing. The guy was massive. And someone was looking for something in his house. What were they looking for?' she said, still watching me very closely. 'You must have something by now. Come on, it's been days. What have you been doing all this time? Do you have anything at all?'

'No. Not yet but we –'

'But what you're saying is that you don't think that there's anything in it.'

'Look, I haven't really –'

'But if there is some link, you can't see it,' she said, interrupting me yet again. She suddenly looked furious. She gestured vaguely as a couple of old-age pensioners, as if on cue, shuffled under the streetlamps past the window. One of them recognized me and waved and I half-heartedly waved back. Emma Forrester looked at my hand falling to my side and rolled her eyes and shook her head.

'It seems to me that your station is far too small to handle something this big,' she said, drawing out the words out as if I were hard of hearing. 'The murder of someone like Miller – it's already all over the papers, and George's too. He was one of us. They're going to be all over it until you find out what happened to him. They're not making as much of a fuss as they would do normally, because he let the side down when he bribed that cop. You're lucky about that. But they won't stop. You and your sergeant Graves might mean well. I don't mean to be rude. I'm sure you're perfectly capable of doing certain things.'

'What, like helping little old ladies cross the street? And rescuing cats from trees?'

Ignoring me, she said, 'But don't you think it might be a good idea to ask for some help?'

Behind me Burton had stopped what he was doing and was staring at me, stunned, with his mouth half open. He looked towards her and then looked back at me.

'Oh, I'm sure we'll muddle through somehow,' I said.

There was a ghost of a smile on her lips. Then it went away. The force of her personality seemed to fill the small waiting room. She looked around the place a little longer, clearly unimpressed, and then looked at me the same way. Her eyes strayed towards the scar on my forehead and she gazed at it quite openly for a few seconds. 'What happened to your head?' she said.

'Car accident,' I said automatically. 'I'll ask you once again: what were you doing at Finn's flat?'

'I was looking for some letters,' she said. 'Personal stuff, like I told you already.'

'Did you find them?'

'No.'

'You didn't go back?'

'No, why would I? Anyway, your sergeant told me off and took my keys.'

'All right, so now you're here. What are you going to do now that you are?'

'I'm not sure yet. Look around maybe.'

'Why don't you tell me why you're really here?' I said. 'You didn't come just to look around.'

She raised her eyebrows and seemed very indignant all of a sudden. 'I don't know what you're talking about,' she said.

'No, of course you don't. But let me tell you something. The men who came for Miller: you're right, they *did* torture him. And Miller was more than capable of handling himself. And they were looking for something. They're still looking for it. I think they killed George simply because he got in their way. So if there's something you're not telling me –'

'There's nothing. I just told you that,' she said angrily.

'Well, if that's all, you should try the Manor if you're staying,' I said, pointing up the road. 'They're not taking any more bookings because of this rain but tell them I sent you.'

'Will I get a discount if I mention your name?' she said sarcastically. She actually laughed and patted me on the shoulder, and looked towards Burton as if he were going to laugh as well. He didn't.

She was already reaching for her suitcase. She turned on her heel and left, uninterested. I watched her brace herself for the rain and put up an umbrella She gave a quick glance to her left, got fed up with rolling her suitcase, carried it across the street and disappeared round a corner.

## 28

Graves stared out at the lights which lined the suburban street and phoned Downes from the warm interior of his car. It had been another long day, and he had spent most of the evening running around hospitals, but it had been worth it. He drummed his fingers against the steering wheel. It had actually been a nightmare getting anyone to talk to him at all. The hospitals in Stratford and Warwick were readying themselves for the floods, and the staff were prioritizing patients with the greatest medical need. Not the best time in the world to try to talk to a hospital administrator.

He could still hardly believe that he had got anywhere at all in the midst of the growing pandemonium, but he had in the end. He felt vindicated and waited impatiently for Downes to answer. A lorry stacked high with sand-bags stopped and men loaded them on to pallets at the end of the road. He watched them as he waited.

Amanda had been phoning all evening, and he realized with a sinking feeling that he was going to give her the boot. It had been good to see her again, but it had raked up old memories of who he used to be and what he used to be like. Someone who had been a bit too carefree and thought only of himself. He was appalled at his own feelings and he knew exactly how it was going to look when he told her: as if he had been out for some kind of revenge all along; but it hadn't been that at all. Then, as he waited impatiently for Downes to answer, he thought of the photos in the chimney and forgot about her again.

'I've got something on Garrett which might cheer you up,' he said when Downes picked up after what seemed an age. 'It shouldn't really cheer you up but it probably will.'

'Go on.'

'I talked to a florist in Chipping Norton this afternoon. Just about to close up shop. She used to send flowers to the theatre and Garrett would come in sometimes personally to pick them up. He had an account there. She mentioned him to one of the girls who'd worked in the shop for a while, though this was years and years after Garrett had gone missing. And this girl told her that she'd heard something about him and that he wasn't all he was cracked up to be.'

'What do you mean?' Downes said.

'I'm getting there,' Graves said. 'She said she'd heard this from her mother. That's all she knew. But I thought it would be worth following it up. So I tried the girl's house. She worked in the shop when she was eighteen. She'd just left school and it was a part-time job. She remembers her mother mentioning Garrett to her and more than once as well.'

'Why? Why bring it up?'

'She thinks it could have been because of something they were watching on TV. Her and her mother. One of these programmes that look at old cases, and it was about Garrett's disappearance on cable, or something like that. She can't remember exactly. But the next day, or maybe later, her mother said she'd heard something about Garrett from a co-worker called Sullivan. Her mother and Sullivan were pretty close friends. And Sullivan was a nurse.'

'So a hospital,' Downes said quickly.

Graves nodded and could feel his own rising excitement echoed on the other end of the line. He tried to keep an even tone to his voice. But it wasn't easy. He felt wide awake, wound up and nervous. 'Both of them used to work in a hospital in Stratford. Her daughter used to be friends with Sullivan's son. Went to school together. They fell out of touch when the girl's mother died, so the number she had for Sullivan was out of date. I tried all the Sullivans in the book. No luck of course. Sullivan could have remarried. Anyway, I tried the hospital in Stratford where they used to work together, but they don't keep staff records that long. I tried the nurse registry but they're not allowed to give out information without a court order, so no luck there either. But I asked around and one of the staff members thought that Sullivan might have gone to work at a nearby hospital in Warwick. She wasn't sure which one. So I tried them all and then the hospital manager in the last one I tried remembered her. Maggie Sullivan. She'd retired early, two years ago, so her records were still on file. I got her address.'

'So you've been around there already,' Downes said.

'Yes. But her husband told me that she passed away last year.'

'So just another dead end,' Downes said.

'No, it wasn't,' Graves said firmly. 'Her husband remembered Garrett well. He lives over in Bourton-on-the-Water now.'

Graves stared at the lights shining from the house. He could just glimpse a shadow of a man behind the curtains. A dog started barking from somewhere and then another dog from far off joined it.

'According to him, Maggie, his wife, used to talk about Garrett quite a lot because she'd had a run in with him,' he said finally. 'She never told her husband about it until they'd been married a few years, but it scared her so badly that when she told him she started to shake all over and it took her a while to calm down. He'd never seen her like that before.'

'Go on.'

'Sullivan was working in a hospital. This was when she was first starting out. So a long time before she was married. We're talking over forty years ago. She never said which hospital it was, but it was a local one and quite small by the sounds of it. So it shouldn't be too hard to find out which one now. Maybe a private clinic of some sort. She was on nights.'

'But it was around here somewhere? He's sure?'

'He thinks so, yes. She lived her entire life in this area, so he thinks it must be local. Garrett was one of the trustees on the board. He did a lot for this hospital as well. Not just the theatre. Raised funds. Spoke to the right people. Gave money himself. But it was much more low-key than his other

238

charity work, the husband reckons. Anyway, she complained but none of it was taken seriously by senior management. And later she found out that she wasn't the only one.'

'Complained about what?'

'According to Maggie Sullivan, Garrett had total access to the place because of what he'd done for it. It sounds like he pretty much had free rein to come and go as he pleased. It's almost like . . . like he bought his way in there. And he'd come on . . . come on a bit strong more than once.'

'To Sullivan?'

'That's right. She'd said no. Quite firmly. But you know in those days . . . I guess things were different and he actually groped her once. He made it out to be a joke whenever he saw her. He was pretty brazen about it. But one night she was working late and had to get some supplies from a store room and he went in after her. Later, she was sure that he must have been watching her and waiting for his moment. He walked in, locked the door and wouldn't let her leave. Luckily someone else came along – an orderly – and he knocked on the door when he couldn't get in. Garrett, while they were in there, called her a number of dirty names. And he pushed her on to a table. She was absolutely sure that if the orderly hadn't come along at that moment, he would have raped her.'

'Christ,' Downes said. 'And it wasn't just her?'

'It doesn't sound like it. The other nurses in the place used to talk about him. She had been warned to watch out for him by another nurse on the ward. I'm not sure how far he took it with the others. Sullivan's husband doesn't know. But, after she complained, the hospital let her go and the orderly lost his job as well. She was sure that Garrett had something to do with it.'

'And the police? When Garrett went missing, did they ever ask her about this?'

'No. That's the other really odd thing. Garrett seemed to be funding this hospital from his own pocket, rather than through any charitable trusts. And she told her husband that soon after she was laid off, the whole place was shut down.'

There was a long pause at the other end of the line. Graves waited.

'Well, it looks like things are finally moving. Thanks to Collinson, we've got some more stuff on Miller. It looks like Miller was gay,' Downes said.

'Gay?'

'Yes. Years ago, Miller committed an assault on one of the members of his gang – a guy called Townsend, who'd been shooting his mouth off about Miller being gay. Word had got back to Miller and he nearly killed him for it. The talk is that when Miller first came to London he was on the streets for quite a while. And in order to survive he worked as a rent boy.'

'But it wasn't on his record.'

'He was never convicted for it. But those are the rumours, and if you ever said anything to Miller about it or even hinted that he was homosexual you were in trouble.'

'So,' Graves said slowly, 'Miller may well have known what that room meant after all. May have even been in that room and survived it. There's no photo of him in there but that doesn't mean he wasn't in it. He seems to be the kind of person who would survive it, if anyone could,' Graves added thoughtfully.

'Yes, but we have nothing to prove that,' Downes said. 'Still, it's all coming together now.'

'It is?' Graves said, surprised.

'Yes, it is. And at the centre of everything is Vine. There's still no sign of him. And Collinson called his supervisors. Vine's on leave. They haven't seen him for over a week and they had no idea he was out here. But this Robert Wilson – when Vine interviewed him recently he discovered that Wilson had served time with Miller.'

'And Vine didn't fucking tell us,' Graves said, outraged.

'No. He's been hiding something from us. This has all been about men's real natures being disguised; we've had to peel them back. Both these men . . . both Miller and Garrett concealed their natures. Now that we know more about them, we'll be able to get to the bottom of what they were hiding. I bet there's a lot more on Garrett,' Downes said. 'Find the hospital where Sullivan used to work.'

# 29

I got home late and carried on working, but it was hard to concentrate. I had closed the box room and locked it, but I kept on thinking about it as I did some work on my kitchen table. The rain fell, and my thoughts darkened. I stood up, walked down the hall, reached for the phone and tried Carlos again. Still no answer. I slammed down the phone and went back to Miller's Police National Database file, which Collinson had passed on to me. It was half open on my table. But I couldn't settle. Here I was, a forty-one-year-old man, still thinking of Pilar after all these years. The sound of the rain faded to a murmur as I thought of her.

And what had I really known about her? Now, after all these years, I was uncertain of what we had shared. Had no way of knowing if it would even have lasted between us. In death she had become almost more real somehow, a more permanent part of my life. More so certainly than if we had just parted ways. But, whatever we had had, *El Rubio* had taken it away without any hesitation at all. I remembered the crowds of people gathered in the sullen heat as they had taken her away and the soldiers with their machine guns hanging nonchalantly by their sides. She had not looked back.

I stared at the rain for a while longer. Then I poured myself a *mate* and made myself think of work. I turned back to Miller's file and went through the pages. Very slowly, Pilar began to fade as I went through the file. The all-encompassing nature of work pulled me back from the past and dragged me reluctantly into the present.

Miller's PND file included 'soft' information such as allegations made against him that may not have resulted in arrest, plus all of the information held by local police forces, including concerns passed on to the police from other bodies. After a few hours' work I closed the file. I thought long and hard about Miles and Garrett. But for a while, before I went to bed, I stared at the photo Powell and my brother had found for me of *El Rubio*, then locked up the box room once again.

When finally I fell asleep, I dreamt of the medical room. The flash of a camera went on and off, and endless photos fell and landed with a cold wet slap on the floor. And when I looked down and picked up the photos, I saw that Pilar, framed by the back window of a Ford Falcon, was in every one.

I woke up gasping, as if under water. I lay in bed for a while listening to the rain. I put on some tracksuit bottoms and a sweater and started pacing around my house. I poured myself a drink and took it up to my study, along with the photos and files. But now, instead of *El Rubio*, it was Garrett whom I thought about.

It was as if Garrett had paid his way specifically to get access to that hospital. I turned the pages of the file until

I had found Freddie Bowman's medical room photo. I looked at it for a long time as the rain beat down on the roof. For some reason I had suspected a more violent end for Freddie. There was a kind of barely restrained control in the photo's composition. A sense of restraint held at the very edge and, once that restraint was gone, everything would be plunged immediately into violent oblivion.

I took all of the photos and laid them out on the desk. After a while the boys' eyes seemed to attain an almost beseeching look as they gazed into my own. Again, that strange light. A caged and underground light. Like stuffed exhibits in a museum. It was the same image that had come to me as I had studied them with Vine and Collinson, and I kept coming back to it. Even then that image had resonated with me on a deep, almost subconscious level. Those photos of the medical room, I was sure, captured the moment between life and death.

My cat Enzo came in and jumped on to the desk and flashed his tail. Hungry as usual, or lonely maybe and sick of being stuck indoors with all the rain.

I had been trying to call Carlos all evening, but he sometimes disappeared for weeks without letting me know. I would get hold of him eventually. Carlos would tell me where *El Rubio* was. But what was I going to do next? If I really took the next plane out to Buenos Aires and tracked down *El Rubio* and took him to an isolated spot, when it was all over would I feel any better? Would the spectre of what had happened to Pilar finally go away?

I thought of Garrett staring up from the white borders of the Polaroid photo. Afraid but still angry in a way. And unbelieving, looking into that camera at the men taking his photo. Indignant. And that was the part that didn't make sense. How could he have been indignant when he knew he was going to be killed right there in that room? It had to be because, despite everything that was happening to him, his role and those of the two other men remained essentially the same.

I tensed suddenly and stared down at the photo. I froze. The answer was in the name we had given the room. It was *right there*. It had been there all along. It wasn't in the physical aspects of the room. It was the psychological imprint of it. In the relationship between Garrett and those men. I whirled around on my heel and ran my hands through my hair. Enzo, startled, jumped off the desk and scurried away. The rain poured outside and for a moment I just listened to it. I was filled with a terrible, unspeakable loathing, beneath which was fear. Fear of the men who had come for Miller.

I thought of Garrett. A powerful man who had been able to conceal his own nature. A public figure in many ways, and he had managed to keep it secret. If it was as bad as I thought it was, he might have needed help to keep it quiet. I wondered about his hotel. Had the other men living there used their power and their influence to protect a shared interest? In the hushed silence of that respectable hotel, amongst the plush carpets and thick fronds of the indoor plants, had horror stalked the rooms? It must have. Outside, the rain began to fall even harder. The floods would come. All of us were waiting helplessly for their arrival. And they would come.

I stared down at the pictures. The moment suspended and kept forever. I felt a kind of awful sadness for all those who had stood in that room. Something bad had happened there a long time ago, and then it had happened again and again for years – and then it had stopped. The years had passed. The weeds and undergrowth had crept in, reclaiming it. But the relief had been short-lived. The men had continued to go back. I stood there thinking of the pictures stuffed up Miller's chimney. And I knew with utter certainty that all the boys in the photos we had found were dead – except maybe just one.

## 30

I managed to get a few hours' sleep. I had a shower, got changed, headed downstairs and made myself another *mate*. Then I drove to Moreton-in-Marsh through the rain. The town was deserted. Everyone was getting ready for the floods; Alex had phoned me over break-fast to tell me that they had had to move the service to midday instead of five. Before calling in at the station I tried the Manor Hotel. Emma Forrester had managed to get herself a room, but she had already gone for the day. I left a message that she was to call me as soon as she got back.

To my surprise, I found Vine at the station, quite non-chalantly smoking a cigarette and staring at the rain from the front steps. He paused, then pitched the cigarette into a puddle.

'This fucking rain,' he said. He looked at my face curiously. 'They really did a number on you, didn't they, Downes?'

'You sure you've got no idea who *they* might be? There seem to be a lot of things you haven't told us, Vine.'

He shook his head and changed the subject. 'I hear half the station will be off to this funeral this afternoon. He was your partner, wasn't he?'

'Look,' I said, and motioned inside, 'you're not even supposed to be here. If Collinson catches you hanging around you'll be for the high jump.'

Vine shrugged. 'I'm through anyway, Downes. I knew it the moment I came here. It's my fault that they got Robert.'

'Your fault how? Look, why don't you level with us,' I said. 'I'm sorry about before. I was a bit rough on you but –'

He shrugged. 'It doesn't matter: you were right about me,' he said miserably.

I walked to the empty canteen and he followed. We sat down opposite each other. Vine unloosened his tie. He looked gaunt and hung-over. Maybe he hadn't slept at all.

'You were at the Southwark archives. You knew all about the caretaker Quint and his supervisor Baines. And you knew about that boy who went missing too. Miles. You were looking for some mention of him in the records, weren't you? Why didn't you tell us?' I said.

'How do you know?'

'We're not stupid. I sent my sergeant up to London and we got wind of it. It wasn't that difficult.'

'No sign of him,' Vine said, looking at me in open amazement. 'They made him disappear. Do you know how much coordinated effort would be involved in making someone just disappear like that? Do you know how many files there are or would have been for Miles?'

'A lot, I imagine.'

'There's the children's home register. Young-persons-being-looked-after files. Looked-after-children client files. Residential-care children's files. Adoption files. Privately fostered children's files, if they are fostered afterwards, which would have been the case with this Miles. The list is almost endless – but it's all gone, Downes, every last scrap of paper is gone. How did they do that?'

'If he existed.'

'He existed all right,' Vine said angrily, 'and you know it. Otherwise you wouldn't be talking to me.'

'But why keep it from us? What are you really doing here?'

Vine lapsed into a moody silence. 'I was warned off it. I was told Robert was probably feeding us a load of rubbish as a way of getting himself off the hook. They expected me just to accept it. Like a good boy. And normally I would have,' Vine said, and looked miserable. 'My career's been on the up until now. I just do what I'm told and it's worked for me so far. There was no proof about Miles, and Robert had been in and out of jail forever.'

'So Robert Wilson was the one who told you about Miles. And he told you only because he was in some kind of trouble?'

'Robert Wilson has been in trouble ever since he was a teenager,' Vine said wearily. 'You know the type. This time he'd assaulted someone who owed him some money in a bar. The whole thing was ridiculous. The guy owed him fifty quid. That's all, and Robert broke his jaw for it. Right in front of a bar full of people on a Saturday. It was the usual stuff, Downes.'

'So he was brought in. And he told you he had something.'

Vine nodded.

'And you conducted the interview I suppose?'

'He was looking at a long stretch,' Vine said. 'Full of remorse of course. Like they all are. In the shit. *Again*. But he said he could give me something. A name. If I could offer him a deal, that is.'

'And could you?'

He shrugged. 'That all depended on what he had.'

'And that was?'

'He said to look for a boy called Miles who'd been in a kids' home. And he bet that I wouldn't be able to find him.'

'He gave you the name of the children's home?'

'Yes.'

'And there was no sign of him in the records?'

'No.'

'But you knew about the fire when you started to look into it?'

'Yes. He told me about that too.'

'So you wondered what a caretaker was doing there at two in the morning?'

'Yes. I talked to the widow.'

'And she told you all about Miles.'

'Yes. She confirmed that her husband had been looking for him, and that it had all been raked up again because of this new story in the paper. I talked to the cold case detective and he agreed to let me go with him when he interviewed her.'

'And asked a few questions of your own?'

Vine nodded.

'So you thought you were on to something?'

His eyes widened. 'Yes. Something big. I couldn't believe it when it all started coming together like that. I went straight to my super with it. I was pretty wound up, I suppose. The Super listened and he seemed to think the same. Said I was in for a pat on the back. Then the very next day he called me into his office.'

'And he told you to drop it?'

'Yes, immediately. And I mean immediately, Downes. I couldn't understand it. It was all laid out in front of them: the answer to the Baines murder and Quint's as well if it all added up. And what had happened to this boy. But they didn't want anything to do with it. I just couldn't believe it. I kept on going back and asking them why. But I never got any answers, and I thought, well, fuck it, they're probably right anyway, so I tried to forget it.'

'But you couldn't.'

'No. I mean, I could understand that Robert may have been lying to get himself out of the shit.' Vine bit the corner of his lip. 'Then something odd happened.' He leant forward, frowning, and lowered his voice. 'I was paid a visit. Two officers came to the station with a photo of this boy Miles. And they said he was all right.'

'You didn't like that.'

'No,' Vine said, leaning in further, 'I didn't. Why go to all that trouble? Why bother to show me a photo? It felt . . . It didn't feel right at all.'

'So you looked into it?'

Vine sighed, obviously wishing that he hadn't. 'Robert was due to appear in court in a few weeks' time. They'd let him out on bail. I got his address and I went to see him. But he wasn't in his house, and when I asked around I found he was living rough nearby. He was sleeping in a park and I talked to him and brought him home.'

'What?' I said surprised. 'You brought him home. To your . . . What about the safe house?'

'There never was a safe house,' Vine said sheepishly. 'I made all that up when you started to grill me, Downes. I didn't expect you to come at me like that. Jesus. I told him to stay put. Robert told me that he'd left his flat because when he'd gone back there the whole place had been turned over. He was sure they knew somehow that he'd talked to the police about Miles and he was terrified.'

'And did you tell anyone at the station?'

There was a short silence. 'Almost,' he said. 'Then I changed my mind. I said he should stay where he was while I decided what to do. And then he told me about Stanley. He said that he would have to talk to him.'

'He didn't tell you what Stanley knew?'

'No. Only that he needed to talk to him. It was up to Stanley to decide for himself what he would say.'

'He told you how they knew each other?'

'Yes. That they'd been in the children's home together at the same time. Anyway, I had to pretend that everything was all right and I went to work. But then the next day, when I came back, Robert wasn't there. I didn't know what to do – and then I remembered that he had told me they used to meet in Trafalgar Square when they were kids. So I thought I'd give it a shot.'

Vine coughed and looked like he wanted to reach for a cigarette.

'Go on,' I said.

He did reach for one, lit it and blew smoke through his nose; I got him a saucer from the canteen and gave it to him.

'I started asking around there first thing the next morning,' Vine said. 'I figured that they must have gone somewhere to talk. I tried all the pubs and cafés and the museums too. Took me all day. I finally found out that a guy fitting Robert's description had been at a café a few blocks away with another man.'

'Stanley?'

'Yes. It must have been. The waitress remembered that they'd had a big argument, the other man rushed off, and Robert went chasing after him.'

'So someone must have been watching your flat. Waiting to see if you were going to take things further, and then, when you did, they must have realized that Robert would lead them to Stanley.'

Vine nodded. He looked around the canteen again, as if he were feeling exposed. 'I didn't know what to do. I reported Robert's disappearance the next day and just kind of found myself going through the motions. I didn't say anything about his staying at my flat of course. Just that he was missing, and I kept my eyes open at the station to see if there was any news on him.'

'But there was none?'

'No.'

'But then you heard about Miller and Stanley. And you knew Miller had served time with Robert, and that we had Stanley in custody. And you were hoping that Stanley could tell you where Robert had got to.'

'Yes.'

'So you called in some leave you were owed and came straight down here.'

Vine nodded. There was a long pause. He stared down at his rumpled suit and put out the cigarette.

I looked at him thoughtfully for a moment and then said, 'All right, I want to ask you about something else. But, before I do, stop feeling so damned sorry for yourself. This might not end up as badly as you think,' I said. 'And don't blame yourself for Robert. Chances are that they would have got to him sooner or later, and he'd be alive for sure if your superiors hadn't lied to you and covered up the whole thing. There're going to be a lot of people held to account when this thing is over.'

I thought for a moment of Garrett and the hotel. It was not the kind of thing we would know about out here, but maybe Vine would. I looked at him for a moment longer and then decided to try him.

'What do you know about a hotel called the Pavilion in London?'

Vine sat back in his chair. His eyes clouded over.

'There are rumours of something having happened there,' I said. 'It could be the heart of it somehow. I think something could have been going on there for years. And nothing's been done about it because the people involved are too high up. You know it, don't you?'

Vine nodded slowly. 'Know of it,' he said. 'But vaguely. Rumours, like you say, that's all.'

From the other end of the corridor I could hear whistling, and Cleaver walked in, his eyes zooming in on an Eccles cake. Then, catching me glaring at him, he walked straight out again.

'What do you know?' I said.

Vine rubbed the back of his neck and sighed and stood up. He stood very still for a long moment. 'You're still remembered in London. They'll never let you back, not after what you did to Havelock.'

I shrugged. 'Havelock deserved it. Anyway,' I said, 'it was self-defence.'

Vine smiled thinly. 'Christ, you don't give much away do you, Downes? Of course it was. Self-defence. Sure, I believe you. What's it like to be exiled? Stuck out here in the middle of nowhere? You know, I'll probably get sent out somewhere like this if I'm lucky.'

'Actually, it's all right. Why don't you tell me what you know? And maybe I can solve this one for you.'

'You think that's what I want?' Vine said angrily.

'I think you want the truth. I think that's why you're still here. They underestimated you, Vine. Maybe they hoped you wouldn't do a thorough job and it would all go away. But here you are,' I said, 'in the middle of nowhere.'

'All right.' Vine took a few quick steps towards the middle of the room. 'There have been rumours. But a long time ago, and yes,' he said suddenly, his eyes widening, 'it's like that damned room. There have been rumours about children being abused and terrorized in that hotel for maybe thirty years.'

'That long?' I said thinly.

'Maybe longer.'

'Any evidence?'

'None. It just vanishes.'

'Vanishes?'

'There was a whole file. Maybe twenty years ago, when the Met started to look into it, if I remember rightly. And they *did* look. The file was handed to the Home Secretary. All of their research, all of their investigations . . . and when we asked for it back –'

'It was gone.'

He nodded. 'And it could have been going on for longer than that. Maybe to the 1960s, even the 1950s. It's well organized and protected. The boys who are taken there are usually out on the streets already. Rent boys or abducted from children's homes –'

'Homes in Southwark, for instance.'

'Yes,' he said quickly. 'Maybe Southwark. Other places, though, as well. Probably from all over London. We've got no real proof. There's more than one location. But that hotel . . . well, that seems to have been the heart of it. But how do you know about it? Is there a connection?'

'I wasn't sure until now,' I said. 'That's why I'm in so early. I wanted to look at it but now you've saved me some time.'

'You're not going to tell me any more, are you?'

I shook my head. 'I'm not one hundred per cent sure myself yet.'

'There've also been allegations about the police in relation to that hotel.' Vine paused, remembering. 'You don't look at all surprised, Downes.'

'Never trust a policeman,' I said, and waved my finger at him. 'That's something I learnt when I was just a little kid back home in Buenos Aires. That's something we all learn there. But it's the same here as it is everywhere else. Just here the corruption goes deeper. So what are the rumours?'

'That the whole thing was dropped because it's too close to prominent people. Statements have been altered. No action has been taken when there was a clear requirement for us to do so. I heard something once about a surveillance operation set up there in the 1970s, gathering intelligence. That was closed down suddenly and for no reason. Another surveillance operation was shut down a few years later. There've been allegations against judges and politicians and MI5 agents. People who actually lived there.'

'What about rich businessmen?'

'Them too. You thinking of anyone in particular? All right,' he said, and shook his head. 'Don't tell me.'

I smiled and then said seriously, 'Has there been word that there are two men who are even worse than the others? Hiding amongst them because they know that they'll be safe and no one will say anything maybe because they know all their secrets? Killing young boys and teenagers and hiding amongst the powerful. Very powerful themselves.'

'Powerful enough to make files go missing from council archives you mean?' Vine said quickly. 'No, I never heard anything like that.' His eyes became thoughtful. He nodded to himself. 'But there is something. This medical room. We don't know where it is. Only that it's not in London. And that every year there's a party held near it. These . . . men, if you can call them men,' Vine said in disgust, 'look forward to it. When the party is in full swing, one boy is taken away.'

Vine put his hands in his pockets and took another step forward. 'The boys are drugged, so no one remembers where it is. Sometimes those who are taken to that room survive, but barely.'

I looked at him and then made up my mind. 'Vine, I'm going to tell you what I think. I don't have much time,' I said. 'We know that there were two of them doing this to these boys because of the Polaroids.'

'Two men?'

I nodded. 'In one of the Polaroids there is a reflection of two men in a tap above a sink in that room. We've identified only four of the boys in the pictures. One of them, called Freddie Bowman, overdosed on drugs. I think it could well have been a type of suicide. The other three have never been seen again and we still don't know who the others are. That photo of Miles, which the detectives made a special visit to show you. Did it match any of the boys upstairs?'

Vine shook his head.

'Well, I do think that his picture is upstairs. But we'll be able to identify him and the other boys only if we can find out where they've been buried. So we absolutely must find them.

'Two men have been working together. They seemed to have been hiding almost in plain sight. I'm fairly certain of it now. They were both part of it and apart from it at the same time. They took things even further than the others. The other men who were at these parties were powerful in their own right. Yet they couldn't do anything to stop these killers, because they needed to protect their own secrets. And the kids who were dying were of absolutely no importance to them at all. They were something to be used. That's all they were.'

I tried to keep as calm as I could and said, 'It's unusual to have two like-minded individuals working together on something like this. They were working together to get those boys into that room. Somehow Miller got hold of those photos and tried to use them to his advantage. But those two men took someone else into that room a long time ago. This man was rich and powerful just like them. And, like them, he was a sexual predator. For some reason, they brought him into that room and punished him. Usually killers like this – men who prey on boys or others who exist on the margins – never have this much power. They are unsuccessful in life. But the addition of great power to their joint enterprise has enabled them to inflict damage that's almost unthinkable. It's also how they managed to get away with it for so long.'

'But why take the pictures?'

'They were an essential part of what they did in that room. Taking them was a huge risk, in case they were stolen. And they *were* stolen. But they had no choice – because I think that they somehow needed to remind themselves of what they were now. They made a mistake though, a long time ago, and it's only now coming to the surface.'

'A mistake?'

'All of those they killed were runaways. Probably on the streets. And they had been missing for some time before they actually seemed to have vanished for good. So there would be no exact record of when they disappeared. But they made a mistake when they killed a boy in care. Children in care are documented every day of their lives. And so they had to make it seem as if he'd never existed at all.'

## 31

I parked the car and bobbed through the rain to my house. I had given myself plenty of time to get changed and ready before Powell's funeral. I wandered towards the kitchen, where I had left a copy of the psalm I was to read on the sideboard near the radio. I picked it up, turned around and then stopped dead in my tracks.

Standing in the sullen silence of my kitchen, I knew immediately that something was wrong. The silence seemed to thicken as I took another step inside. The kitchen was colder than it should be. I stared long and hard at the kitchen door, then moved towards it and examined it. Someone had been in my house. I whirled around and stared wildly in all directions. Christ, if it was them. For a moment I didn't know what to do. I almost reached for the phone but didn't.

I could see two deep grooves where a crowbar had slipped inside near the latch and finally gained purchase, and there were a few other marks where they had tested out some other weaker points on the door. But once the crowbar had snapped the lock, the sound would not have been all that dramatic. It had probably taken seconds. The crowbar, which I recognized as my own from my garage, was resting neatly against the door. I stood trying to listen for them, wondering if they were still in the house.

I grabbed a knife from the kitchen drawer. I walked quickly along the hallway and checked the living room and then the dining room and the downstairs bathroom. Nothing as far as I could tell had been moved and there was no sign of them. I took a long deep breath. I ran upstairs. No sign of disturbance up there. I moved to the study. The door to the box room was still locked. Then I tried my room and flung open all the wardrobes and checked under the beds; then the upstairs bathroom. Finally I pushed open the door to the spare room.

I stood stunned on the threshold. The bed was always unmade in here and had not been used in many years. Now the bedroom cupboards were open; sheets and the duvet lay in a tangled mess on the bed. I switched on the light. There was a fresh glass of water on the side table near the window and even a hot-water bottle lying on the floor where someone had kicked it from the bed in their sleep. Some muddy trainers were sitting beside the doorway. I pulled the duvet back and threw it on to the floor.

'Jesus Christ,' I said. Stanley was fast asleep in my spare bed. And he didn't even move or stir when I grabbed him by the shoulders. Then his eyes slowly opened and fixed immediately on the knife. He sat up in bed and yawned. Then he pushed the duvet to one side and stretched his arms.

'Put the kettle on, will you?' he said.

I stepped back and watched in silent amazement as he got out of bed and wandered along the hallway, scratching his backside and heading to my bathroom. He locked the door. I waited a while and then the toilet flushed. I heard running water and when he came out he was still bleary-eyed. His clothes were filthy. Covered in mud, pieces of grass and what looked like cement or lime.

'Sorry about your door. Didn't think you'd be coming back so soon. Are you skiving off or something?'

'How the hell did you know where I lived?'

'Your little pep talk in that car park ... Not many Guillermo Downeses in the phone book.' He shrugged.

'You knew you'd be safe here,' I said in awe.

'As safe as anywhere.' He stared for a good while at my face. It seemed to reassure him and at the same time make him more nervous. 'I thought you lot were supposed to be trained for that sort of thing. You know, self-defence.' He did a quick fighting stance and smiled. 'Hand-to-hand combat, martial arts, that kind of thing.' He shook his head in disappointment.

For a moment longer I stared at him, speechless, then I managed to say, 'Where the hell have you been and how did you manage to get away from that hospital? We had it locked down in minutes.'

'You don't have a cigarette, do you?' Stanley said, ignoring me.

'I gave up.'

'Shame.' He reached in his pocket and pulled one out of a full packet. 'Well, there was no way out. I knew that. So I sneaked back in. It's massive, that place. I got some clothes. Nicked 'em from one of the staff rooms and hung out in the canteen. Nobody even looked twice. Then, when it was all over, I got the bus out of there. Been sleeping in fields and old barns for the last couple of days. And it hasn't stopped fucking raining.' Stanley eyed the knife.

I put it down on a side table. 'Those men: do you know who they are?'

'No. I never saw them before.'

'But how did they know you were there?' I said.

'You tell me. I didn't tell anyone.'

'But you were ready for them when they came, though.'

'I let the bastard have it with the vase.'

'But how did you manage to find your way out so fast?'

Stanley waved his cigarette in the air. 'You should always know exactly where you are and always know your way out of a place.'

'In case there's a fire?'

He looked up at me sharply. 'If you like,' he said. 'Anyway, all you need to do is follow the red line to A & E. Then you're out. Simple, really. I heard your little speech and then legged it down the tunnel. My knight in shining armour.'

I stood still, not sure what to do. 'All right. I'm kind of in a hurry. Let's just get a few things straight before we go any further.'

'Sure,' Stanley said reasonably.

'You were staying at Miller's. You saw what happened in there, so you ran. But you went back to the house to get something.'

'He was driving me bonkers,' Stanley said. 'I just had to get out of that awful house and out of the countryside. So I took the bus to Cheltenham. I knew Lee would be angry about it, but I went anyway and got the bus. I did some window shopping, had a coffee and then went back. I got the last bus back.'

'So this was when?'

'Around seven.'

'And you used the spare key he had given you to get in?'

'Yes.'

'And you saw what was in there?'

'I walked in and . . . well, there was this man lying on the floor.'

'You didn't know who he was?'

'No. I thought the poor sod had had a heart attack or something, the way he was lying there. And then I saw . . . that he'd been cut. I went into the living room and Lee was in the chair. The fire was nearly out but I could still smell . . . something, but I didn't know what it was.' Stanley shivered.

'You didn't go upstairs to get your stuff?'

'Fuck no. I just legged it to the pub. I had my wallet with me of course. Not much in there. Tried to get a lift. None of them would give me one. They hate me in there. I thought about going back and seeing if Lee had any money on him. But I just couldn't stand the idea of going back in there. So I hitched as far as Oxford and got the bus.'

'And you stayed in London but you knew that you were going to have to come back eventually?'

'Yes. Well, London . . . nowhere is really safe for me any more. But I know London.'

'Where did you stay?'

'Nowhere. Slept rough. I've done it before. Plenty of times. It was too dangerous to go back to my flat. I didn't see anything about it in the papers. I thought someone would have found them by then. I knew I should go back while I had the chance, before all hell broke loose and the whole place got mobbed with journalists.' Stanley took a few steps towards the stairs and leant on the banisters. 'I wasn't exactly over the moon about coming back but I had to risk it. I got a bus to Oxford and managed to hitch as far as Stratford. Then I had to traipse the rest of the way to that village again. By the time I got there it must have been around . . . I don't know, around two in the morning. I was knackered. I walked down the hill, saw the police tape but decided to let myself in anyway.'

'You knew Miller had something hidden up the chimney?'

Stanley nodded. 'I'd heard him up there once. I crept out of bed and followed him to the attic; I could see him kind of reaching for it. I tried to do the same but it was too high up, so I had the bright idea of climbing up there, didn't I?'

'Did you know what was there?'

'No. He never told me.'

'But you knew it had to be something to do with what had happened, right? To those boys?'

Stanley looked at me as if I had just said something absurd. 'I was hoping for something a lot better than that, mate.'

'Money,' I said quickly.

'Or jewels. Lee was a thief. A professional. So stands to reason he had a hiding place in his house. And a pretty damned good one. So I went up there and found it. But there was just this envelope,' Stanley sighed and shook his head. 'An envelope, after all that. I knew it wasn't money, I could tell straight away. But the bricks. Lee must have had some way of getting to it. I don't know, some kind of technique. And as soon as I got up there, they just started to move all over the place. I didn't know what I was going to do. And then I could hear you yelling from downstairs. Then . . .' Stanley looked strained suddenly. 'I remember you and that other man looking up at me. The other one. The good-looking one. No offense,' Stanley said quickly, 'you're just a bit old. Sorry.'

'I'll try to get over it,' I said.

Stanley didn't seem to have heard me. 'Then I remember falling. It all gets a bit hazy after that, and then I woke up in the hospital.' Stanley paused. 'Look, how about that cup of tea? And I'm starving. I tried your fridge but all you have are steaks. Don't you ever eat vegetables?'

'Stanley, I have to call someone. You did the right thing in coming here, but we're going to have to call someone else. Because I'm going to need help. We both are.'

'Someone else . . .'

'Don't worry. It'll be the idiot who risked his neck trying to get you out of the chimney. The good-looking one. He might not want to help us. I wouldn't blame him, especially after what you put him through. You know he fell in after you?'

'Did he? I can't remember a thing.'

'He was stuck in there with you for a good hour. I'll have to leave the decision to him.'

Stanley frowned. 'You're sure you're not going to call anyone else?'

'No, I'm not. Not yet. But the only way this will work is if you tell us exactly what's going on and who you think we might be up against. It's something to do with that children's home. The one you were in when you were a kid.'

Stanley didn't say anything but he followed me as I walked downstairs to the hall. I reached for the phone, called Graves and told him to drop whatever he was doing and come straight over.

Then I went upstairs and put some fresh clothes for Stanley in the spare room. I changed into my suit, and checked my watch again and started to pace up and down. I was cutting it *really* fine. Stanley made a tea for himself and a coffee for me, and we waited while I carried on walking up and down and staring at my watch.

'This place isn't at all tacky, you know,' Stanley said.

'Gee, thanks,' I said.

'Look, there was someone else,' Stanley said, taking a long gulp on his tea. 'A man. Robert. I've been trying to reach him on the phone for weeks. But I haven't heard from him. Do you know anything about it?'

'I'm sorry, Stanley. No one knows where he is.'

Stanley hunched over his cup.

I took a quick swig of coffee and a few moments later I peered out of the window as I heard gravel crunching outside. 'Wait here,' I said.

'Aren't you supposed to be somewhere?' Graves said, stepping inside and out of the rain.

'I've found Stanley. Well, he found me.'

I motioned to the kitchen.

For a moment Graves was very still. 'Here? What the hell is he doing here?'

'He trusts us. And if we take him into custody, I think that one way or another they'll get to him, just like they got to Robert Wilson. And then we'll never know what happened or what any of this is about.'

'But don't you think we should call it in?' Graves said, in growing agitation.

'Let's hear what Stanley has to say first, shall we?'

Graves sighed and rubbed his hands over his face. 'God, I knew you were going to get me in trouble. You know that's why they sent me out here to work with you in the first place. The Super warned me about you back in Oxford. I was to let them know if you pulled anything like this. They're looking for a way to get rid of me and this could be it. If they find out that you've got Stanley hidden here and I'm helping you . . . well, it's curtains for me.'

'You still planning on sticking around?'

'How did you know I wasn't?' Graves said indignantly.

I shrugged.

For a moment Graves was very still. Enzo appeared from nowhere and wrapped himself around his legs. Graves, surprised, looked down at him and stroked his ears.

'Don't worry. They won't find out,' I said.

Graves sighed again. 'All right,' he said.

'Are you sure, Graves? I'll understand if you decide you can't be part of any of this.'

'Yes. I'm sure. Go on. Bugger off before I change my mind,' he said.

## 32

The funeral was in the church in Stow-on-the-Wold. I drove like a demon despite the rain. They were now issuing dire warnings on the radio about flash floods. I couldn't find anywhere to park because the road leading up to the church was lined with cars and I ended up parking outside some sandbagged shops in the town.

Rain plastered the skulls and dampened the coats of the mourners packed tightly under the domed roof. Collinson was there and she nodded in my direction when she saw me, and there were a lot of other people I recognized from over the years.

I made my way to one of the pews near the front and listened, and made sure for about the hundredth time that I had the psalm I was to read in my pocket. I rubbed the rain out of my eyes. Powell had not wanted a eulogy, so there would be none. And the committal of his body would be carried out with just family and a few close friends.

I stood up when I was supposed to, and mouthed along with the hymns Powell had chosen, and listened as Alex stood up and read. Then I went and read my piece.

When it was all over I followed the procession out into the rain while the others darted towards their cars. I watched them lower the coffin into the ground. The rain gathered at my feet and beat amongst the graves. I listened to the vicar and felt immensely grateful to him for taking his time over the words despite the weather while an altar boy held an umbrella above his head and got soaking wet.

Powell had done something for me. He had done something immeasurable, and now I would never be able to thank him for it. Alex and everyone else turned around, but I stared for a while and watched as the men came and started to put earth into Powell's grave. The rain started to pour down even harder than before and the men made quick work of it, then sprinted towards a van parked outside the graveyard. I remained exactly where I was.

He was down there. Hard to imagine somehow. What would Powell make of what I was up against? What would he have advised me to do? I tried to conjure up his voice, as if even now he could guide me. But there was nothing. I suddenly felt out of my depth. I rubbed the top of my skull and felt along the old scar beneath my hair.

The rain poured and soaked my feet. I was after the kind of people who could take a little boy from care, make him disappear, use their influence to make it all go away and keep it that way for over twenty years. Maybe even longer. The idea of it contaminated the very air around me. They had erased Miles from the records. Erased him out of history, like he'd never existed in the first place. There would be no grave for Miles. No ceremony, unless we could find him. He had simply been discarded after being used. It was the same way Pilar had been made to disappear by powerful, ruthless men.

*Pilar Fernandez.* Her name, after all these years, was a distant whisper from so far away on this fading Cotswolds afternoon. What had they done with her? Where was she? Would *El Rubio* tell me where she was? Would we be able to bury Pilar at long last?

The rain fell on the graves. It pounded on my umbrella. I remembered Powell asking me about her in that insistent friendly way of his. *So those men came for you because you'd come looking for Pilar's sister, right? You tried to help her. But they came for you after they took Pilar. And then they found you. And you did something about it? You didn't think twice, did you? You grabbed the driver and the car hit the water. Then what happened?'*

For a moment I stood completely helpless as I looked down at Powell's grave. What did Powell want me to do? Did he want me to go back home after all these years? They had hunted us down like animals, murdered Pilar somewhere in the camps, probably after weeks of torture, and then found me hiding over in Villa Urquiza. It was all so long ago now. I remembered Powell's look of utter horror when I had told him everything. And it was *El Rubio* who had sent those men after me and made sure they'd put me in the back seat of the Ford Falcon. And he was still walking around somewhere even now.

The light from the graveyard began to fade. The rain fell so hard that my umbrella began to sag. I thought of the Ford Falcon. It had rolled, tumbled, hit the water.

'One of them big old things, wasn't it? A Ford,' Powell had said when he had asked me about it.

'With a big boot good for putting subversives in, and they never broke down. But they put me in the back seat because they didn't think I was going to make any trouble.'

'A mistake,' Powell had said quietly.

'They tied my hands in front of me. We had been driving a long time. And then we were near the river delta. They were going to take me to a camp. I knew it. There was no other way. Once I was in the camp I knew I'd be finished. I did it without thinking. Grabbed the driver. And the car left the road. We went straight into the river.'

The rain fell. I closed my eyes. The memory was as vivid as if it had happened yesterday. For a moment I tried to push it away, but it was no good. *The car jumped and for a moment the river rose up before us so that it filled the whole windscreen. The car swerved, bounced another time as it hit the kerb and made an awful metal screech as the undercarriage gouged and tore at the pavement. The right passenger window at the back gave and then exploded as we hit the water. There was the sound of breaking glass, groaning metal and the engine turning and bellowing. Muddy black water poured through in frantic, billowing waves. The right headlight was still shining out crazily, showing our descent as if we were in a submarine. The driver's head was lolling against the steering wheel. The other passenger was scrabbling wildly, trying to get out.*

*The car sank. The windscreen split all along in a jagged line of cracks and splinters. The water, rolling black, burst in, hissing, through a thousand gaps and cracks. The Falcon made a muffled roar as it shuddered and sank deeper and deeper into the dark swirling water. Lazily, it began to flip over on to its roof and then, lurching, gained momentum and shuddered forward.*

*Ahead, a brief crackle and a spark of sizzling electricity as I pushed through the broken passenger window. The driver's body was lolling face down. The other militar was stuck, his seat belt jammed. He was twisting desperately as the water rose. His eyes huge and terrified. His arms reached out helplessly in front of him, pushing against the roof. I propelled myself out of the broken window and left them there. There was still some light from the car. The wheels were still spinning. A face was caught in the reddish smouldering glare of the headlight. Then the light went out. I was never quite sure, but above the deadened wailing howl of the car I thought I heard a scream.*

I thanked Powell under my breath as I finally left the graveyard, headed down the hill, and back towards the deserted town and my car. Maybe I could put an end to it, thanks to Powell. All the shops were closed. The floods were coming. But even now, in the rain, I was grinning as I remembered those two men dying, and I was glad that they were dead and glad that they had died by my hand. They were still down there at the bottom of the River Plate on the other side of the world, right where I had put them. They were rotting skeletons perhaps, lying in the rusting wreck of the Ford Falcon. Powell and my brother were the only people who had known I had killed two men. I wondered suddenly if Powell had suspected all along, as he had searched for a name, that there would eventually be a third.

# 33

I phoned Graves to make sure Stanley was still at my place and told him I would be back as soon as I could. Then I phoned Alex and told him that I would miss the wake and told him why. He said Len would have understood. I said I'd call him later. Finally I phoned the Manor. The receptionist told me that she had given Emma my message but that she was out already. She had been asking for directions to Broadway Tower.

I drove out there. The roads were beginning to flood, and the wind was picking up speed. I slowed down and took the small road which curved and then widened. The rain was pouring so hard now that it was hard to see. A tree had fallen over and was blocking half the road, and pieces of broken branches and leaves were scattered everywhere.

A police car was standing at the road, its lights blurred in the rain, and a policeman in wellingtons waved as I shuffled past it and up the steep long hill, one car in a long, slow procession. Smoke rose from the exhaust of an old lorry ahead of me. The flood warnings were becoming more dire by the minute. The rain poured down the hill; the drains overflowed. The tower now rose up in the distance. I rubbed the condensation from my window with the edge of my fist and peered outwards.

The truth had been in plain sight all along, but I had not been able to see it. Len had asked me how I sometimes seemed to see things. It is my job to examine the worst parts of human nature. To actively seek it out if I can. But this was so unthinkable that I had not taken it into consideration. A part of me even now hoped that I was wrong, and now, when I thought of it, I felt a knot of deep anguish and horror. But it had to be it. It was the only way it could have played out. Why had Freddie Bowman been allowed to live? Others had walked out of there in one piece, but they weren't like Freddie. In a way Freddie had suffered more than any of them. I knew that now. But someone else – someone close to him – had known it and in their own strange way had taken pity on him.

And I thought of Finn. How had he known? Why had he suddenly decided to drive out to the Cotswolds? Why had he become so interested in the Baines case after so many years? There was only one way that could have gone down, and Emma knew. That's why she was here. Someone had been guiding Finn all along. Someone who had pieced together almost all if it before us. Someone who knew about that hotel and the rumours that had surrounded it for years. And he had sent Finn like a missile straight to Neil Baines. Guided him to the fire and then led him straight to Miller as well.

It had to be somebody who was quite aware of what they were up against. Finn must have had only a vague notion about how it all tied up with Garrett. He might even have figured that bit out by himself once he had been put on to Miller. Sooner or later he was bound to have pieced that all together, just as Graves and I had done.

The gate to the car park was closed and the doors of the large tea room beyond were shut as well. I grabbed my umbrella and crossed the car park, walked along the narrow lane and went across the bumpy grass towards the bottom of the tower. Emma was walking in my direction and she stopped in her tracks when she saw me.

'The jobsworth in there won't let me in,' she said, as she peered through the gloom under her umbrella. 'Whole place is locked up just because of a bit of rain.'

'What are you doing here?'

She didn't say anything.

'You want to go to the top?'

'Not if you plan on pushing me off.' She smiled.

I didn't smile back. I left her and persuaded the gruff elderly security guard to open it up for us and we walked upstairs.

Broadway Tower was a folly built in the form of a small castle and stood in the centre of a park. It had a Saxon look, and the windows and entrance were set into arched openings in the stone. We climbed straight to the top, up the narrow winding stairs, and then pushed open the door. I opened up my umbrella again, rather pointlessly, and both of us sheltered under it. For a moment she stood at the top looking down at the dark hills rolling off into the distance. Her long hair blew out in the strong wind and a strand of it touched my face.

'So you came all the way out here. Sightseeing?' I said, turning around to look at her. She was beautiful all right and I could smell her. Clean, like she'd just got out of the shower. Her eyes narrowed when she saw me looking at her. She probably saw the same look on men's faces every single day.

She didn't seem to mind. She crossed her arms and peered at me sideways, perhaps really seeing me for the first time. Then she turned around and stared out at the rain falling on to the hills. 'It's quaint around here,' she said, 'but not nearly as quaint as I thought it would be.'

'Long way down as well.' Below, the rain fell in a thick sheet. Soon the roads would be completely impassable. 'Why did you come here? Finn had something else, didn't he? That's why you went back to his flat.'

She stood very still.

'I think Finn knew that he was heading for jail, so he must have been told to get his affairs in order and store his stuff somewhere – am I right?'

'You suspected that when you saw me yesterday, didn't you?' she said. She didn't look quite so sure of herself any more.

'A friend of George maybe?'

She nodded. 'I wanted to check his flat but your sergeant was there. I phoned his friends and one of them told me that George had asked if he could store some of his things in a spare room. George had already asked me and I'd said no. Not enough room and why should I? We split up ages ago.

He just wouldn't let it go. You know what men are like,' she said, looking at me. 'Sentimental lot. So I found George's friend and asked him if I could look through George's stuff.'

'And of course he let you.'

She shrugged.

'It's something to do with a burglary, isn't it? And Freddie Bowman.'

She looked at me sharply. 'How do you know?'

'It can't be anything else,' I said.

After what seemed a while she said, 'After Freddie Bowman died, do you know what happened to his father?'

'He killed himself. Came here to do it.'

She crossed her arms. 'There were five people up here. Three Italian tourists and a couple on their honeymoon. He went right to the edge and threw himself off. Didn't hesitate. It made all the papers. He was a big shot around here.'

'An MP.'

She nodded.

We walked inside. There were a number of small round windows which looked on to the hills below.

'So what did Finn have?' I said finally.

She reached into her pocket and handed me the pages of a crumpled form. I sat down on one of the small benches set inside the window and looked at it.

'This was with his things?'

She nodded. 'It was with a bunch of his old articles, in a box.'

'You know what this is?' I looked across at her. She looked worried. Her pale green eyes shone in the half-darkness of the room.

I looked at the form, baffled. I knew what it was but couldn't understand how it tied in to anything. I turned it over in my hands and flicked through the pages. It brought back a lot of memories. As a police constable, when I had first been starting out, I had filled in thousands of them. It was part of the daily existence of policemen all over the country, and a common complaint was that they took far too long to complete. 'So what is it,' I said, 'if you're so smart?'

'It's a form. A form police have to fill out. An E & A form, I think it's called.'

'So why didn't you tell me about it yesterday?' I said angrily.

'Because there's something going on. And it's to do with you lot.'

'The police?'

'Yes. Police constables have to take notes. A constable is required to carry a notebook in which they write down what happens while they're on duty. It has to be comprehensive, accurate, credible, and made at the time of the incident or as soon as it's practical to do so.'

I looked up at her. 'Right so far,' I said.

She stood up and started to pace up and down like a lawyer in a court room. 'A notebook, though, can't be used in criminal proceedings as evidence of events.'

'Go on.'

'As a result, all constables are compelled to fill in an Evidence and Actions Book after the event.' She stopped and looked at me. 'That's what that is.'

I checked the pages. 'So George had another contact,' I said, looking up at her. 'Another policeman who was feeding him information and who gave him this form. That's why he came here. And it was for serious stuff this time. Not celebrity phone numbers or number plates or any of that stuff. This one is different, isn't it?'

She nodded. 'A whistleblower, I think. Probably anonymous and not in it for the money. That's why he was never connected to George.'

'You didn't know anything about it before?'

She blinked and shook her head.

'If this goes in your paper –'

'Oh, come on, will you? Just *please* read it.'

'A burglary,' I said. 'In London. A long time ago.'

'Check the date.'

'It's 15 May 1983.'

'Mean anything?'

'The day Freddie Bowman was found dead of an overdose,' I said.

I looked at it and read it. Then I said, 'So the day Freddie was found dead someone broke into his parents' house in London. Looks like they went straight to the study upstairs. But they were gone by the time the police got there.'

'Yes. They got in by a side window. The alarm didn't go off but a neighbour heard glass breaking and alerted the police. Daniel Bowman was informed and inspected the property with the police present. There were signs of disturbance, but they hadn't had time to take anything.'

I stared at the form a little longer, then I tapped it gently with the tips of my fingers.

'This burglary occurred on the same day that their son was found dead,' Emma said, pointing her finger at me. 'Yet there is no mention of the burglary anywhere. The son of an MP is news, Downes. There's nothing about the burglary in any of the papers. Mrs Bowman didn't even know there had been a burglary at their house in London until I told her yesterday. Her husband had never mentioned it. So why hide the burglary?'

'Maybe he didn't want to bother her with it. Not with everything else that was going on at the time.'

'You don't believe that for one second, Downes,' she said, and leant in and pointed at me again. 'The fact that George had it means something. It means that the break-in was suppressed. Someone high up must have known that it had been reported and didn't want it on record. But why? Why go to all that trouble to make the report disappear when nothing was even taken? And that's not a copy, it's the original. I checked. Once signed, they're kept in records under lock and key, in the middle of a police station. So why, decades later, would someone just decide to give it to George?'

She seemed tired and cold suddenly. Her hands were trembling and her shoulders slumped. 'Almost twenty years ago a council worker announces he's going to the police with what he's found. Next thing we know at least two men are seen hanging outside his building and taking files out of his house while he's probably lying there dead in his flat. George prints the story about Baines and then a few months later he's discredited, out of a job, broke and facing jail. When he does actually try to do something about it, when he comes out here, what happens to him? He's murdered hours, *literally hours*, after he steps inside that village. And Miller, a criminal who has spent years in London and has no doubt had plenty of contact with the police over the years, is killed too.

'George ... well George drank too much and was in a bad way and would have been easy. But not Miller, from what I'm hearing. You really think I'd write about any of it until I was absolutely sure? And what about you? Do you think you can handle them? I asked you about that before, but you just thought it was all some joke. You know what I think. I think you're too proud or maybe too stupid to admit that you're out of your depth. And look at your face. What the hell happened to you anyway?' She suddenly looked defeated. 'Whatever it is that's happening, it's going to get buried forever – unless you stop it. You could be the only person who can.'

I looked at her. She was relentless and persuasive, just like someone else I used to know. 'So you've been asking around,' I said mildly. 'And you know you could be in danger as well if all this is really true.'

'You might not like us or think much of us, Downes. And maybe George's techniques were a bit suspect – but the only reason why this is going to come out is because of us. That's why someone contacted George. Word must have got round that he could be trusted. Eventually he would have got to the truth and they knew it. They wanted the truth. They wanted it all exposed, but they're afraid to come forward with it themselves.'

'You still want the story?' I said.

She blinked. 'Of course I want it.'

'How long would it take you to write it up and send it?'

'It could be in tomorrow's paper,' she said surprised. 'It could be everywhere, tomorrow.'

'So you still want it?' I said. 'Are you sure?'

'God, of course I'm sure.'

Looking at her, I knew that there was only one place where she would be safe and only one way I could get her to do what I told her. 'All right,' I said. 'Then it's yours.'

# 34

Graves opened the door, saw Emma standing behind me and then let us in. He nodded when Emma slipped past him. I'd persuaded her to leave her rental car where it was. We were soaking wet from the walk back to car. I fetched some towels from the airing cupboard and chucked one at Emma; she dropped it, then picked it up.

'Charming,' she said, and started to dry her hair.

I turned around and let her get on with it. Then I went into the kitchen.

'Stanley's in the bath,' Graves said. 'Been up there for hours.'

Emma came in a few moments later and looked up sharply when she heard footsteps coming down the stairs. Enzo, bewildered at having so many people in the house all at once, slinked off somewhere.

We waited for Stanley in the kitchen in silence and a few moments later he walked in. My clothes looked too big for him. I saw that he'd raided my wardrobe and was wearing one of my cashmere sweaters which I'd worn only once.

'Who the hell are you?' he said, looking at Emma.

'She's press,' I said. 'We have to get this out in the open somehow. In case something happens.'

'Happens to me, you mean,' said Stanley.

'Not just you.'

'All right,' Stanley said. 'Very dramatic, isn't he?' he said to Graves.

Graves gave him a wary smile as Stanley sat down at the kitchen table. I turned on the electric fire, turned off all the lights in the house, shut the curtains and checked all the doors.

Stanley reached for his cigarettes; I found an ashtray for him and gave him a beer out of the fridge, and gave one to Graves and Emma as well. I had a feeling they were going to need it by the time Stanley was through. Stanley lit a cigarette and watched the smoke drift into the air. The rain was still thundering outside.

'Are you ready?' I said.

Stanley nodded. 'Yes, I'm ready.'

Emma hit the 'record' button on her phone and pointed it at Stanley.

He began with Robert.

# 35

Of course Stanley had seen Robert from time to time over the years. Once, many years ago, he'd seen him from the top of a bus as it had been making its way slowly through the traffic. Stanley had sat back, feeling the coarse material of the seat through his jacket, and shaken his head. Amazed that Robert was still around. That he had survived somehow.

He had never really thought that he would see him again – not to speak to him anyway. And when word had got round years later that Robert wanted to meet with him – and word was not hard to get round in the circles Stanley still moved in – it had taken him a good couple of weeks to screw up the courage to actually go and get the number. But in the end he'd got it from a barman in Soho, whom he knew well, and tucked it deep into his wallet and tried not to think about it. More than once he had taken the number out and stared at it and rolled it into a tight ball and then tossed it into the bin, only to go rushing after it; and once, when he'd been drunk, he almost set it alight in an ashtray.

He told himself that if he did call and if they did meet again, it would be a short reunion. If Robert needed money or was in trouble, he would try to help him the best way he could. After all, he owed him that at least. But if Robert tried to bring up the past or to talk about what had happened to them in any way, in any way *at all*, he would politely ask him to stop and leave it at that.

This was because the past for Stanley was something that was muddy, black and terrible. A kind of hole that would swallow him up. When he thought about it, his face would go completely blank, and his jaw and his mouth would slacken. The middle-class accent he had tried hard to cultivate over the years, his hard-earned refinement reflected in his small supply of elegant clothes, the act which he knew people saw through straight away and made him a joke to everyone who knew him, everything he had struggled to learn about while walking through innumerable museums and sitting through thousands of hours of evening classes . . . it would all just slip away. And he would again be the same teenage boy who had sat on the edge of his bed sobbing, with Robert at his side comforting him.

When he could feel the past come rushing towards him, he would go to the small, very neat bedsit he kept in Streatham and close the door and go through it all again. There was no other choice. Everything would just fall away from him and it was as if he could feel the carpet under his bare feet and could hear the sound of steady conversation and laughter in another room. A silence falling. A door closing.

It was always bad, but it was worse when it came and he was not ready for it. On Christmas Eve, sitting in Lee Miller's living room, he'd been half watching a game show when he suddenly felt as if he were suffocating. He'd rushed to the toilet downstairs and heaved, but nothing had come up, and so he had bathed his head in the cold water and then gone marching to the pub up the road. But poor old Lee had caught up with him and taken him stumbling down the hill and then back across to that awful dreary house of his. It hadn't been the first time.

So Robert's card had waited in his wallet, scrunched up and flattened out again and scorched at one corner. And one day, after a few drinks at a bar in Soho, he had plucked it out of his wallet and called and kind of watched himself do it. Robert had answered straight away. There was that slightly hesitant effeminate murmur on the other end. And so polite. He'd forgotten about that. After all that had happened to him, Robert was still polite. It was an essential part of him. It had taken Stanley's breath away and he'd heard himself say, 'Robert, it's me.'

They had met near the lions in Trafalgar Square, as they had when they were kids. Where they could merge with the tourists and the students and smoke their cigarettes and then go to the park and drink beer from cans.

Robert was staring at one of the fountains, and he had turned around and smiled and waved. And they had held each other just as they had so many years ago as the children's home had burned all around them.

They went to a pretty awful café. They made small talk, and for a while Stanley thought, well, this isn't so bad. Actually, it was good to see him. Robert looked a little heavy under the eyes. He was no longer the waif-like creature Stanley had known in his teens. He had put on more weight even since he had seen him on the bus, and he was losing his hair.

Stanley was putting milk into his tea when without warning Robert started to tell him that he had made up his mind, and that he was sorry that he hadn't told him before. Robert had been waiting for weeks for Stanley to call him.

It might all be in the papers soon so it would be better for him to hear it from Robert first. Stanley must have known that one day this would be coming. Stanley had looked at him, frowning. Robert's mouth was moving, but it was as if he could not hear him beneath the rattling of the saucers and cups and the radio in the background. The noise of it seemed to rise. An inane pop tune was buzzing in his head. A builder was staring at a paper as a baked bean dribbled down his chin. He could not seem to breathe. Panic and fear overwhelmed him.

Robert was reaching for his arm. He was saying, 'Are you all right, Stanley? I didn't think that . . .' Beyond his shoulder a large black fly was feeding on the counter. It rose into the air and then flew against a window pane. 'I'm sorry, Stanley. I'm sorry. Look, mate, I didn't –'

And then Stanley was pushing against the table. His chair clattered to the floor. Something fell. He looked down. A sugar bowl had fallen off the table. People were turning around. He reached for the door handle, but he couldn't open it and he was scrabbling at the door and trying to push it open. But it wouldn't budge and he couldn't get out. He pushed uselessly and then the door, thank God, suddenly opened and he was out into the light.

He breathed in, gasping. There were people every-where, crowding all along the steps of the museum. He reached for the collar of his shirt and undid a button, feeling the wind blow against the sweat on his chest. He started to walk. He didn't know or care where he was going. He could hear Robert behind him. Reaching for him. Robert seized his arm; Stanley pulled it away.

'Stanley, it's going to be all right,' Robert said. 'It's not like it were before. Don't you see what it can mean? They were going to have to know sooner or later. You must have known that. Oh, come on, Stanley.'

Stanley wanted to turn around and scream at him. Wanted to say, 'Don't. Now don't say his name. *Please* don't say his name. *Please. Please. Please* don't say his name. If you don't say his name, maybe it's not too late.' His heart was thundering in his chest. He was covered in sweat. Everyone was staring at him, wondering what was wrong with him.

He staggered through the people. He was back near the middle of the square. He slumped on a bench and listened to the steady pounding of the fountain. He put his head in his hands and stared at the ground and the endless pieces of chewing gum sticking to it. What if they were here right now? Watching. Or listening. He was shaking uncontrollably.

Robert sat next to him. 'I'm sorry. I didn't mean to get you all worked up like that, Stanley. I thought you'd be happy about it.'

He looked at him in utter disbelief. 'Happy?'

'Well, all right, not happy. Of course not happy, mate. But, look, you've got to trust me. Things are different now, you know. It's not like it were before.'

'Different!' Stanley yelled. He could not seem to help himself. 'Different how? How are things going to be any different? What's changed?' He lowered his voice. 'The people. Those men. Don't you remember the kind of people they were? You remember what they looked like? You remember the types of places they took us to? Well, *do* you? You think they've stopped?' He reached for his cigarettes and, with trembling hands, lit one. 'You,' Stanley said. 'You really think someone like you can make a difference?' Stanley laughed. 'A difference to them?'

'Yes, I do. It's too late for us, mate. We never had a chance. We've had it. They made sure about that. But there will be others. There have been others. There must 'a been. Think about it for a sec, Stan. I . . . I have these awful dreams, right. I don't know how to explain it, but it's like I can't never get away from it *ever*.' He got to his feet. 'It's in here. In here somewhere,' he said, pointing to his head. 'And I know it. I always end up doing stupid stuff and I never get anywhere. If someone says the wrong word to me or looks at me in the wrong way, I go fucking spare. I always hoped that one day there would be some way that you and me could –'

'You want to see them punished, is that it?' Stanley said in disbelief.

'Yes, of course I want them punished. Don't you? We got away, didn't we? There were others who didn't and you know it.'

'But they're not going to believe us. Just look at us, Robert.'

'They have to believe us.'

'Who says?'

'I say. They are going to believe us. They do already. We're not the only ones. I've told someone about it. And he believes me and all. He says he's going to help.'

'You've gone to the police,' Stanley said very quietly.

'Yes. That's what I was trying to tell you before you threw a fucking fit in there. He's going to help. I'm not even supposed to be here now talking to you.'

Stanley rubbed his face with his hand. 'And what proof do we have? I'm in trouble, Robert. I've been in jail. More than once. They're not going to believe what I have to say. There's no proof any of it ever happened at all.'

'Are you sure about that?'

Stanley sat very still.

'He has to be out there somewhere,' Robert said quietly. 'He's still there. If they can find him. Then it's proof, ain't it? If we can find him. Then they will have to believe us. If they can find Miles.'

'I'm leaving,' Stanley said. He stood up. Very calmly he heard himself saying, 'Don't ever try to contact me again, Robert. *Ever.*' And Stanley walked away from him.

*

As he crossed the square, moving towards the steps of the museum, he remembered that cold, damp afternoon when they had finally taken him away to London, away from the seaside town where he had grown up, and put him in the room with Robert. And for a while he had been allowed to sleep soundly in the room they had for him. Then it had been like before: rough hands shaking him out of the dark, so when he woke he was sure that somehow he was back there.

He had gone quietly enough. Part of him had never really expected to get away. He had taken the bottle they had given him and let the vodka burn down his throat, knowing that it would make things a little better as he had sat on the leather seats in the back of the car.

Then it had been the men staring at him as he had stood barefoot with his toes digging into the carpet. He looked at the other boys, who were already draped around the place, laughing at the men's jokes and sitting smoking their cigarettes on the edges of chairs. An arm moved along his. A lean shadow watched from a sofa. His legs were neatly crossed in front of him.

He had wanted to run. A clammy awful sickness came over him, as it had before, back home. The men who had come for him were standing on either side of the sofa, watching: the driver, a well-built man with a moustache, and the man who'd sat in the passenger seat, leaner, older, more elegantly dressed. He glimpsed a number of obscene photos lying in a scrapbook on a coffee table and recognized the type of grimy suburban rooms in the background.

There was a seriousness to the men now. Their faces were very still. Eyes focused on him as the others paired off and disappeared. And then he was moving as a man led him roughly by his hand into a room. There was laughter after him. A shout of encouragement.

But no, he wouldn't. No, he couldn't. Not again. He was sorry. He didn't want to cause any bother. He just wanted . . . He watched with his head hanging low as the man padded angrily out of the room, and then he heard the door swinging open, and a moment later the two men who had come for him were standing in the doorway. The driver's hand whipped across his face so hard that he reeled back, falling. Blood from his mouth dripped on to the floor. The driver yanked him to his feet. He handed him a handkerchief and told him to clean up. Then they left. The older man came back in and closed the door. And when it was all over, they drove him home as dawn broke across London.

After a while, and it hadn't taken long, he approached it almost like a different person. Robert made things better. Robert had told him that the only way was to do what they told them. He had tried to fight them at first as well. Had even tried to run away, but it was no good. Playing along was the only option. And sometimes, when they took them both in the car, it wasn't so bad. Robert would smile from across the room. To be in a place like that and still have kindness was almost a miracle in a way. Robert was not like the other boys that they brought into those places.

There came a time when they didn't have to wake him up any more. He was lying there, waiting for them. Without a word he would take the pills they gave him and drink the vodka they handed to him. Wear the clothes they wanted him to wear. Play the role they wanted him to play. Reality would recede from the cone of darkening light, so that though his body moved, he still felt very far away; he watched what they were doing to him and heard their voices, but it was as if it was all happening to someone else, in a different room. If you drank enough; if you took the things they offered you; if you were nice to them; if you did what they told you, however bad it was; if you went along with whatever games they had come up with, no matter how vicious or savage or absurd they were: then it wasn't so bad. The mask would stay in place and he knew that he was safe. That he had survived, and that, as Robert kept telling him, was all that mattered. And then it would be dawn rising over the statues in the square again or over another grey park, the frost clinging to the windows, and then into the back of the car, to fall eventually into sleep. And weeks later, though sometimes just days, and it would be the same silent men in the front of the car and someone waiting for them in a doorway or near a lift or ushering them into a flat or a house or that hotel.

Within weeks he was like the other boys. He began to steal money from their wallets, and he began to take the drugs they left on tables and on sideboards, and telling the new boy, Miles, what he would have to do, just as Robert had told him. Miles was a little younger than the rest. His arms were frail and spindly, and he had a delicate elfin face that brought out the worst in them. Stanley would stand trembling as Miles was led away and he would think, *That was me*. And the realization that it had taken hardly any time at all was somehow worse than anything. And so it went on.

Then it was summer and all three of them were taken away much earlier than usual on a much longer drive. The car slipped through the streets and then finally picked up speed and headed out on to the open road.

They were each given a pill. All three of them took it. Its effect was almost immediate. From time to time Stanley's eyes would open and the landscape would loom up in the distance, then run away from him, and his eyes would slowly close. A small village and then a town. Fields rolled off into the horizon. Then the colours of the fields merged and blackened, and when he came to the car was moving up a hill. It went over something metal on the floor and bumped. Then there was the sound of gravel crunching under the tyres. The doors opened, letting in a warm breeze and the smell of long grass.

He felt sick the moment he opened his eyes because of the pill. They were led along a dim passageway to the far end of a house and then downstairs to a small room. The lights danced in front of his eyes. He could barely stand up. Shrubs and bushes covered the broken window outside.

He managed to change into the clothes he was given. They were led up a crumbling old staircase to what might once have been a living room. There were candles everywhere. All the windows were blacked out. A sudden squeal of delight greeted them when they walked in. And then they started to move through the men gathered there.

But whatever they had given him would not wear off. He walked with a sluggish urgency. His whole body seemed numb. He took a drink and then another from the trestle table at the side of the room. He felt feverish and sick. The whole room was spinning. He closed his eyes and opened them, swaying on his feet, and looked around. All along the walls were bottles of champagne in ice buckets. Grass had taken hold in places, and ivy reached in beneath the windows, and moss covered the walls.

Even before it began, he had somehow known it was going to be bad. The driver and his passenger had been tense as they'd left London. Out here in this remote spot, it seemed that there had been a sense of awful anticipation. Now it was rising to some dreadful crescendo. It was like being hit by a black wave. There was a strained, desperate look to many of the men as he walked past them and a kind of suppressed bristling anger aimed at him and the other boys. And he saw that it wasn't just them this time. There were other teenagers, girls and boys whom he did not recognize. He moved warily through the crowd, ingratiating himself as best as he could along with Robert and Miles. But the words he said came out half formed.

The driver stared at him with flat, hard eyes. Music played softly in the background. There was loud raucous laughter. He was hurled from one pair of hands to the next. A man built like a bull stared at him with disgust but could not seem to look away. In the half-darkness, the flickering and sputtering candles created shadows on the wall that danced and shuddered. Pockets of darkness in the corners lengthened and stretched outwards. He poured more vodka down his throat, heard himself laughing in a desperate kind of way, and saw Robert staring at him, worried, across the room.

Everything began to fall away from him. Suddenly he had to be sick and he pushed through the men, looking for a toilet. There was a bathroom further along, but it had not been used in years. He turned back and made his way through the men and ran down the stairs and was sick outside amongst some shrubs. He heard movement behind him and turned around.

The driver grabbed him, looked into his eyes and dragged him back to the room where they had changed. He disappeared and a moment later the other, older man came down. They started to talk. Something about the pill they had given him. He didn't care. He felt his eyes closing again. Could feel himself drifting off to sleep. He felt something smash against his cheek. He opened his eyes and then closed them again. The whole place was spinning. He was thrown to the floor, and, as he fell, his eyes opened and he saw the ceiling spinning again. The blackness was waiting for him like a blanket.

He woke up in a corner of the room where he had changed. Freezing. He had been sick again. More than once. He pushed himself to his feet and staggered outside, shivering. He wiped his chin. He trudged upstairs. A smell of stale cigarette smoke. Empty upturned glasses. Bottles in buckets and melted ice. A man with a boy curled up next to him was fast asleep on an old sofa. There was a coat hanging on the back of a chair; he looked around carefully before going through the pockets and taking the money, careful to snatch only a little, so it would not be noticed. He stuffed it into his pockets, then drank melted ice out of a bucket through his cupped hands.

He went back downstairs. There was a great stillness over the place now. Beyond the trees the hills rose off into the distance. It was the first time he had been alone for months. Everything looked so pristine. It was as if he could at that moment simply step out and walk amongst the fields in the sun. He had not felt such a moment of peace since his mother had held his hand so long ago before she went away; and now it was as if she still held his hand as he walked away from the house and amongst the trees.

He was not sure where he was going. But if he could somehow get away from them. Find a village or someone whom he could trust, and maybe escape. Far ahead, the ground began to rise. There were just a few cars now, tucked deep in the shadow of the house. He walked beneath the greyish arch of shrubbery. Then quickly he headed through an old orchard, climbed over the wall and pushed to the other side of the undergrowth.

He moved quickly amongst the small copse of trees that lay beyond the orchard and then into the woods, all the time keeping away from the small lane which led to the house. Very far off he could see a village rise up from beyond the trees. He headed towards it. Sometimes there would not be a way through. Blocked off, so go around. Find a way.

He stared down and wiped the moisture from his eyes with the back of his sleeve. The trees were fewer, and the soft wind came rippling the grass. He had already come a long way, or at least it seemed that way. His pace quickened when he suddenly heard something coming to him from beyond the trees.

He peered at a grey building encircled by trees that stood in the middle of a stretch of long grass. It was hard to make out what it was. An old private house. But too big for that. Standing abandoned in the middle of a field. Again, rising from somewhere within it, came a noise. It was muffled. Then it came again. It reverberated around the fields and then abruptly ended. A long scream of agony, ending in three words: 'No. Please. No.'

It was Miles. He recognized the voice immediately. Everything told him to run away. But instead he ran towards the building. Every single fibre of his being begged him and pleaded with him to go the other way. But he would not. All he could think of was Miles. Maybe he could somehow take Miles with him. They couldn't be too far from the village now. He saw the grey roof peeking above the branches and then the doors rose up before him.

He paused and then ducked inside. He went running along a corridor. Some glass-panelled doors led to an empty room. There were ancient-looking radiators, and the painting on the walls had peeled, leaving wide strips of paint lying along the floor. Paint was peeling everywhere. The hallway coiled ahead like a snake shedding its skin. Tangled wires poked out of the walls. Windows looked out on to a small courtyard, and two dead trees stood in a walled garden.

The sound came again but more quietly now. A quiet gurgling murmur. He followed it. There were some footprints outlined on the dusty ground. Ahead was a tall archway; he went through it, down some stairs and then along another narrow corridor.

On this level were a number of strange abandoned pieces of machinery. There was a broken armchair with its springs showing. A dust-covered chair stood on its side. An old heater, which may once have been fixed to the wall, lay smashed at the bottom of the stairs. A thick open door was in front of him. He peered in: the room behind it was covered in white tiles that ran all the way across the floor and along the walls. On the wall facing the door was a sink and next to it a long black stretcher.

There were two stirrups hanging from the bottom of it. A porcelain sink beside it had broken, and water tinged with red was flowing all along the tiles. It ran through the open doorway and over Stanley's shoes as he crouched down in the darkness and watched.

It was a room he had heard of before. Word of it had got around, whispered amongst the other boys, the ones who drifted, like him, through that night-time hellish world. They called it the medical room. It was where the wet work was done, a place with walls that could be scrubbed clean. Where there was a stretcher in the middle and a harness and other objects.

In the middle of the room was a heavy ceramic structure built in the shape of a long slab. It stood on a round-ish ceramic base, and thick white pipes led from its base directly to the floor. Lying on top, his eyes staring, his arms outstretched, was Miles. There was a splash as a man's out-line was suddenly framed in the doorway. His naked back was facing Stanley. He stood over the porcelain slab. He cradled Miles in his arms. Miles's arm slapped against the man's cheeks as he held him tighter. He let him go suddenly, and Miles fell back on to the slab. Then the man began to walk away. Stanley ducked further into a corner and did not move a muscle. But from the corner of his eye he saw Miles's arm twitch.

The man's head swivelled slowly to one side. He was overweight. His skin was pale and flabby. He was naked. He had black smooth hair which had been ruffled. He had bags under his eyes and a wide nose. His movements were unhurried, measured and languorous. He turned around and paused, listening. Blood was flowing and curling into the water. The taps were still running. There was a long pause. The man bent down and reached for Miles's shoulder to try to get a better hold of him. For a moment it looked like he was going to embrace him. Miles's arm flew up in the air, slapping the man limply in the face as if he were still trying to fend him off, and his legs shot out, slipping on the slab. There was a squeaking sound as his feet pressed against its wet surface.

Then, without any hesitation at all, the man slammed Miles's head against the edge of the slab. Red on the tiles: a splash of it big enough to cover an entire wall. Stanley covered his mouth and bit down hard on his hand. Then the man did it again. He stood looking down. Then he turned around and reached for a towel and held it over his stomach. His footprints left wet marks on the floor as he headed towards the door.

Stanley looked away. He pushed himself further into the corner and waited. Moments later the man padded past him and moved towards the stairs. Stanley listened until there was no sound and then he fled back up the stairs. Out into the light he ran, and he didn't look back.

## 36

'They picked me up in a village,' Stanley said, putting out a cigarette. 'Brought Robert and me straight back to the home. Just us of course.'

'You have no idea what they did with Miles's body?' I said.

'No. None.'

'What about where you were taken? It was an abandoned house in the countryside somewhere,' I said. 'But the village they picked you up in. Is there anything about it that you can remember?'

'Yes,' Stanley said straight away. 'It was really small. And there was this long stone bridge – like, well – like stepping stones going across a small river. It was really strange. And there are two churches – kind of facing each other.'

'You know it?' Graves said.

'Eastleach, I think,' I said after a while. 'That could well be it. They're two villages. Right next to each other, but people just call it Eastleach. That's the parish, I think. Eastleach Martin and the other one Eastleach something . . . I can't remember now. But there are two churches and they're separated by that old bridge. Powell took me out there once because there's a good pub and we had a look around.'

'There were just three possibilities remaining,' Graves said, reaching for his notes. 'I was going to check them out this afternoon. But now we know it must be this one.' Graves flipped a page. 'I've got one down as near Northleach, which is on the main road, but not Eastleach. But Eastleach must be nearby, am I right?'

I nodded. 'That's the town nearby and it's not too far from Cirencester and Cheltenham, and not that far from Burford either. If the hospital was there, it makes sense, as it would have been close enough to large towns. But it's sufficiently off the beaten track to have suited their purposes.'

'So it fits?'

I nodded.

'So you must have headed towards Eastleach, then,' Graves said, 'when you were trying to get away.'

'And when you got back to the children's home, the only person you told about what you'd seen was Robert?' I said to Stanley.

'Yes. Just Robert.'

'And how does Lee Miller fit in with all of this?'

'Robert called me. After we left each other in Trafalgar Square. I didn't answer it but he left a message. He sounded scared and said he was heading towards the Tube. He said that he was being followed, that I was to go straight to a house in the Cotswolds and that I was to get rid of my phone. I was not to go to my flat. He told me to get on the next bus, go straight there and Lee would take care of me. And that's exactly what I did.'

'And he didn't say anything else? He didn't tell you what his connection was to Miller?'

'No.'

'You didn't know that Robert had served time with Miller?'

'No. I didn't.'

'Well, Robert must have told him,' Graves said, standing up. 'Told him about you, Stanley.'

'Did you tell Miller what you knew?'

'I told him I was a friend of Robert's.'

'And that was enough, was it?' I said.

'Yes. He didn't want to talk about it. He said that I should lay low. He would take care of me for as long as he could.'

'What did the people at the home say about Miles?'

'They told us that he'd been moved.'

'So they were involved, obviously,' Graves said.

'Yes. They were the ones who got us ready for the men.'

'Jesus,' Graves said, horrified.

'And the caretaker, Quint – he was the only one who noticed? Who actually said something?'

'Yes. He wanted to know where Miles was. He started to ask around.'

'So you knew you were in trouble,' I said.

'Yes.'

'And the fire?'

'We were asleep.'

'You didn't know Quint was there looking for records of Miles?' I said.

'No. He just came running in and woke us up. There were some other men in the building. He kept them away and gave us enough time to get outside.'

'So you ran?'

'Yes. We both did. Robert and I. We split up, and we knew we could never see each other again or mention it to anyone. We would just have to survive any way we could on our own.'

'And nobody reported you missing,' Graves said, 'because no one wanted you found.'

'That's right,' Stanley said.

Emma was sitting very still. The colour had drained out of her face. She hit the record button on her phone, ending the audio recording. 'What are you going to do?' she said.

'We have to find it,' I said. 'It's the only way.'

Graves looked at the rain pouring outside. I had hardly noticed it as I listened to what Stanley had to say, but when I looked out I saw that the water had now covered my driveway and the flower beds on the other side and would probably reach my door in a matter of hours if it kept on like this.

'We have to discover where Miles was buried,' I said finally. 'He was probably buried near that spot. And there are no doubt others there as well. We don't know how many yet. And we can't tell anyone until we've got absolute proof, because the chances are they'll make anything less disappear, just as they've been doing for years. These are powerful men we're dealing with. And without concrete evidence it will all go away again.'

I reached for the crowbar which was still lying by the door; it made a loud clang when I put it on the table. 'But for years nobody cared about those boys. They were disposable. They were taken to that room and murdered there and nobody came to help them. You, Stanley, are the only person who ever tried to do something and you were just a kid. You went running down there to help Miles; almost everyone else would have gone the other way. You should remember that the next time you start having one of your panic attacks. You're still the only hope for Miles and the other boys who died out there.'

'And what are you going to do?' Graves said, suddenly nervous. 'Don't you think we should call it in?'

'No. Definitely not. Look what happened to Stanley,' I said, catching Graves's eye. 'They knew. Somehow. We can't take that risk. Get out there with Stanley and see if you can find it. You've got only three places to try.'

'And what are you going to do?' Emma said.

I reached for my jacket and put it on. 'I'm going to find every single person who knew what was happening and never did anything about it. I'm going to track down anyone who was ever at one of those parties they dragged you to, Stanley, or anyone who knew that they were happening and looked the other way. Every single one of those men who ever attended an event like that: I'm going to find them all and they're going to pay. I'm going to bury them in a hole that's so fucking deep that they'll never climb out of it.'

## 37

The floods were finally upon us. I drove out into the surging rain and followed the road to Mrs Bowman's house. Staring at the water on my driveway, I hadn't realized how bad the rain had become, and when I climbed uphill, away from my village, I saw in shock that the water had risen to the tops of the swings and the climbing frames down in the park.

It took me an hour to get anywhere near her village, and as soon as I arrived I knew I was going to have to turn around and find another way. Locals were staring forlornly out of windows, while others were braving the rain and converging near a fire engine which had blocked off the square. A bright green tractor ploughed through the dirty-looking water, and there was the sound of generators pumping out the water from a long black pipe. The water was brown and rippled as rain pounded on its surface.

I could hardly see for more than a few feet because of the rain. It was falling so fiercely that I went straight past her house without even recognizing it. I parked, and knocked on the door, and waited. A light quickly came on in the hall and she ushered me inside.

She looked just as immaculate as she had before. This time she was wearing a long blue skirt and a white blouse and a string of pearls around her neck. She was holding a drink and she offered me one. I nearly accepted it after the drive but said no. I took off my coat, and this time, instead of me dripping all over the carpet, she led me back to a very large and modern kitchen overlooking the garden. She had a portable television on in a small alcove near the window, and both of us watched the news of the flood in awed silence for a while.

In some places in southern England two months' worth of rain had fallen in just that day. Whole areas had already simply vanished under water, while thousands of people looked like they might be driven from their homes. A bewildered villager was talking about how the water had come rushing in like a tide. Possessions gone. His business ruined. The thunder rumbled overhead. She turned down the volume, and we both sat at the kitchen table. I looked at her for a moment longer.

I pushed my hands out in front of me. I felt nervous and on edge and I couldn't seem to look her in the eye. 'I need to go over what we talked about before,' I said finally. 'I need to talk to you about Freddie. Did you know that there was a burglary in your house in London the afternoon of the day he died?'

'Well, not until yesterday.'

'Because a journalist came to see you and told you.'

'Yes, that's right.'

'Can you think of any reason why your husband didn't tell you about the burglary?'

She stared at me, thinking, and then said, 'I'm sure he didn't want to worry me about it.'

'So the day before your husband died, what happened? Let's go through it. Your husband was up in London?'

There was a momentary pause before she said, 'Yes, he was working and I stayed here. We decided that it was better if one of us stayed here and one of us stayed in the house in London. In case Freddie decided to come back. Daniel came back that evening. He took the train from Paddington and then drove here.'

'Were you surprised to see him?'

'Yes, I was, actually. He said that he wanted to come home and needed to be out of London. He'd had a hellish couple of days at work and just wanted to come home for a night and that he'd take one of the first trains back to London the next day even though it was a Saturday.'

'And how did he seem?'

'Well, worried sick of course. Freddie had been gone for almost a month by then. He was very quiet. We tried to have a normal type of dinner. But he said he wasn't hungry. He ate something, I think, and then he went upstairs to his study and spent most of the night working. It was the only way he could try to keep his mind off Freddie.'

'Was he was on the phone in there?'

'In his office? I imagine so – why?'

'Talking to who? Shaw maybe.'

'I suppose so.'

'They used to work together, didn't they?'

'Yes. Charles used to be his adviser.'

'He's still in politics?' I said easily.

'Oh, yes.'

I moved forward in my chair. 'And Shaw . . . he's always lived alone?'

'Charles,' she said confused. 'Yes, as long as I've known him, yes. But what –'

'And when you phoned him a few days ago,' I said, interrupting her, 'when you got the call from the police, he was at home, was he?'

'Yes. I don't understand why you're –'

'Has he been around here a lot lately?'

'Quite a lot, I think, with Christmas. He always comes back from London for Christmas.' She was watching me closely. Behind her on the television were more scenes of chaos and growing pandemonium. She stood up suddenly and switched it off and made herself another drink. She looked confused, and her eyes were watchful and tense. She took a sip on her drink and then took a larger, almost defiant gulp.

'All right, let's go back a bit,' I said as she sat down. 'I know that it must be difficult to go through all this again. I know that the next day must have been . . . well . . . unbearable,' I said, knowing that the word was inadequate. 'But I do need to ask these questions.'

'But *why*?' she said, looking very small and fragile all of a sudden. 'I can't . . . I don't understand why. I want to help you but I don't know what any of this is about. I mean, Freddie's been gone for decades now. What good can come of digging up any of it now?'

I looked at her and wondered if at some deep-down level she might have known or suspected. But I didn't think so. No. She seemed far too trusting for that, and maybe there was a lack of something . . . a lack of curiosity and even imagination, I thought unkindly. It made her more innocent somehow, and it still persisted after all these years. I wondered if that had been one of the things that had drawn her husband to her.

'Your husband came home,' I said finally. 'He spent the night here and he had intended to go back to London the next day in case Freddie came back. But something made him change his mind?'

Mrs Bowman sighed deeply. She prepared herself for the memory and her face hardened and her eyes attained a far-away look, as if she could see the events of that day laid out in front of her. 'Yes, he woke up quite early. I stayed in bed. And there was a phone call.'

'What time?'

'Around seven or eight o'clock. I heard him talking on the phone and then hanging up.'

'You couldn't hear what he was saying?'

'I asked him who it was and he said it was just work and that they wanted him to go back to the office.'

'How did he seem?'

'Well, angry. He couldn't face it and he had told them that he was going to stay for the morning. It was a Saturday anyway, and he said he'd head back up at lunchtime. Then he brought me up a coffee and said he wanted to go for a drive and get a bit of fresh air.'

'That's the last time you saw him?'

'Yes. I . . . I had breakfast. And I waited for him to come back.'

'But he didn't come back.'

'No. It was . . . God, what happened next,' she said. Her face crumpled. 'God, I didn't know anything at the time. It was only later. He couldn't face it, you see. Couldn't tell me. He paid for his ticket, climbed to the top and then he –'

'It's all right, Mrs Bowman,' I said. 'I know what happened next. But you didn't find out until later?'

She shook her head. 'No. They couldn't identify him straight away.' She paused. 'His face, you see.'

I nodded. 'So the phone call he'd got that morning . . . It hadn't been work at all.'

'No, it was the police. They phoned the house because they'd found Freddie's body.'

'But you didn't find out about Freddie until later?'

'No,' she said quietly.

'But,' I said as gently as I could, 'you don't know for sure that it *was* the police who called that morning, do you?'

She looked up sharply. 'Well, no, but . . .'

'But when you heard about what had happened to your husband you assumed it was them? You assumed that he'd heard the news about Freddie earlier that morning and then decided to take his own life?'

'Yes. At around lunchtime I heard someone coming up the drive. I thought it was Daniel.'

'But it was Shaw, wasn't it?'

'Yes,' she said, and looked at me with sudden suspicion. 'And he asked where Daniel was and I told him I didn't know.'

'He seemed surprised when he wasn't there?'

'Look, how do you –'

'Please, Mrs Bowman, this won't take much longer. Just tell me what happened.'

'All right,' she said reluctantly. 'We waited and when he didn't appear Charles said that he had something to tell me.'

'He told you about your son?'

'Yes. He said that the police had found Freddie. And he'd come to see if we were all right. Then the phone rang.'

'And that's when you both got the news about your husband? That he'd committed suicide.'

'Yes. Then it was just . . . well . . . it was policemen knocking on the door and after that . . . I don't really remember much at all.'

I looked at her sitting alone in her big house as the rain poured hard on the roof. I think the first time I had seen her I had known something was wrong, but I just hadn't been able to understand it. Now that I did, some part of me wished that I didn't.

'Your husband and Shaw have known each other for a long time, haven't they?' I said.

'Yes,' she said.

'How did they meet?'

'It's a story they used to tell quite often,' she said. She suddenly seemed cheerful again. 'They'd known each other for years.'

'How many years?'

'Ever since they were boys.'

'They went to the same school, did they?' I said.

She smiled. 'No, but they were in a rugger match. That's the funny thing. Opposite teams. Both captains. Daniel was injured in the game. Broke his collarbone, and Charles broke his arm. They were sent to the same hospital because it was nearby.'

'A hospital?'

'Yes, for children.'

'You don't know where this hospital is?' I said, as calmly as I could manage.

'No. They were there for over a month, though, in the end. That's how they became friends. They caught an infection while they were there and had to stay. One of those hospital bugs, I think it was. So they had plenty of time to get to know each other.'

I didn't say anything for a moment. I felt old. My jaw and head ached. I wanted to stand up and leave that beautiful house and never go back. But there was one more thing to do first. It was a long shot of course. 'Have you got a photo of your son?' I said.

'But I thought Charles had already given you one.'

'It's just in case,' I said.

'Of course. But we didn't really have that many,' she said, standing up. 'Freddie never liked getting his photo taken.'

I watched as she left the kitchen and stared at the rain. She returned with the photo, which she'd removed from its frame, just as Shaw had done. She handed it to me and I looked at it. Freddie Bowman was staring at the camera. He looked brown from the sun but he wasn't smiling.

'Daniel took that while we were on holiday,' she said happily. 'Cornwall.'

I sat very still at the table. I didn't look at it again for what seemed a long moment. Then I took a deep breath and turned it over slowly in my hands and then traced the white borders on either side with my finger. It was a Polaroid of course.

# 38

I rang Shaw from the Bowman house, but there was no reply. Either the lines were down or he wasn't in. Then I phoned his office in London. They hadn't heard from Shaw in days. They didn't know where he was or when he was coming back and they had not been able to reach him on his mobile and they were worried.

I decided to chance it with the rain. Shaw lived near a small village ten minutes away. I asked Mrs Bowman for precise directions to his house. Then I got in my car and I headed fast down the hill and phoned Graves as the car pushed through the rain.

'We're having trouble finding it,' Graves said, his voice rising as he tried to make himself heard above the din. 'It's not . . . can you hear me, sir? All I know is that it's probably somewhere between Northleach and Eastleach. It's a small children's hospital called St Joseph's, but it closed down years ago. The roads are terrible. Moreton-in-Marsh is under water, and we've have to avoid heading along the main road: there's been an accident and the road's blocked in both directions for miles. We're trying the back way through all these small villages, but it's tough going and we're not quite sure where the hospital is exactly.' Graves began to yell. 'I can hardly hear you. Can you hear me?'

'Yes. Yes. I can hear you.'

'The car's almost had it as well. We had to swerve into a ditch. Fucking tractor came the other way.'

'Wait for me once you've found it and try and get someone else out there. It will be pandemonium in the station, I think, but we need as many people as we can.'

'But –'

'Just do it, Graves. I'll be there as soon as I can.'

The brown hedgerows rose up on either side of the narrow road. Ahead the fields were all waterlogged and water now lapped at the edges of the roads. Before Shaw's village there was a bridge which crossed the railway tracks below. The water had risen to the edges of the platform. For a moment the church spire and the whole village disappeared out of sight behind a thick hedge as the road dipped. Then, as it rose again, the spire, the walls of the church and finally the uneven rows of houses that lined the square slipped once more into view through the falling rain. On the other side of the village, lorries, vans and cars lined up, blocking the road, their lights smeared through the windscreen.

What had once been a stream was now a lake in the middle of Shaw's village. It pushed against the trees on the green and benches. Swathes of vegetation had been flattened in the water. Traffic cones were floating in the road. An old couple were trying to make their way unsteadily across a street. There came a surreal moment when ducks were actually swimming in front of them, and then a kid sitting on his knees in a yellow inflatable went careering across the surface and the ducks flew off with an indignant squawk.

I parked my car as high on the verge as I could. I stepped into the water and waded past a sealed-off petrol station and down a small road beyond the line of shops. The water soon began to rise over my boots, to my knees. I found the lane and kept going and pushed through the water. The water began to subside as the road sloped upwards, and I broke into a fast, heavy-footed jog when I finally saw his house.

It clung to the edges of the village down a small winding lane. It was big but it lacked the charm of the rest of the houses in the village, which stood in almost perfect yellow-stone harmony. The walls looked slightly too thin, and the windows were too large, so that you could see in quite clearly from across the lane. I looked for the bell and found it under a door knocker and rang just in case, but there was no reply. I went around the back and inspected the window in the back door; and then I covered my elbow with my coat and smashed through it. I reached in, undid the latch on the other side and let myself in.

The alarm went off straight away, as I knew it would. There was no way of turning it off. No one would care with everything else going on. It wailed and the sound of it reverberated off the walls as I switched on all the lights and began a thorough search of his house. I had no proof. Just a vague half-formed theory. And knowing how well Shaw had covered his tracks, I realized now might be the only opportunity I would ever have to find anything.

The house was immaculate. There was not a single dirty cup or plate. The carpets and rugs had all been vacuumed recently. There was a faint, pleasant smell of fresh flowers drifting along the hallway. No dust anywhere. No real signs of life. His cupboards were stocked with healthy-looking organic food. Bottles of water were laid neatly on top of one another in the larder. No alcohol anywhere. The kitchen was sparse and the worktops gleaming. A cloth lay at an exact angle by the side of the sink. The washing-up bowl had been turned over and scrubbed clean. There were some files from work lying in a neat pile on top of his kitchen table.

My boots thudded and squelched on soft carpet as I made my way upstairs. All the while the alarm rang out. I stared out of the window for a moment. No signs of life out there.

I grabbed a towel from Shaw's bathroom and wiped the back of my neck and began to search. I overturned bookcases. Went through each one of the books and flipped through the pages. I shook out magazines. I looked through boxes on a chair by the door; I tipped out drawers in every room. I took off my coat and tossed it on his perfectly made bed. I went through the cupboards in his room, rifled the drawers by the telephone and found folders and papers and photocopies and endless spreadsheets. I pulled back magazines from shelves and ransacked the cabinets in his bathrooms. I let it all pile up in each room. More files and more paper. More boxes which I overturned and pillaged.

Address books. More photocopies. Linen drawers. Sock drawers. Underwear. Shoes. Golf clubs. Racks of clothes in wardrobes. I knocked over a lamp which fell to the floor. I inspected underneath desks and tables. I turned over chairs and mattresses and hurled out blankets from a cupboard underneath the stairs. And then I began downstairs.

By the time I was finished there were overturned bookshelves, tipped-over furniture and loose papers all over the place. Cutlery and food and bottles of water were rolling along the floor. Not a thing. Then, as quickly as I could, I went through it all again. Rummaged in the chaos I had created. And then, finally, just as I was about to give up, there amongst the wreckage in his study, a single picture had fallen to one side. He had needed it near him of course.

It had been concealed amongst the pages of one of his books in his study, although now I didn't know which one. I took it over to his desk and switched on the light and took a deep breath and had a look at it.

It was a photo of Garrett after they had finished with him in that room all those years ago. I stared long and hard at the photo. It wasn't easy to look at. Shaw had needed that photo: when the nightmares came, the only way to rid himself of the memories of that room was to relive what they'd done to Garrett. The picture was worn and ragged at the edges and was almost falling apart because it had been handled so often. Garrett lay in the middle of the floor on the tiles. The shadow of a large structure loomed above him, although I could not make out what it was. His face was pointing towards the camera. Blood pooled around his broken mouth and all around his legs. The beating had continued in that room for what looked to be a very long time, but that wasn't the worst part. He was bleeding from below the waist, where they had unmanned him, and, as he had tried to crawl away from them, he left a wide trail of blood all along the tiles. I felt a spasm of disgust when I realized what they had done to him.

I put the photo in a book so it would not get wet, found a plastic bag in the kitchen and wrapped the book tightly inside. Then I put it on the sideboard. I decided to have another quick look. I kept looking, and this time went through the books collected in the study more gently. And then froze. Another final photo. Face down.

I turned it over. This one was newer than the others. And, looking at it, I remembered Irwin mentioning the local missing boy, Conrad. For a moment I simply froze and felt a lurching sickness right down in the pit of my stomach. I had not made the connection. Conrad had been discounted pretty much straight away as not being one of the boys in the photos because he had run away only recently, and it had not been the first time. Irwin had checked it out. And teenagers went missing all the time, as Shaw had so rightly pointed out when I met him, and we didn't have the resources to follow up on them all. The Polaroids had been taken so long ago as well. But this one looked brand new and was not worn like the others. The borders glistened in the light of Shaw's study as the rain pounded on the roof.

The boy cowering in the corner of the room was wearing clothes which looked new and modern. The medical room looked older, as if it hadn't been used for many, many years. Part of the ceiling at the far end had fallen in and there were large mounds of dirt and rubble piled up beside the sinks. There was no pose this time. The boy was simply cowering in fear and the photo looked as if it had been taken quickly. With trembling fingers I added the photo to the other Polaroid in the plastic bag.

I thudded down the hall and used the phone to ring Graves, but there was no reply. I slammed down the phone and tried the station. I was put on hold. I hung up again. I began running and all the while the sound of Shaw's house alarm followed me as I plunged through the rain and down the street.

# 39

I put the photos in the glove box and then retraced my way out of the village. I drove as fast as I dared, thinking of the boy, hoping to God that there might be a chance to save his life. I tried Graves on the radio but it just crackled. I tried his phone, but got no answer, then I tried again. No luck. I tossed the phone on to the passenger seat and grimaced, hunched over the wheel. I picked up speed. The car roared and surged forward.

I remembered Irwin mentioning the runaway Conrad again. Already it might be too late and it would be my fault. His blood would be on my hands as surely as if I'd put him in that room myself. The road uncoiled and the water whooshed on either side of the car. The windscreen wipers struggled against the force of water hitting them from every side. I felt a hopeless tide of rising panic and anger. If something did happen to him . . . Christ, it must have happened already. His chances were next to zero if he had been brought into that room.

I picked up speed, nearly hydroplaning twice, and managed to steer my way out of it at the last second both times. Then, just as I was getting close to Northleach, I went around a bend too fast and nearly went spinning into a tree. The car jarred to a stop on the muddy verge and the engine died.

I slammed my fists against the steering wheel and forced myself to wait and then tried the ignition. It worked on the third try and I kept going. I snapped on the radio. The army had been deployed to help emergency services. The relentless rain had left hundreds of homes and businesses under water, and countless drivers and travellers were stranded as road and rail routes were inundated by fast-rising flood waters. I saw the sign to Eastleach and took it.

I stared outside with growing desperation. It was as if I had travelled back in time somehow and it had all taken place within a matter of hours. The water rose amongst the fields and lapped on the roads. It climbed towards the verges until they crumbled. Trees stood marooned. Abandoned cars were now dotted along the side of the road.

Then suddenly, out of the darkness, Graves emerged, waving frantically in the rain. I pulled over and nearly landed straight in a ditch. He ran towards my car. He was soaked to the skin and white smoke was pouring from the bonnet of his car.

'This is it,' he said. 'Up there's the house Stanley told us about.'

'Have you been up there?'

'I left Stanley in the car and had a quick look. We were lucky as hell to find it. We missed it and then went back, but Stanley thought he recognized the road that leads to it and it's up there, we think. The damned car died on us and I tried you on the phone but couldn't get through. There's something wrong with the radio as well. I've never seen anything like it.'

The water pounded through the trees and raced along the hills. The wind roared and the back of Graves's coat flapped out behind him.

'I think the only route we can take is back up towards the house and then across the fields,' he said. 'I can't find the original road to the hospital. It must be overgrown by now. And there's no backup available. Before the radio died, I heard that the emergency services are at breaking point. The only person in the station is Burton, and he can't leave because he's manning the phones. Everyone has been called in to help out. It's absolute chaos everywhere, sir.'

'What about Vine?' I said.

'Vine?'

'Yes. Give my mobile a try. He might still be at the station.' I reached into the back seat and passed him my mobile through the open window. 'I don't have his number but see if Burton can find him in the station. Try as many people as you can and get someone else out here right fucking now.'

I opened the door and ran towards Graves's car. Stanley was sitting in the back. I thumped on the window and he reluctantly opened it.

'Stanley,' I said, 'you all right?'

He shrugged and flinched from the rain as it fell through the open window.

'We need you to show us where it is. I'm sorry. I don't want to have to put you through it again, but there could be another boy up there right at this moment.'

'Another boy?' he said, shocked.

'Yes.'

'Oh, God, all right.'

He stepped gingerly out into the rain and his feet landed in a puddle. He winced, bracing himself for the rain, and we stood outside. In seconds he was soaked. Graves reached into the front seat and passed me a torch, and I took the crowbar out of the boot of my car.

'Another boy,' Graves said, sounding rattled. 'What do you mean?'

'The Conrad kid. It was in the local papers and Irwin talked to his old man. But Shaw had a photo of him in his house.'

'That's where you were? In his house?'

'Yes.'

'He's not there?'

'No.'

'And where's the kid?'

'No one knows where he is. He ran away from home a few weeks ago, but I didn't make the connection,' I said helplessly. 'I talked to Mrs Bowman and apparently Shaw was here for Christmas, and he was here when we spoke to her the first time. So that's where he might be if he's keeping someone here. But there's no reason why he would leave him alive indefinitely.'

We closed the car doors and then headed as fast as we could towards the house, staring from time to time at the hill rising up into the distance. Then we moved along the side of the muddy track. The water was slack here. It drifted against the trunks of the trees. On its surface floated tendrils of vegetation and leaves which had been stripped off by the fierceness of the water. Above, the hill rose and beyond it I could see the gate leading to the abandoned house. The water seemed to dominate the entire landscape. It seemed impossible that so much water would ever go away.

We moved towards the crest of the hill. Stanley trailed in our wake, moaning and cursing the weather, but trying to hide his fear well. I knew I had taken him back to the one place on earth he had never wanted to go.

'So it's Shaw,' Graves said.

'Yes.'

'But I don't get it,' Graves said. 'How on earth did Finn know about any of this? What was he after out here?'

It was hard to make myself heard over the rising din. 'This has been going on for a long time. There were certain things that Finn knew, but he couldn't have known all of it. I think he was only just beginning to piece it all together. He knew that he might be on to something big but he couldn't know for sure until he heard it direct from Miller or at least managed to talk to him. Someone high up had been tipping him off about it.'

'Who?'

'A policeman.'

'Christ.'

'Yes,' I said, as we started wading through a large expanse of water. 'This one is much higher up than the police officer he bribed years ago. And the link was never made because this one didn't want money and they probably never even met. He'd been moving up the ranks quickly because he was a good boy and did what he was told. And when he was told to suppress a piece of evidence regarding a burglary in London, he did so. No big deal. But then something happened the very same night the burglary occurred.'

'Freddie Bowman happened,' Graves said.

I turned back and we waited for Stanley to catch up. The wind was blowing hard. Water was rising everywhere. We carried on walking along the narrow road and up the hill.

'Hours after the burglary Freddie is found dead in a squat,' I said, making sure Graves was close enough to hear me above the rain. 'The burglary had already been suppressed; orders must have come from high up. Whoever was told to hide the evidence kept it. And I think they looked into it because they wanted to know what they'd got themselves into. Because if they had been told to suppress the burglary at Bowman's house in London, then it had to be important.'

Behind us, I could hear Stanley cursing and muttering under his breath. The trees shook in the wind. I wrapped myself deeper into my coat, feeling my shirt sticking to my skin.

'You found something and you were told to keep a lid on it, Graves. Something in Oxford. And what did you do?'

'I told the IPCC.'

'And what reward did you get for doing that?'

'I got sent straight out here,' Graves said glumly.

I rubbed the water out of my eyes and we fell into single file. The road dipped, and we skirted another mass of water. 'So this police officer . . . they're not as dumb as you or me,' I said over my shoulder. 'He or she does what they're told but that doesn't mean they're completely dishonest or corrupt. From the sounds of it, we're talking about someone who is ambitious enough not to step out of line but who might later have regretted it. So instead they leak it to a top reporter on one of the bestselling papers in the country, and only then, many, many years later.'

I turned around. Graves nodded and looked up through the trees. It was still quite a way to the top. Stanley pushed a branch out of his way and then stared down at his soaking wet shoes and trousers. Graves started to walk beside me again.

'No one was ever arrested for selling Freddie the drugs, for letting him die like that and taking all his possessions,' I said to Graves. 'This was the son of an MP after all. So why wasn't more done to get to the bottom of what had really happened? A few people were rounded up. But for some reason the Met couldn't take it further. Why, Graves?'

Graves sniffed and pushed back his hair. There was a long streak of mud along the side of his face. The trees and shrubbery were thinning out as we climbed towards the top of the rise. 'Well, there could be a hundred reasons for that.'

I felt in my pocket to make sure that my torch was still reasonably dry, turned it on and off, and glanced back down the hill. 'Someone very high up wanted this hidden. Miles was made to disappear. Quint and Baines were silenced. The truth has been suppressed. And only someone with power could do it. Whoever has been doing this has hidden themselves amongst powerful men and used their secrets as leverage. They've got enough on the police to bend them to their will, and when they call in favours they come through. And they're big favours, Graves. They even managed to discredit Finn, but that just made him more determined to prove his story was true. They underestimated him. The same way they underestimated Vine and the same way they underestimated Stanley.'

The path had widened slightly. There was an old gate further up and what seemed to be the orchard Stanley had mentioned. Large pieces of Cotswold stone were buried here and there in the undergrowth. We stopped for a moment, waiting impatiently for Stanley again.

'I think our whistleblowing policeman had a good look at Freddie's case and did a bit of checking on his own,' I said, facing Graves. 'Maybe he asked a few of Freddie's mates up in London and I think they would have given him a name sooner or later or an address or something. And it could only have been one name. Freddie runs away. Goes to London. We know Miller was gay. And we know that Miller's dad wasn't exactly enlightened about that sort of thing. Maybe his dad kicked him out and they met up later in London or met before somehow. We'll never know. But we're talking about two young men alone in a time when being gay was very different to what it is now. I think those two became close. Freddie – a sensitive boy unable maybe to fit in and I think despite everything Miller was sensitive too in his own way. I talked to Miller's aunt yesterday. Miller was abandoned by his mother, who walked out on him when he was just a kid. Got pregnant pretty much as soon as she got married. His father blamed him for his wife leaving. Miller and Freddie were from the same area. And those two were in London at the same time.'

Graves gestured for Stanley to hurry up. Stanley muttered under his breath and angrily splashed through the water.

'And we also know that Miller was back here in the Cotswolds before going back to London,' I said as we carried on walking again. 'The police were looking for him. He was arrested but was never charged. I checked the records yesterday and the date is days after Freddie was found murdered. So why was he never charged with anything? Because it's all linked to the burglary,' I said. 'The burglary of Bowman's house in London. Whoever went in there knew that the alarm wasn't working. Mr Bowman is told of the burglary. And he comes straight over to inspect it. From the report at the time we know he went straight to the study and checked.'

'All right, sir,' Graves said, sounding unconvinced. 'So you think it was Freddie. But if Bowman knew it was his son, or suspected it was his son, he wouldn't necessarily announce it. He wouldn't have wanted to get him into any more trouble. And why not use the front door? He must have had a key.'

'Freddie didn't take it with him when he left. I asked his mother just now. He only bought a single ticket when he took the train; he wasn't planning on returning to his family. But he probably ran out of money. So he waits until his father is out at work and then he breaks in. But he probably had help.'

'Miller,' Graves said quickly.

'Yes. When the police show up, Bowman doesn't point the finger at his son and if there is anything missing like cash or any valuables he doesn't say.'

'But why? Why go to all that trouble to make the incident report disappear over a simple break-in when nothing was taken. Unless . . .' Graves stopped walking. 'Something was taken and he didn't want anyone to know about it.'

'Exactly. I think there was a safe in there somewhere and Freddie knew the combination. It sounds like whoever it was knew the layout of the house well. They went straight to the back door and smashed through the window and then let themselves in. No alarm to worry about. They went up there and took what they wanted and left.'

We had finally reached the top of the hill. Stanley stood for a moment, looking at the old house beyond the gate, and then pointed through some trees. From the top there was a wide-open view of what the floods had left behind. Everywhere was the constant sheen of black water. The rain poured down in a steady roar.

'That's the house,' Stanley said.

'So which way now?'

'Over here, I think,' Stanley said, and began to take the lead.

'So if the burglary was suppressed,' Graves said thoughtfully, 'it would have to have been by someone who could pull strings. Someone like an MP. And that means Bowman had something to hide. So the photos,' he said quickly. 'The photos were in his house and if they were in his house it means . . .' Graves suddenly looked sick to his stomach.

'His own son.'

'My God,' Graves said loudly.

Stanley turned around briefly. He seemed determined now to get to the house. He carried on trudging through the rain and we had to walk faster to keep up with him.

'I'm afraid so. Bowman took his own son into that room,' I said. 'Freddie became addicted to drugs and ran away from home shortly afterwards. And either he told Miller all about the medical room or Miller would have heard rumours about it when he worked as a rent boy.'

'But they went to the flat for money?'

'Yes, I think so,' I said, as I looked up through the trees. Stanley was really picking up the pace now, eager to get it over with. We caught up with him. For a moment we all walked in single file again, not saying a word. Then I said, 'They must have gone there for money and then gone through what they had taken back in the squat. There must have been an envelope along with whatever else they took. And Miller must have seen what was inside. So he knew that Freddie – the boy he may well have fallen in love with – had been taken there, and by his own father too.'

I wiped the water from my face and blinked into the falling rain. It couldn't be too long now, but it felt as if we had been out here for hours. 'The way Freddie died was gentle in a way, and it never fitted and I couldn't figure it out,' I said. 'I think the first thing he did when he got the money was to buy drugs. Oblivion was the only way he could forget what had happened to him. He could well have opened the envelope when Miller had gone off somewhere. And the moment he saw those photos he had to forget straight away.'

'So he overdosed. On purpose.'

'It could be, or it could have been an accident, but Miller didn't get to him in time. When he came back and saw Freddie dead, he took the envelope and everything else with him. He probably knew that he was going to be arrested sooner or later because he'd been seen with Freddie more than once. So he goes home and hides the envelope. Then he's arrested.'

'But never actually charged.'

'Miller knew he had a card to play. Several of them in fact. Those photos were a guarantee of his own safety. That's why he kept them. And he went home to hide them. Don't forget: the hiding place in the chimney was right up at the top. I think it was a hiding place Miller must have had when he was much younger, when he was small and able to get up there easily.'

The path narrowed again, and we had to push our way through undergrowth which seemed to be getting thicker all the time. Graves was shivering and he put up the collar of his coat. It was even harder to make myself heard over the din of the rain now.

'So Bowman didn't kill himself because of what happened to his son?' Graves said.

'No. He killed himself because he was a coward and he thought he was about to be exposed and deep down I think he'd had enough. He tried to suppress the news of the burglary, because if the photos were found he could simply deny that there had been a burglary in his house. There would be no official record of it. It wasn't much. A holding action, I imagine, to give himself time. But he knew that it was over for him if they ever came out, and it must have looked at that moment as if they would.'

'He knew he would break down when he was interviewed.'

'He might have known. And I think that part of him wanted to die as well. It could have been something that he'd been planning for a long time. He seemed to have picked out the spot in advance. He went home, spent one night there. His last. Then the next morning he drove straight out to Broadway Tower.'

'But he could have denied everything of course.'

'Yes – and he doesn't appear in any of the photos himself. There was no way for sure that they could have been conclusively traced back to him. But we know that Freddie was hanging out with other boys in London and he might well have figured out that if Freddie went to the house to break in, someone else would have probably gone with him. Whoever it was would have had a damned good chance of proving that he had been there. There could have been his fingerprints, and he would have been able to describe the safe, if pressed, and tell them where it was. Bowman probably knew that. He didn't know how much Freddie had told anyone else either.

His influence could only stretch so far; and the police and the press were going to want to know why he had a photo of his own son standing half naked in that room, along with photos of other boys, all of whom had disappeared. Not to mention a photo of Joe Garrett. He didn't know that his son was dead, and that Miller had the photos and was ready to make a deal with Shaw. But when he thought there was a good chance of his being exposed, he climbed to the top of Broadway Tower and jumped.'

We trudged in silence for a while, and there, encircled by trees and rising at the edge of the fields, was the old abandoned hospital. Stanley had stopped dead in his tracks. He turned around and I saw that he had gone as white as a sheet. I put up my hand and Graves stopped as well.

We all crouched down low. The rain pounded around us and swirled at our soaking feet. Stanley sat shivering and staring wildly at a car perched at the top of the hill. I gripped his arm and told him to go back into the trees and wait for us. We skirted along the sides of the field. The hospital rose up ahead. The rain fell.

'Oh, Jesus. They must have come up along the old road to the hospital,' Graves said. 'What are we going to do?'

'We're going to have to get rid of them somehow,' I said.

'But how? Look at what they did to you last time. And that was just one of them.'

I held the crowbar close to my leg and pushed the water away from my eyes. There was a sour feeling in the bottom of my gut. 'We've got no choice, Graves. I'm sorry. We're on our own out here. There's a possibility that the boy, Conrad, might be alive. If he's dead, Shaw's come here to bury him. But he might still be alive.'

'It's definitely them?'

'It's the same car. So it's them.'

'The same guys who took out Miller and Finn,' Graves said quietly.

'We'll get the jump on them this time,' I said with more optimism than I felt. 'It'll be all right. Is there anything around here you can use?'

Graves moved towards the trees and came back with a big branch and swung it a few times in his hands.

I took it and held it. 'You take the driver and I'll get the other one. I'll use the crowbar to get rid of him and you just hold the driver off for as long as you can. Then I'll come and help you with this. Follow my lead. Once it starts it won't be too bad. This is the worst part, Graves. The part before it all starts. But if it all goes wrong and you get a chance, get the hell out of here.'

I walked back to where Stanley was safely hidden in the canopy of trees and asked him if he could drive. He couldn't. So I told him to go straight back to where we had left the car and flag down the first car he saw and then get away.

I moved back and stood next to Graves. Then we ducked down beside a hedgerow. I thanked God for the rain. Inside the car, two men sat in silence at the front. We crouched down low and skirted along the crest of the hill, approaching the car from the side. Graves's eyes glimmered in the dark. He swallowed his fear and we moved up silently along the grass.

They didn't want to hear what was going on in that abandoned hospital. That's why the radio was on, which meant that the boy might still be alive, and I hastened my step as we got closer. Behind them was the entrance to the hospital. I felt anger beginning to replace the fear. I pointed and Graves went to the other side, ducking down low. He didn't hesitate. I drew to a slow stop.

I made my way towards the front door. The music grew louder. The window cracked open and then went straight back up again. I took a long deep breath, but before I could breathe out again there was a startled shout from the other side of the car. The car rocked and jolted on its axis. Immediately the door on my side was thrown open, hitting me hard on my shoulder. I looked up. It was the man from the hospital. His eyes took on an air of cold decision when he saw it was me. He pushed the door open. I sprang to my feet and slammed my body against the door. He pushed again. He was unbelievably strong and fast. His other hand was scrabbling towards the glove box. The glove box opened and something slipped out and hit the floor. He swore and reached for it.

He heaved his shoulder against the door. My feet slid along on the grass. His left hand slipped through the gap in the door. I eased off. From the other side was a muffled bellow and then a grunt and I glimpsed Graves flailing and then falling to the ground.

I glanced down. The man's hand had slipped through the gap as he'd tried to push forward. I took a deep breath and pushed against it with all my strength until the door gave and slammed on his fingers. He screamed and tried to move his fingers away. I rammed my shoulder against the door and pushed down hard, then let go. He whipped his hand back and howled in agony. Then he leapt out of the car and shoved his broken hand under his armpit, slipping in the rain. I lunged at him and swung the crowbar towards his face.

The water splashed and churned in our wake. We moved clumsily in the mud. There was no gracefulness to him here, as there had been in the hospital. Now it was just blind rage. He caught me in an ugly tackle and I went flying. The crowbar spun out of my hand, hit the bonnet of the car with a dull clang and fell to the ground. I hit him on the back of his shoulders and went diving for the crowbar. He threw himself at me. I slithered out of his grasp on my back and turned him over and wrapped my legs around his chest. Then I put my arms over his head and reached for his throat and with all my strength squeezed. He let out a choking, stifled grunt, and spittle began to fly out of his mouth. I released my grip to get a better hold. In desperation he punched me hard in the side of my face with his elbow. Then he did it again.

But I only leant in closer and ignored it. I could smell the leather of his jacket; I could see the stubble on his chin bristling in the dark. Then I opened my mouth and bit down hard on his ear.

My mouth instantly filled with warm gushing blood. The man screamed and screamed. It was fear, pain and panic, and the scream came out wet and gurgling. I sunk my teeth deep into cartilage and flesh, and like a dog I moved my head from side to side. The blood began to pour down my chin and soaked my shirt and sprayed on the grass.

Then I let go and scrabbled for the crowbar. Already I could feel him moving after me. I snatched it from the water, scrambled to my feet and then swung it in the air. The sharp curved end of it landed straight on the front of his open mouth. He reeled back. I hit him again. He crumpled to his knees. He stared, gargling blood and spit and choking, and then collapsed to one side. For a moment all I could feel was pure rage at what he had done and I very nearly ended his life right there on that wet patch of grass, but instead I glanced to the right and saw Graves stumbling backwards and then rising to his feet.

I raced around the car, slipped once near the boot, fell and then got to my feet. Graves was lying on the ground. The other man was pinning him down with his knees. Then he changed position, reaching for his throat. He scrabbled around on the ground, trying to get Graves into some kind of choke hold with his legs and using the front tyre to gain traction, but he slipped in the mud. Graves by some miracle managed to push him off and rose, gasping, to his feet. There was a wild look in Graves's eyes. They circled each other. Graves pounced, diving for him, and flung him against the side of the car. The driver hit the bonnet.

I scrambled after him and rammed down the crowbar. It missed as he rolled away from it. I fell on top of him. He punched me hard in the face. I shook it off and dragged myself on top of him. Almost immediately I felt another hammering blow as the back of his elbow came down on the back of my head. With a huge shove with his knees he pushed me off and I was on my back on the ground again in front of the car.

'Stop!' Graves shouted. 'Stop!'

He whirled around and stared at the gun which Graves had got from the floor of the car. For a moment I was sure he was going to make a move for it. He stood still. I had dropped the crowbar and, gasping, I stood up and went and got it. Then I rammed it hard on to his right knee so that he fell forward. Then I did it again.

Graves looked on, appalled. There was blood in my mouth and I spat it out. I searched his pockets and the inside of the car and then I searched the other man, who was writing on the ground, clutching his mouth. There was no other gun.

We stood above them. Breathing heavily, gasping and bleeding all over the place but secretly quite pleased with ourselves. Blood was dripping down Graves's head and on to his coat and mingling with the falling rain. He wiped his forehead with his sleeve and then rubbed the blood off his knuckles.

'You all right?'

'I don't know. I think so.'

'You can keep an eye on them?'

He nodded.

I took a moment to catch my breath. There was no telling with those two men. They looked defeated but I didn't want to chance it. So I let Graves keep the gun. Then I started to move again. I took the crowbar with me, thinking it should be enough for someone like Shaw. The area in front of the hospital was completely water-logged. It rose above my knees and I moved through it, still gasping and trying to catch my breath as best I could. The walls of the hospital were grey. The windows had all been smashed in years ago and were now empty and dark.

For a moment I didn't want to go in there. I stood very still. I could not face what might be there or what Shaw might have done. I could not face the sickness which had compelled him and Bowman to come here over and over again. But their sickness lay there waiting for me in some dark corner, down amongst the rot and filth. I could smell the moss and the peeled paint. There would never be enough rain to wash away the blood from those white tiles. I gripped the crowbar and watched in fascination as blood dripped from its end. I moved through the rain and stood at the doorway much as Stanley had almost twenty years ago. Then I walked in, knowing that the graves of dead children awaited me.

## 40

The only light came from my torch. There was a stench of enclosed darkness and musty decay. Shrubs poked through broken windows. I sniffed at the dark. My nerves were wound as tightly as a spring. The rain fell through the holes in the roof and dripped all along the corridor.

There were overturned chairs and a number of wooden crates and metal tables and old cabinets. The beam of my torch caught a picture in a broken frame of an ocean liner sailing off into a distant horizon. I peered into another room and saw the shapes of cabinets. There was a slab of thin concrete covering a door. Mounds of old rubbish were piled into corners.

I went down the first staircase I came to. More rubbish and broken pieces of old furniture blocked part of the way. I sidled past. The narrow hallway was waterlogged and beyond it came the sound of someone murmuring. The voice rose and fell. I walked quickly along the corridor and approached an open door. I took a few steps further in.

The thick heavy door stood open and I noticed that a number of large padlocks had been attached to a series of bars which slotted into the wall. I peered in and saw at once what the medical room's original purpose had been.

The room was bigger than it had looked in the photos, and the large structure which had covered Garrett as he had tried to crawl away was a mortuary slab. They had made sure that the rest of the room had always been bathed in darkness when they had taken their photos. The equipment, including the black stretcher, had probably been removed years ago.

Thin black pipes ran all the way along high walls. There was a broken glass roof high up. A shattered lamp hung overhead. The floor was covered by almost half a foot of flood water.

I took another step. The boy was in the corner of the room, standing with his back towards the sinks, which I now saw ran all the way along the far side of the room. He had been in that room for at least two weeks and the remains of the food Shaw had brought him were rotting in the corner. There was another smell too, which was even worse.

Conrad was seventeen but small for his age. He had a big shaggy mop of blond hair. He looked pale and skinny in his clothes, and his hands were bloody from where he had tried either to crawl his way to the top where the ceiling had fallen in slightly or beat his way out of the room. Shaw was standing above him, shining his torch in his direction. He was wearing a large overcoat. His umbrella stood neatly in the corner. He was soaking wet and rubbing the water out of his eyes as he paced up and down in his wellington boots. He was holding a large metal bar and not a gun. The bar looked like it had come from somewhere in the hospital – maybe a piece from a broken bed.

And he was tapping it gently on the side of his leg. Every time the water splashed and touched the boy he would flinch away from it. The boy's eyes flickered towards my own.

Shaw didn't want to kill him; but, at the same time, he very much wanted to, and he wanted to do it slowly. Otherwise he would have taken the gun with him and got it over with. He was telling the boy, in a tight reedy voice, that he had no choice but to kill him, and was almost pleading with him to try to understand that now it was too late and he was sorry.

'It's been a long time since you were last down here, hasn't it, Shaw?' I said.

Shaw wheeled around. His eyes stared at me in the doorway. He took in the crowbar in my hand and for a moment I sincerely hoped that he was going to make a move for it, but he didn't. He stood very still as the rain pounded on the roof and cascaded down from the broken tiles and broken gutters.

Conrad took a few faltering steps and then gripped the edge of the slab at the far side of the room. I motioned to him. But Shaw moved fast for his age. He swung the bar in the air. It glanced off the boy's shoulder. The boy reeled backwards. Shaw darted forward, grabbed him and then pulled him tightly towards his body. The boy struggled and pushed against him with a huge shove. It took Shaw by surprise; he lost his balance, fell into the water and dropped the bar. I scrabbled for it as the boy ran. Already Shaw was getting to his feet, but then all strength

350

seemed to leave him. He sat back down in the water and suddenly looked resigned. Then, with a nod of his head, he motioned to the door. 'Get out of here,' he murmured, then screamed. 'Just get out!'

The boy took a few paces, looked at him with wide eyes and then within seconds was through the door. I grabbed the metal bar and threw it to the other side of the room and waited until I could hear the boy's feet pounding up the stairs.

Shaw listened until the boy's footsteps had faded. His shoulders hunched. Then he pushed himself up. His torch was in the water and he picked it up. He shook it and turned it back on. He looked relieved. There was a slackness to his face in the velvet shadow. He was shaking. He stared around the room, his eyes expressionless. It was over and he knew it. And he was glad about it too. But now I was going to have to hear it. *All* of it.

For a long moment I considered dragging him out of there. We could wait and then talk to him in the safe confines of the station, where it would have been more bearable. But I knew that once out of this place the old Charles Shaw might return. Right now his face looked raw and vulnerable. He looked younger somehow.

'So you know?' he said finally.

I nodded. 'Not all of it. But I know what happened to you and your friend Daniel Bowman.'

'Daniel.' He said the name, drawing out the word lovingly. He looked around as if expecting to see him standing by his side. The word was like a whisper which reached out through time and crossed the years, so that for a moment it was almost as if the room was as I had seen it before in the photo: the walls scrubbed clean, the windows full of glass, no shrubs invading dark corners. For a moment the hospital was full of people. People were moving upstairs. Nurses were bustling around a busy, brightly lit corridor. And then night fell and the little boy who had been brought here was standing before me.

'Garrett brought you down here, didn't he?' I said. 'You and Bowman. You were injured. Playing rugby.'

He looked at me for what seemed a long while. There was a moment of indecision and right then I knew it could go either way. It was up to him now. Then he made up his mind.

'Yes, that's right,' Shaw said brightly. 'I suppose Mary told you, did she? Poor Mary. Well, we got stuck here actually. I should have been here for only one night. Got infected with those damned viruses you get in hospitals and had to stay for six weeks in the end. Daniel got it too.' He took a step towards me and, seeing the expression on my face, stood very still.

'And that's when Garrett came?'

'Garrett. Yes.' He paused. His voice had become less strident and more hesitant. He glanced up and looked deeply puzzled. 'But I never remembered. Never remembered any of it until much later. It only came back when I saw him. Otherwise I might not have remembered any of it at all.'

'When you were older?'

'Yes.'

'Near here?'

A thoughtful expression crossed his face. 'I was at the theatre. Back here for the holidays from Cambridge to see my parents for Christmas. It was the Christmas panto. *Cinderella*. And he was there as well . . . Garrett. He was in the audience, near the front. Laughing. I saw him and I just went into this awful, terrible panic. I had to leave straight away. My mother didn't know what was wrong with me. I didn't know either. After that I kept on seeing him. I would see him suddenly silhouetted over in that doorway where you're standing right now. I could be anywhere and it would come to me and I couldn't breathe. And I thought I didn't know what was happening to me. I couldn't sleep. I thought I was going to break down completely. I couldn't even remember who he was. I'd forgotten I'd even been in hospital or why. And I didn't know why I kept on seeing him like that. There was no way I could stop these . . . these pictures in my head. And sometimes, when it was really bad, they seemed to come all at once. And sometimes they would just . . . I don't know . . . flicker like a film but with no sound. Pictures,' he said, looking very seriously towards me. 'One after the other. Hundreds of them and all at once in my head. All of this place. And it got worse. I had a seizure,' he said in a matter-of-fact way. 'I woke up on the floor in my bedroom. I'd scratched my skin all over so deeply that I was bleeding.' He paused and took a step forward and I raised my crowbar and he stayed where he was.

'Joe Garrett,' he said. 'You see, we played games up there in the ward when it was late and he used to come to visit us. Good of him to visit us like that and cheer us all up. And then he'd draw the curtain across and it would be another game, one with different rules. Yes' – his voice began to fade – 'a game. I remembered the game and then later, when I was in the toilet, it was as if he was standing beside me in the mirror. I saw pictures of his face standing in doorways, holding himself. And ... and ...'

'And you didn't tell anyone?'

'Tell anyone? I was only twelve, Downes.'

'Were there others? Did other men come here?'

'Yes. Sometimes.'

'He brought them here? From that hotel where he lived?'

'Yes.'

'So you contacted the other boy? The one who was in the hospital with you, to make sure?'

'Yes, I didn't even know his second name. We'd only spoken to each other a few times when we were here. But I phoned his old school. And got his address and then I phoned him. He knew why I wanted to see him immediately.'

'And Bowman was experiencing the same thing?'

'No. Daniel remembered all of it, unlike me. We talked all night and in the morning we knew that there was only one way we could make it end. If we told anyone they would not believe us and what good would it do us? It was all so long ago and Garrett was famous. We had to make it end and the only way for it to end –'

'Was to bring him back here.'

'Yes.'

'How did you know where he was going to be?'

'Oh, that part was easy.' For some reason Shaw seemed disappointed. 'It was the anniversary of the theatre. We knew he would be back for that and we knew his mother lived nearby. We watched his house and then we followed him in Daniel's car. He stopped off by those stones. You're not supposed to walk your dog around there, but Garrett let his dog off, then put it back in the car. We were alone. He didn't even recognize us. We asked if we could take his photo. He was pretty well known, you know. And he said he could do one better. He had a camera in his car. A Polaroid,' Shaw said thinly.

'So he was still doing it?'

'*Of course* he was still doing it,' Shaw snapped, as if I'd asked him something ridiculous. 'He said we could take his photo and then he'd sign it. So Daniel took some pictures of us together.'

'But you left one of the photos.'

'That was an accident. We heard someone coming along the road and we had to move fast, you see. It blew away. There was no time to go back for it.'

'So you brought him in here and you punished him for what he'd done to you?'

'That's right,' Shaw said, again speaking matter-of-factly. 'We brought a spade with us. He was pleading with us all the time. We brought him up here and then I think

355

he must have known what we were going to do to him. But he still didn't know exactly who we were.'

'Because there had been so many others?'

'Yes. He had photos. Photos of them ... of us ... in his hotel in London. We found them when we got inside his room, and we knew some of his friends would have them too. Garrett tried to get away. Daniel had a gun from home – a rifle from his father's house. That's how we got him in the car. All the way in the car he still didn't know who we were. He kept on asking us what we wanted. Then, when we arrived here, he knew. Just a game, we kept on telling him. If you want to play, you have to play by the rules.' Shaw giggled. 'It was raining and we led him to the back and we watched him dig a big hole back there. He was crying all the time, begging us for forgiveness. Just like a little baby. It was *pathetic*. He said we'd had our fun and that if we let him go we could forget all about it.' His eyes hardened. 'But we watched him do it. Then we had a bit of fun with him outside. We brought him in here, and then ... well ... then we started on him. We made it last as long as possible. You understand that, don't you, Downes?' Shaw said seriously. 'That was important to us. We discussed that in advance. He died right on that slab over there and we watched him. This is where he used to bring us. And sometimes there would be ... a child right there. A dead child on the mortuary slab.'

'And the camera?' I heard myself saying. 'Whose idea was that?'

'Oh, that was Daniel's. He only had the idea when we saw Shaw had it with him. Daniel said it might help us. He thought that if we had something that could help us remember, we might be able to use it – so that if we were afraid again . . . if I had any more of my little panic attacks, it would be something to look at that would make it go away. Not forget, but know for sure that it was over and that he could not hurt us any more. We knew what he was when we brought him here. We found out very quickly that he was really just a sad little man who begged and cried and snivelled right up until the end, when he knew what we were going to do with him. And the photos. They would help us remember that.'

'The same way he remembered. He made you pose before he did what he did to you.'

'No, that was different,' Shaw said angrily. 'We took the photo because it would help us. It would help us know what he was. We weren't trying to be like him.'

'But after it was over. You knew that it might not be it. You knew things weren't going to get any better for you. It was worse somehow, wasn't it?'

'It didn't go away. I could still remember each detail, and the only relief was the thought of him dying here in this room, screaming like an animal. And then . . . then I saw him again.'

'Who, Daniel?'

'No, not Daniel,' Shaw snapped. 'Daniel and I were friends by then. We saw each other all the time. I'd decided to help him with his work. He needed someone he could trust up in London. No, I saw Garrett. I was at home watching television and they put on this old documentary about how he'd gone missing. And there he was, smiling. And it all came back worse than before.'

'So you had to kill Garrett again, but Garrett was dead,' I said. 'So someone else had to die. *You* had to die. How many have there been, Shaw?'

He looked at me with an expression as empty as a shop window at night. 'I don't know,' he said helplessly. 'We used to put them in the little courtyard, out by the trees. But I think Daniel came on his own sometimes. Some things had been moved around. He'd been here on his own.'

'Rent boys. Runaways. Boys living on the streets that you brought here from London. But not Miles, right? The one from the children's home. That was a mistake, wasn't it? Some of the boys you brought here walked out alive, didn't they?'

'Yes, some of them.'

'But not Miles?'

'No. That was Daniel. Daniel knew he had gone too far.'

'Gone too far?' I shouted. 'Christ, Shaw. Wake the fuck up! We're talking about a little boy here. You had to make him disappear. Erase him as if he'd never existed. Because, unlike the other boys, there would be records of this one.'

'Yes, all right, yes.'

'So you used Bowman's connections?'

'We used *our* connections, Downes.' And for a moment there was a glimpse of the other Shaw I had first met. 'We knew their dirty little secrets. So they had to help us. They knew that.'

'Other men in power, like you and Bowman. Men working in Whitehall. You sent those two men after Robert and they took care of it. The same two men who came for Miller afterwards. They're security services. The same kind of men who no doubt killed Baines and set the children's home on fire years ago.'

'Ex-security services. Discharged.'

'Dishonourably no doubt. And men like them have always been told to help clear up after you.'

'Yes.'

'But Miles wasn't the only mistake you made, was he? Miller was a loose end as well, wasn't he? And it all started to unravel in the last two weeks, when Robert came forward and then there was the story about Baines in the paper. It was all being brought up again. Why? You needed to know. You figured out someone must have put Finn on to the story, after all these years. Someone who's been too scared to do anything till now.'

'Yes. It was time to end it once and for all. I had to chance it that Miller would tell us where the photos were.'

'But he wouldn't?'

'No. My men worked on him for hours. He wouldn't say a single thing to them.'

'Did you know that Bowman had brought his own son here?'

Shaw's face became expressionless again. 'No, I didn't know that. Not until later, when Miller and Freddie broke into his London flat. We were sure that it was over for us then, but Freddie was found dead later that night.'

'You didn't know he was dead until the next day. But you phoned Bowman in the morning.'

'I told him that there was still no news on the burglary, only that we'd managed to suppress it.'

'So you went to see Miller over in the Cotswolds, where he'd been picked up.'

'Yes.'

'And you made a deal?'

'I didn't actually have to say anything, but he knew quite well where we both stood.'

'You pulled strings so that Miller was never charged with anything. You could never come back here. But you couldn't bring yourself to destroy this place.' I took a step towards him. 'I want you to think about this very, very carefully before you answer, Shaw. Since Daniel Bowman died, have there been others?'

'No, I swear it. Things got a little better after Daniel died. I don't know why.'

'And then you saw him. You saw that boy.'

'Yes. I gave him a lift. It was all coming back to me because of Finn and the paper and Robert going forward to the police. It was all coming apart and I knew it. I stopped off and we got talking. He said he wanted to go

360

to London. He said that he was going away. That he'd got fed up and was leaving this time for good.'

'So you took him straight here?'

'Yes.'

He turned away and took one long look at the room. His tone and whole demeanour had been almost dreamlike at times, as if he was unsure how he'd arrived there. Now his expression changed to one of acute concentration. His eyes seemed to absorb and reflect back the very darkness of the room itself, so that each dark contour was buried deep within his gaze. His eyes rested almost lovingly on the long sinks in the corner and the porcelain slab set in the centre. He paused suddenly, his head cocked to one side.

'It's not raining anymore, is it?' he said. He paused, listening, and I realized that he was right.

He took a few steps away from me. He made the decision with ruthless, breath-taking speed. He dropped the torch and it hit the ground. With a quick movement he reached into his pocket. I took a step forward, knowing that I had made a terrible mistake and knowing that it was too late. The crowbar lifted in my hands. I dropped my own torch and it landed with a splash, but it did not go out. Shaw's hand moved swiftly and without hesitation, not towards me but towards himself. For a moment there was a dull glimmer. An edge of something, moving in an arc. It moved up to his neck, and I saw the edge of a handle and then a blade and then the knife was gone, plunged deep beneath his chin.

He moved it across as far as he could with such force that I could see the muscles of his forearm pop as his coat-sleeve rolled up. For an awful, hideous moment the gaping wound opened to reveal the inside of his neck. He remained all the while as expressionless as a porcelain doll. He tumbled forward on to his knees. The knife clattered to the ground. His hands fell forward. His head hit the floor. He made a choking kind of cough. He instinctively reached for his throat, trying to cover it and perhaps put it back together, but the blood burst hissing through his clenched fingers.

I dropped the crowbar and rushed forward. Shaw fell to his side, writhing and shuddering convulsively. I put my arm under his body and without thinking drew him closer to me. I tried to cover the wound with my own fingers but they only slipped through the tear in his throat. He clutched at the collar of my jacket, pulling it and ripping the collar with slick hands.

The room rose up above us. My torch lay on the ground, illuminating his face through the water. He pulled at the back of my neck, trying to draw me closer. His eyes began that glassy stare and looked into my own while his legs kicked out against the cold wet ground.

I held him and watched the life slowly ebb out of him. Maybe it was something about that room. It was a place from which all light had been sucked out, like a void. I found that I was trying to comfort him as best I could. He struggled and writhed in agony. But I told him that it was all right. That it would be over soon, as the walls of the medical room slowly faded out of his sight. But I knew none of it was any good. Because Shaw in that moment was a lost and frightened little boy. His lips began to tremble. He let out a final wail of hideous despair. A wail that had been heard too many times in that room. And then it died into nothing. And, as he stared over my shoulder, it was if a cold shadow was rising above us both, and his eyes clouded over in appalled horror and fear. I knew then that Garrett's shadow loomed over him still. Then it was over.

I pushed him away and his arm splashed in the water and his head rolled back with a thud. The water coiled red around him. I stood up. I reached down and picked up the torch. I took off my coat and walked back towards him and threw my coat over his body. It was more than he deserved. I picked up the crowbar. Then I moved away from him. I closed the door behind me and I did not look back.

I followed the beam of my torch as I finally left the long empty corridors behind me. Then I was standing in the broken arch of the doorway. I leant my hand against the crumbling bricks. I felt sick, and the awful stench of that room would not leave me, and now there was no rain to wash the blood away from my clothes. I breathed in long and hard like a man emerging from deep under water.

The forest seemed to be waiting for the rain to begin once more. It didn't. Instead the wind blew the water, pushing it and creating small whirls and eddies. I reached down and cupped my hands and washed the blood away from my face and from my arms and my hair and then looked up.

There was a great silence after the rain. And then in the silence sounds slowly began to emerge: the drops of rain falling from countless branches of the trees and from the broken roof of the hospital. The reflection of the moon, unexpected, spread, was shattered and then became whole again as I pushed my way through the water.

I stopped once. I turned around and stared at the ruin of the hospital and its broken roof and broken windows. I felt a huge wave of complete and utter despair when I thought of all the boys who had died here. For a moment I had an impulse to go back in there and burn the whole place to the ground. But of course it wouldn't burn now. The crowbar slipped and dropped through my fingers.

Beyond the waterlogged trunks of trees, Graves was still standing over the two men. I started to wade back across the flat black water. When I was halfway across, I saw that Stanley had not gone back to the car as I had told him to do. Instead, he was helping Conrad, leading him gently away down the hill. Vine appeared out of nowhere, rushing through the trees, and when he emerged and caught sight of me he just stared.

What could I do for the boys who had been made to disappear? Nothing. It was too late. They had died out here alone and in fear. All I could do was pray. But what good would that do? I tried anyway. What else was there? So I prayed for all those who had been brought here to die in dark turmoil. I prayed for the sleepless ones. For Miles and for Freddie and all the other boys who had sat waiting in the strange artificial light of the medical room. And before I left the shadow of the hospital, before I began the long journey through the flooded fields to my car, I looked back once more, and I said one final and reluctant prayer for Charles Shaw and his hell-bound soul.

# Epilogue

Around six months later, when I got home early from work one evening, I saw a letter waiting for me on the doormat with my brother's familiar handwriting on the envelope. Inside it was a first-class return ticket to Buenos Aires, valid for a year, and no letter. I held it in my hands for a moment, put it in my pocket, turned around and walked through the warm evening sunshine to the pub. I started thinking about Powell and his funeral and then of the medical room in the middle of the night and all that rain. But already the events of that long week and that abandoned hospital were fading, especially since someone had gone out there in the middle of the night and burned the whole place to the ground.

Emma had got her story. But, despite everything, my big speech to Stanley had amounted to nothing. Of the guests who'd once frequented the hotel, not one conviction was secured due to lack of evidence, and no one was ever identified from Stanley's account of what he had seen.

An inquiry that was supposed to gather evidence on the missing boys had made headlines for months, but it found nothing new. Stanley was portrayed by members of the committee as a convicted felon. And he couldn't provide them with names. When it was all over, the spark in Stanley that had kept him alive for so many years had simply gone. Day after day I watched as the committee bullied him until there was nothing left of him at all.

His memories of where they had taken him had been too vague. The hotel had closed down many years before, and he could not even remember for certain that he had been taken there. Its permanent residents had included a QC, a number of actors, a judge and three high-ranking civil servants, none of whom were ever convicted, as it had all happened so long ago and half of them were already dead anyway.

They had hauled me in front of the committee too and tried the same thing with me, although they had appeared friendly enough to begin with. Then I had got tired of them and stood up halfway through and told the Chairman and all of them that they could go to hell for all I cared. It was thanks to Emma's coverage in the paper that I didn't lose my job. Vine did, though. He was sacked the moment the story broke. As for the men Graves and I had dealt with, they claimed to have no knowledge of the whereabouts of Robert Wilson, and no trace of him was ever found.

Fifteen bodies had been buried in the grounds of the hospital, and we were able to positively identify eight, including Garrett. They cremated what was left of him and scattered his ashes. We managed to trace Miles through his biological mother. It turned out that the only photograph left of him was the one which had been taken of him in that room. It was the second photo I had seen. The one of the boy with the thin face and the trail-looking body and blue eyes. It ended up being buried in some archive in London.

I took the envelope out of my pocket, looked at the ticket, waggled my glass at the barman and he poured me another. It had taken two weeks before I managed to get Carlos on the phone, by which time I had calmed down, although not much. Carlos was still keeping an eye on *El Rubio* for me. I was going to have to face it all again: I had known that the moment I saw his picture. I couldn't put it off much longer. One way or the other he was going to tell me what he had done to Pilar. But it wasn't about punishing him. Not any more. The idea of making him pay for what he had done now seemed absurd. I just wanted to know where Pilar was buried, and it was up to him how hard he was going to make it for us.

I turned around in my seat. The pub windows were open and through them I could just hear the distant and steady drone of a far-off lawnmower. A single bee hovered lazily amongst the flowers in the window boxes. I put the ticket back in its envelope and put it in my pocket.

Quint, Baines, Stanley and Vine had all tried to help. They had all believed, in their own way, that you could make a difference. Yet *El Rubio* still walked. The men who crowded around that living room with Stanley and Robert remained unpunished. Does it make any difference? Any of it? Sometimes I wonder.

I don't know when I will be going back to Buenos Aires, but it will have to be soon. And when I have finished with

*El Rubio*, I will return to my home nestled in this quiet village. For there is a darkness buried here amongst these ancient hills, and when it comes to the surface I must be ready for it, because Pilar watches me and silently judges me still.

# Acknowledgements

I would like to thank Helen Heller for all of her help and guidance, as always, during the writing of this novel. I would also like to thank Rowland White, Viola Hayden and Nick Lowndes at Penguin Books and Celine Kelly and Donna Poppy, and Camilla Ferrier and Jemma McDonagh at the Marsh Agency. Thanks also to Gerke Haffner at Bastei Lübbe.

# dead good

*For all of you who find
a crime story irresistible.*

Discover the very best crime and thriller books on our dedicated website – hand-picked by our editorial team so you have tailored recommendations to help you choose what to read next.

We'll introduce you to our favourite authors and the brightest new talent. Read exclusive interviews and specially commissioned features on everything from the best classic crime to our top ten TV detectives, join live webchats and speak to authors directly.

Plus our monthly book competition offers you the chance to win the latest crime fiction, and there are DVD box sets and digital devices to be won too.

**Sign up for our newsletter at
www.deadgoodbooks.co.uk/signup**

Join the conversation on:

# He just wanted a decent book to read ...

Not too much to ask, is it? It was in 1935 when Allen Lane, Managing Director of Bodley Head Publishers, stood on a platform at Exeter railway station looking for something good to read on his journey back to London. His choice was limited to popular magazines and poor-quality paperbacks – the same choice faced every day by the vast majority of readers, few of whom could afford hardbacks. Lane's disappointment and subsequent anger at the range of books generally available led him to found a company – and change the world.

*'We believed in the existence in this country of a vast reading public for intelligent books at a low price, and staked everything on it'*
**Sir Allen Lane, 1902–1970, founder of Penguin Books**

The quality paperback had arrived – and not just in bookshops. Lane was adamant that his Penguins should appear in chain stores and tobacconists, and should cost no more than a packet of cigarettes.

Reading habits (and cigarette prices) have changed since 1935, but Penguin still believes in publishing the best books for everybody to enjoy. We still believe that good design costs no more than bad design, and we still believe that quality books published passionately and responsibly make the world a better place.

So wherever you see the little bird – whether it's on a piece of prize-winning literary fiction or a celebrity autobiography, political tour de force or historical masterpiece, a serial-killer thriller, reference book, world classic or a piece of pure escapism – you can bet that it represents the very best that the genre has to offer.

**Whatever you like to read – trust Penguin.**